CRYSTALS AND CONTRACTS

A LE FAY ROMANCE

A. A. FAIRVIEW

Copyright © 2023 by A. A. Fairview

All rights reserved.

No part of this book may be reproduced in any form or by any electronic or mechanical means, including information storage and retrieval systems, without written permission from the author, except for the use of brief quotations in a book review.

This is a work of fiction. Name, characters, locations, and incidents portrayed are the work of the author's imagination.

Copyediting by Gabriel Hardgrave.

Interior illustration by Savanna Meyer @nightmaskart.

Cover at by Sophie Zuckerman @dextrose.png.

Cover design by A.A. Fairview.

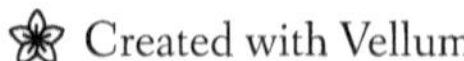 Created with Vellum

CONTENTS

CONTENT WARNINGS

This Novel contains the following content: Violence, Death of a parent, cancer, discussions of death and terminal illness, slut shaming, reference to street harassment, infidelity (not involving the main couple).

This novel features sexual content and is not suitable for readers under the age of 18: BDSM elements, impact play, pegging, public sex, praise kink, blood play, breath play, size kink, monsterfucking.

CHAPTER ONE

MINNIE

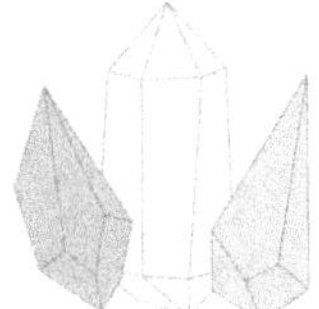

The glass pen glides along the thin, almost translucent paper. I dip the glass nib into the ink once more, finishing up the detailed margins of the magic circle. Amber sits across from me on the floor, a pastel braid between her eyes as she bends her back to watch me work. I finish up the design and set down my pen. Amber reaches to grab the paper and check my work but I touch her hand.

"It'll glow red if I did it wrong," I remind her. She's my teacher, but I still remind her.

"I want to study your work. You understand this summoning stuff better than me."

It sounds contradictory, that Amber could be the one teaching me summoning spells while I'm the one who understands the material best.

I smile at her. "You're better at plenty of other magic." I nod to the array of plants on her windowsill; rosemary, parsley, ivy, and others I've forgotten the names of. "Except for that one time your magic seed pod exploded and knocked us both out."

Amber snorts. "And mom thought we were just stoned out of our minds."

"Which is funny, since neither of us smoke."

She looks over the magic circle once more before setting the paper back down on the floor. "Alright. Go for it."

I hover my hand atop the piece of paper, whispering an incantation. The ink goes from black to glowing blue. The runes and circles disappear, burning the paper as they leave. The remaining paper folds in on itself as embers lick at its edges, eventually burning out and leaving nothing but ash.

Amber and I both look up from the paper at the same time, smiling like we've pulled a fast one on her mom. In a way, we have. Usually magic is taught by family members, but seeing as all the would-be-witches in my family are dead, I've had to learn bits and pieces from Amber. It's a safety issue. The more people who know magic, the more chances there are for someone to slip up and make a scene. It doesn't take a historian to know magic is frowned upon by those who lack it.

"If I had included an offering–"

"You would have summoned something." Amber nods. "A gnome, I think?"

"You think."

"Maybe a pixie. A fae of some sort. You summon it, give it a task, and when it's done–*POOF!* Back to its original plane."

I tilt my head. "What... sort of offering do I need in a spell like this?"

"Depends on what you're summoning. Fae like sweets, I know that. I think someone said celestials like parchment and flowers."

"What about devils?"

Amber makes a face I wholly expected: a nervous mix of a grimace and a frown. "Nasty shit. Blood and bones and viscera. But I think devils also accept precious metals and gemstones."

I can make that work.

There's a knock at the door, and Amber and I scramble to hide the evidence, her putting the glass topper in her bottle of magic ink and me shoving the parchment under her bed. Once we're settled, Amber calls, "Come in."

Her mom opens the door and doesn't say a word. Her braids are strung with bright wood beads and piled high atop her crown. She puts her hand on her hip and shoots us a soft, closed-mouth smile. "Just like high school. You two, hanging out doing who knows what."

"It was usually studying," I remind her, very intentionally avoiding the detail of what subject we would study together during our sleepovers.

"Amber, I need some help preparing for the coven meeting tonight," her mom says.

She stands up, "Alright. I'll be there in a second."

Her mom, the coven Supreme, frowns.

"Minnie's package came in," Amber explains. "It would be bad customer service to have her leave without it."

"Fine. Make it quick."

We leave Amber's childhood bedroom and head out of her family apartment, down the steps that lead to the store. Some kids had a childhood playground, but I had Lucky Witch Readings, a metaphysic shop in the heart of Highland Park. The shop is filled to the ceiling with everything a witch could ever need: incense, oils, crystals, prayer cards... Sure there are some lay customers, but most of them are coven members.

We walk past the cluttered shelves to the front counter, Amber disappearing behind the countertop for a second before popping back up with a box in her hand. As soon as she sets it on the counter she leans forward, blocking the box with her body.

"I heard some talk that you're single now." She rests her hands in her peachy palms. "Spill."

I play coy and reach for my box. "I don't know what you're talking about."

Amber pulls herself and the box back, grinning like a cat. "So I get to break Emmanuel's heart and tell him you're still dating that walking legal pad person?"

"Really? Legal pad person?" She's talking about my ex, Alexander, who is indeed my ex-boyfriend, making me, in fact, single.

Amber lets out an exasperated sigh. "Girl, he is so boring."

"He has a good job! And he's tall. Buys me nice things without me asking..."

The fact I still need to defend him either says a lot about me or him, and I don't want to know which. Officially, we've only been broken up for a few weeks, but I haven't felt anything real toward him in months. Nothing, except the things I've already mentioned: his high paying job, his height, and all the nice things he would bring me just because he could.

"I forgot that's all you need. Money and a man you can climb like a tree."

I roll my eyes, annoyed that she's right. "Wow, guess I'll take my business elsewhere, then."

Amber snorts. "No one else has our level of quality," she points out. "And you're seriously not going to spill to me, of all people?"

"Don't you have to go help the Supreme?"

"Oh, she wants to know, too."

I guess if Alexander and I were still together, if we made a life together like he wanted, there would be a possibility of him finding out about magic. Despite being human, my Gramps knows magic exists. Which is a bit of a point of contention for the Supreme, even if it was Amber's Grandmother who allowed for Gramps to learn the big, scary secret we all try to keep. Witches, werewolves, vampires–things that go bump in the night–are real.

But humans have always had the upper hand. They've always been the majority, with armies, governments, and faith at their disposal. So we stay hidden.

"Stop by my apartment sometime, and I'll give you all the gossip." I reach for the box again.

Amber playfully slaps my hand away. "Last time I saw your apartment, it was a cardboard city. Does your offer mean you've finally unpacked everything?"

"Well, I don't know about *everything*." My eyes trail off, looking at the display of candles kept next to the register. If she knew I had been practicing magic at home, that I knew from experience how gnomes and pixies will do just about anything for a little treat, well... I don't know. She's my best friend and teacher; I'd hope she would be proud of me. "But I promise we won't eat off cardboard boxes this time." I smile. "We'll eat off the coffee table I found on the side of the road."

"Hey, that's where the best stuff ends up." Amber holds my order out for me to grab, only for her to swipe it away as soon as I reach for it. "Now, if I did come to your apartment, would a certain will-o'-wisp of a man be there?"

"You are so annoying," I tell her, rolling my eyes. "Fine. The rumors are true. Alexander and I broke up."

"Yes!" Amber practically jumps for joy, following her exclamation with a little dance and humming to herself. "Byyyye, biiiitch!"

I understand her excitement. I mean, *I* broke up with Alexander, after all. But not because he was boring. We were too different–him, a transplant from the East Coast who calls his parents once a week, and me, a local whose only living family is my Gramps. My Gramps, who I recently moved into an assisted living facility. It's the first time the two of us has ever lived in a different home.

That had really been the nail in the coffin for our relationship. Alexander didn't get what the big deal was, kept talking about how he would visit his grandparents in the nursing home all the time as a kid, and they seemed to love it. I know he was hoping I would move in with him once my family home sold. I knew that was never going to happen but I stayed, maybe hoping things would get better–or maybe I had gotten a little too used to being showered with gifts.

"I'm not planning on dating again any time soon," I tell Amber. "If you could pass that on to Emmanuel? *Gently.*"

"Good!" Amber claps her hands. "That means I get you to myself." She reaches out and takes my hand, her acrylics decorated with glitter and stars sparkle in the shop lights. She laces her fingers with mine. "Forget your apartment. Let's go to a club."

My face scrunches. I like dancing enough for clubs to have been worthwhile in my twenties, but I'm getting closer to thirty now, and the appeal of loud music and getting covered in stranger's sweat has melted away. Though any time I've said that to Amber, she's been scandalized, emphatically insisting, *"We're not that old!"*

"Oooor," Amber adds, seeing the distaste on my face, "we could do facemasks and anime." I start smiling, and Amber snorts. "You are such an old lady, you know that?"

"I prefer the term 'mature.'" I flutter my eyelashes.

Amber snorts at my declaration. "Old, mature, grown–whatever you wanna be Minnie. I'm just glad you're focusing on yourself."

I finally manage to grab the package from Amber, who laughs as a rebuttal. The package is a little beat up and covered in about a dozen different shipping stickers. Poking out from under the stickers is a skull and the letters "TO–" before being cut off by a shipping label haphazardly slapped onto the package. In the back of my mind I wonder if Amber noticed the skull. Though if she had, she would have prodded me for answers.

"Need to pick anything else up?" she asks.

"I'll get out of your hair. Don't want to keep the Supreme waiting."

"I swear if I get up there, and she just has me doing dishes..."

I laugh, though in the pit of my stomach, I wish my mom or Gramps were still around to nag me about chores.

The silver bell over the door chimes as I leave, and I notice Amber locking up out of the corner of my eye. Sometimes it feels like she's the only family I have left. Except, a few months ago, I found out the ugly truth about my Father. Though, are any absentee Fathers ever really pretty? Either way, I know who my sperm donor is, and he knows who I am.

Which means I need to act before he does.

I MAKE it back to my apartment and get to work. I put the package on a countertop in my modest kitchen and grab the first sharp thing I can find, a chef's knife I left in the sink. I cut through the labels and tape, opening up the package to find a slab of wood; it's a beautiful shade of brown with hints of red running through it. Despite its beauty, I read that, when cut, it bleeds.

I angle the tip of my knife to one of the block's edges to see if it's true. It takes a lot of pressing, but the knife cuts into the wood, and a substance begins to ooze out. Normal tamboti wood secretes a white and poisonous latex when it's cut. This wood isn't that different, but instead of white sappy ooze, the same warm red that runs through the wood grain drips from the cut, like cutting into the vein of someone's forearm.

"Gloves," I think aloud before setting down the knife.

I look under my sink and find a pair of rubber gloves meant for washing dishes. It's not the perfect protective gear, but I imagine so long as the sappy-latex doesn't get directly on my skin I should be fine. I've carved enough wands that I doubt I'll cut myself.

I take some time to prep: changing into an old pair of sweats and a shirt, pulling my curls back with elastic and clips for the flyaways. I lay an old towel on the hardwood floor. Then I get to work carving.

Wands aren't especially popular. They're pretty obvious, and the last thing any witch wants is to turn heads. A lot of people see them as a novice tool, as well, since they're a very precise magic conductor. But I like them, and while I'm not a novice (at least I don't see myself that way), I don't have the training other witches have.

Learning magic from a non-magic user goes about as well as it sounds.

My Mom tried, taught me what she learned from her own Mother before she passed. She read cards and built altars; she practiced for personal peace or maybe connection to her Mother. But she had no control over magic. If she drew a magic circle on practice paper as I had hundreds of times, it would have just been a drawing. Nothing more.

It's not enough to be born a witch, nor is it enough to study witchcraft. They go hand in hand like the components of a spell.

I lose track of time, and soon the wood is shaped into a stretched out cone, thicker at the base and thinner as it extends. I've carved sigils into the wood, symbols specific to the practice of summoning, symbols like the ones I drew back at the shop. I rather like drawing sigils and symbols, designing my own for exactly what I need. The more obvious the magic, the more I gravitate toward it–an unfortunate moth to a dangerous flame.

The cloth underneath me looks like a crime scene, and my clothes and gloves aren't much better. I toss the gloves before I move to the next step, grabbing a jeweler's kit containing gold wire and various crystals. I wrap some gold wire around the base of the wand to secure it, then start winding the wire up the wand, stopping occasionally to wrap a crystal in wire before attaching it to the wand.

The type of crystal matters. It all matters; every little detail put into casting a spell has an impact. Moldavite is my first crystal, a swampy green color, it reminds me a bit of sea glass but nowhere near as smooth. As I wrap the crystal and affix it to the wand I take a second to admire how nicely the colors all come together, brilliant gold pulling out the natural reds of the wood and complementing the green crystal.

I keep wrapping the wand and add another crystal, this time cinnabar, a brilliant red that rivals the wood. It's so beautiful, I feel a bit sad that I won't be able to show it to Amber. She teases me for still using wands, but she's also my biggest supporter when it comes to me performing magic. The rest of the coven is a lot more wary.

I'm finally near the end, which means it's time to put on the final crystal at the very tip of the wand: a rich purple charoite, which might be my favorite of the crystals. Though I am biased. Purple is my favorite color, has been ever since I was a kid and read that purple was considered a royal color for most of history.

I wrap the last bit of gold wire several times around the wood and charoite, making sure nothing will slip. My fingers, red and tender from all the work they've been put through today, run along the cool metal and stones affixed to the wand. Rich purple, reds, and green reflect the light in my apartment.

The sun is starting to set, alerting and alarming me as to how much time has passed. I should set the wand aside, give everything some time to settle. But I can't. I lay the wand down on my bookshelf before going to grab some candles and chalk from the box in my bedroom where I keep my magic supplies.

My landlord is going to hate me for what I'm about to do.

I pull my coffee table and rug aside, opening up the center of my tiny living room. I stand in the center of the room, then mark that center with a little "X" in yellow chalk. I take three steps from the center, then mark that. I do that a few times, creating different points on the outside of the center mark. This is the sketch for the summoning circle, but it has to be right. There's a lot of math involved, though I might be the only person who sees creating magic circles as math projects. Designing the sigils reminds me of geometry homework. But witches don't like to compare the art of magic to the strict sciences–save for alchemists, who are basically wizard chemists.

I create small blocks inside the outline to lock in the various symbols I'll need. The intent is for the magic to bounce off each symbol before it reaches the edge of the circle. I'm about halfway done with my sketch, when one of the symbols looks funny to me, and I second guess everything I've drawn up to that point.

I huff before standing up and taking a moment to double check my work. I'm aware I'm much too deep in the process to really be a reliable critic, but better for me to double check than to wing it and blow up my whole apartment. I mean that *shouldn't* happen anyway. The symbols aren't meant for offensive magic. Though summoning spells aren't exactly defensive, are they?

With my palms yellow and dusty, the magic circle sketch is finished. Standing at the edge of the circle I smile with pride looking at my work. "Okay..." I reach to grab my wand, only to remember what a mess my hands are. I dust them off on my sweatpants before picking up the wand. I point the charoite tip at the center of the circle, then map where the magic should go once the circle is activated, going from one symbol to the other, like electricity lighting up a switchboard.

"And all I'd need is a candle and an offering."

I shouldn't. This is all just prep work. I can't actually cast the spell now.

Well, I *could*, but it would be a bad idea. I'm full of ideas, but they're good ones. At least, I like to think so.

Still, I run to my room to the chest where I keep all my supplies and grab a red altar candle. "Offering, offering..." I mutter to myself.

Amber said devils like gross things and precious things. Still holding the wand, I open up the wooden jewelry box I keep on my dressing table. I riffle through my jewelry; most of it is too precious to leave as an offering: my Mom's old heart shaped door knockers that are still my favorite pair of earrings, bangles left behind by my Grandmother, my Gramp's class ring he gifted to me when I was accepted to college.

I find the pair of dangling flower earrings Alexander bought me for our three month anniversary. I was absolutely floored by them when he first presented them to me. He informed–or maybe bragged to–me that those were real teardrop diamonds hanging from the intricate flower posts decorated with what I recognized as citrine. I wore them exclusively on date nights with Alexander. Now looking at them, all I can think about is his long face and his long frown looking at me and saying nothing while I cry.

I grab both earrings and return to my living room, setting

the earrings down at the base of the candle before lighting the wick. Looking at my work, I realize I have everything the spells needs. Well, I want to clean up my sketch more and go over it with white chalk. Maybe I should put the candle and offering on a proper altar instead of on the floor? But still, it was pretty impressive work for one day and all by myself. Light from street lamps pours through my windows.

The last step is the incantation, a spark to start the reaction. I lazily point the wand at the center of the circle and whisper the incantation, as if speaking in a low voice could hide my words from the universe.

This was ill advised, I realize a second too late, as the flame of the candle plumes past the wax wall that contained it. I stop speaking, but the flame keeps growing. The candle melts like it's inside an oven, red rivers of wax pouring onto the floor and onto the offering.

The *one time* I want things to stop, it's too late. If I don't keep speaking, the spell will still...occur. Not the spell I intended to cast, but *something* will happen. I keep my wand pointed at the center of the circle and continue the chant, not letting myself dwell on my mistake. It feels like the magic circle is pulling me in, trying to consume me along with the offering and the candle. I brace myself, digging my heels into the wood floor.

Then, the candle extinguishes. Once brand new, it's now over halfway burned, with arms of wax around it like a spider web. The earrings left as offerings are lost in a river of wax. Smoke hangs in the room; at first, I think it's from the candle, only to see it's the chalk lifting and disappearing off the wood floor returning to the air as dust. I hold my breath, not wanting to get chalk dust in my lungs. The dust swirls, though there's no breeze in my apartment and begins to gather at the center of the circle surrounding the candle.

Then, nothing.

I huff, accepting the spell failed. Then the candle is alight again, now with an eerie purple flame. A sound like a garbage truck hitting a semi rips through my apartment. I cover my ears and shut my eyes trying to drown it out. When I open my eyes, it's all gone: the chalk, the candles, the offering. And standing in their absence is a man.

A very naked man.

CHAPTER TWO

MINNIE

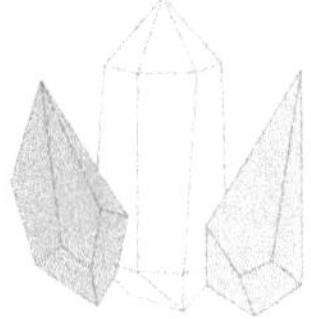

I HAVE NEVER BEEN MORE GRATEFUL TO SEE A STRANGER'S bare behind, because at least that means the man hasn't seen me yet. I stare–more like gawk–at the figure with olive skin like aged parchment. Black curls brush his shoulders. My eyes wander further down, and I try to focus on the dimples right above his rear instead of looking any lower. But damn it, his butt is perfectly toned without losing its roundness.

He clears his throat. My eyes jolt up and are caught by a single golden eye glaring at me over a shoulder. Not golden like brown with hints of yellow, but golden like his eyes are solid gold coins. The contrast of his inky black curls and his warm eyes is breathtaking enough, but the way his eyes bore into me takes my breath away.

Finally the figure turns to face me. "Oh–" I wince, covering half his body with my hand. I like the view, sure, but I'm not really ready to see this stranger's family jewels.

A low, smokey voice speaks. "You summoned me."

I blink, and it hits me that the spell worked–too well. "I was practicing," I breathe.

He doesn't seem to hear me. "*You* summoned *me?*" his gravelly voice repeats, though this time it's a touch mocking.

I furrow my brows. "It appears that way, doesn't it?" The figure scoffs and starts to walk away, right to my front door. "No, no, no–" I panic, running to block his exit and press my back against the door.

This doesn't stop the man, who walks right up to me. "Move," he commands.

"Absolutely not!" I respond, shaking my head. "You are *much* too naked to be going anywhere–"

He lifts a brow. "Naked?"

"A-and I summoned you here!" I straighten my back and lift my chin. "Which means you have to listen to me."

The figure chuckles, showing off bone white teeth. "I listen to no one, little witch."

I hadn't taken in the entirety of his face before this moment. Lips so full I'm jealous rest on a square jaw with a jutting chin. His nose is curved, long, and distinct like the rest of him. Though his eyes are striking, they're probably his smallest feature, almond shaped and cat-like. He towers above me like everyone else, the joys of being 5'1", but his broad shoulders somehow make me feel more trapped than if he had just been tall.

"Look, if you leave this apartment looking like you do, you're going to get arrested."

"What?" he snarls.

Somehow that's the most polite thing he's said so far. "You're going to be attacked if you leave, but we really need to talk about–" There's a knock at my door. I freeze–more than freeze. Ice pumps through my veins. If I could shatter like a lake in March, I would.

Alexander calls through the door. "Minnie?"

Yup, shattering into a million little ice cubes sounds great right about now.

"Minnie, I know it's late; I just need to grab some things."

I pinch the bridge of my nose and mutter, sounding like an annoyed cat in front of this tall guest I've summoned into my living room. I pull my hand away from my face and glare up at him, my jaw tight. "Stay. *Quiet.*" I turn around and open the door a hair, peering out to see Alexander.

He stands there in his usual suit. Must have come straight from work. His flat brown hair looks a touch messy, and his blue-gray eyes look bored. The only nice thing about seeing him is realizing he's taller than the man in my apartment by maybe three inches. But he's also lanky like a sapling. Amber always teases me for liking sickly looking skinny white boys. Which is true, but she doesn't have to say it so loud.

"Alexander, what do you want?"

"Can I, uh, come in?" he asks.

"No," I tell him.

Alexander scoffs. "Wow, okay, didn't realize things had gotten that bad."

We didn't sleep together for three months, and you were surprised we broke up? I don't have the energy for that conversation. Not tonight and not ever.

"Are you serious?" I ask. "Look, can't you pick up your stuff tomorrow?"

"I'm here right now. Come on, Minnie."

Sighing, I say, "I'll bring it out to you. What did you even leave here?"

"My toothbrush..."

"Oh, are you being serious?" I want so badly to open the door wider, so I can slam it in his face. "Buy a new toothbrush."

"I was thinking, okay? I have other stuff. Let me in, please?"

"Now's not a good time." I don't want to beg him to leave,

but it's looking like that's my best option. "I had a long day, and I just want to sit and read and forget about the world, alright?"

A voice growls behind me. "Minnie?"

Oh, good, the naked-man knows my name now.

"Um...who is that?" Alexander asks, now craning his neck to try and look into my apartment.

Before I can even come up with an excuse, the man I've been trying to hide pushes the door open further, almost hitting Alexander right in the forehead. I stand there, no doubt looking rather guilty, with a massive naked man looming behind me.

"Rosier," he says with the confidence of a man not showing his dick to the entire hallway. "You must be Alex."

Alexander hates when people call him Alex. Rosier–I guess that's the man's name–has no way of knowing that, yet still vexes my ex in a way few people know how.

Alexander's white skin goes red. "Oh, so *that's* why I can't come in?"

"Please don't shout," I hiss. I've only lived in this apartment for a few months and don't need my neighbors to make a noise complaint.

"You're the one who started shouting!" he insists.

I know I wasn't, but my saying so isn't going to help the situation.

He stares at me, his top lip twitching. "I can't believe you're already sleeping around! Or did you get a jump start before we broke up?"

"If you're accusing me of something, say it, Alexander!" Now I *am* shouting, but I'm not going to let him say I'm sleeping around, never mind him implying I cheated on him.

I slam the door shut. Alexander keeps shouting nonsense in the hallway but I ignore him, marching into the single bathroom in my apartment. I hear tall, rude, and handsome follow me.

"Now I *have* to ask..." he says in a smooth yet rumbling voice. "Did you summon me to fuck me?"

The hairs on the back of my neck stand up, and I my face grows hot. In the bathroom mirror I can see him smiling to himself as he leans against the doorframe. I don't bother with a response, scoffing and grabbing Alexander's toothbrush. I brush past Rosier and go back to my front door, opening it wide enough to toss Alexander's toothbrush at him. Then I shut and lock the door, praying Alexander hears the bolt turning and gets the message.

He must have, because he shouts, "You're a heinous bitch, Minnie!" Then, silence.

With my back against the door, I slide down to the floor, feeling like I've chased a feral animal out of my home.

Again, tall, rude, and handsome appears, following me like a duckling. He looks down at me, and his burning eyes are... curious. "So, Minnie–"

"Minerva," I correct him before pushing myself up off the floor. "Only my friends call me Minnie."

"You *wound* me, Minerva," he replies. I purse my lips into a hard line to keep myself from smiling. "If you didn't summon me as a companion..." He smiles wider, showing off his teeth once more but with an air of menace like a shark swimming towards me. "Then you must want to make a deal?"

I take a deep, shaky breath, still processing what I had actually achieved–even if somewhat accidentally. My summoning circle worked. Which meant the man standing naked before me isn't a man at all.

He's a devil.

CHAPTER THREE

ROSIER

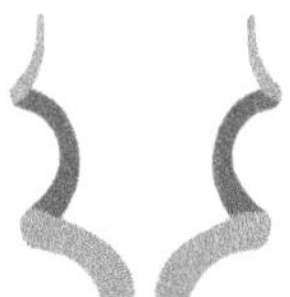

To be ripped from the Hells and dragged to the Mortal Plane was unexpected but not unwelcome. If I were older, one of those leathery winged fucks that sits higher in the ranks than me, getting dragged to the Mortal Plane would be commonplace. Everyone's heard the stories: a deal with the Devil and all that. But over the centuries, it became harder and harder to get humans to agree to sell their souls. Almost as if people didn't live in the dark anymore.

I'm glad those practices are antiquated. The idea of being dragged out of Hell on the whim of some scholarly mortal who can't fight for himself is obnoxious. Yet here I am, on the Mortal Plane, standing in front of a mortal woman who'd summoned me the same way I summon my servants.

She's a tiny thing, a good foot smaller than I am in this form. Her brown curls are pulled back from her face, showing off cheekbones dotted with dark spots like grains of mica in granite. Her eyes are green, not a color often seen in the Hells, and I admit I'm captivated by them. The longer I look, the more flecks of gold I spot floating around her irises. Her lips are a deep clay color that pairs well with her bronze skin. If she were only a bronze statue in some palace, she would be perfect.

Alas, she's a mortal. And wasting my time.

Minerva shakes her head and buries her face in her hands. "This wasn't supposed to happen so soon," she laments.

I raise a brow "*You* summoned *me*, witch. Not that I fully believe it yet."

She pulls her hands from her face. "What?" She sounds like a confused imp, small and floaty. Then her face scrunches like crushed metal, her brows a deep crevice down the center of her forehead. "How can you doubt that I summoned you? You're here, aren't you?"

I don't entertain her with an answer.

"Look, let's get one thing straight." She lifts her chin, as if that will make her taller. "I brought you here, so you have to listen to me."

I chuckle, shaking my head slowly. "You're much too cocky. Until we have a deal, I am free to do as I wish. I listen to no one, certainly not a mortal."

If we do make a deal, we will be bound–and not solely on this plane or in this life. Once the contract is signed, her soul will be forever tied to me: Rosier, Prince of the Hells. I hold out hope she did summon me for a romp in her bed. Afterwards I could explore this plane of my own accord, leave without any entangling strings.

Dragging a mortal soul around for an eternity is asinine.

"O...kay," Minerva stutters. "I, uh..." She starts to pick at her nails.

Though I have no interest in deals, she's piqued my curiosity, entertained me thus far. "Well?" I press.

Mortals usually want one of six things: power, wealth, revenge, transformation, adoration, or apathy. Money and power

I understand. Adoration and glamor, sure. But why anyone would sell their soul for revenge, for mutual destruction, I cannot comprehend. Even if I could, it would still be a waste of my time. Nor do I understand the desire to kills one's emotions, but I'm not meant to understand it. Humans sometimes feel too much, to the point of madness. Empathy, I think they call it.

Minerva looks up, her eyes so wide, the veins of gold trailing through the green shine. "I want revenge."

I roll my eyes. "Such a boring option."

"*Excuse me?*"

"Details." I snap my fingers, wanting to see her dance further.

Her mouth falls open, and she makes a sound like she's being lowered into the freezing pits of Hell. Finally, she composes herself. "My Father is a witch named Arthur le Fay. He abandoned me and my Mom; he's a terrible person."

"Because he abandoned you."

"No. Well, kinda."

"You're *extremely* convincing," I drone. "I'm dying to rip his head off myself."

"Can you do that?" Minnie asks.

I'm delighted to know she has a pension for violence behind that sweet face. "Terrible isn't a reason for revenge. Not where I'm from."

"Arthur le Fay is a criminal, a drug runner." She knits her brows, her voice turning serious. "And he works with humans. Casting spells right in their periphery. He's a danger to all witches."

I've read enough histories written by mortal souls to know what happens when humans find out about witches. But if witches are burned in the public square, well, that's humanity at its finest, isn't it?

I pinch the bridge of my nose. "How exactly would you have me go about this revenge?"

"Well..." She hesitates. "Isn't that where *you* come in?"

"You waste my time, witch," I spit.

Her face curls in on itself, looking disgusted. "Okay I would rather you call me Minnie than witch, if that's how this is going to be."

"You are a very confusing and vexing little thing." I step closer to her, and she jumps but holds her ground stays. "Revenge is vague. You say he abandoned you? So, do you want his family to abandon him?"

"S-sure? I don't know."

I huff, now bored of this game. "I refuse your proposal."

Her face falls. "But–you can't just say no!"

"Yes I can," I inform her. "I heel to no master. You chose to forget this."

"But–but I summoned you to make a contract." She frowns in an attempt, I think, to look intimidating. "I want to make a contract. You're standing in my kitchen butt naked–"

"You used that word again." She cocks her head to the side as if not understanding my words. "Naked," I clarify.

"People usually wear clothes. You know." She tugs at the cloth that covers her chest. "Clothes."

I looked her up and down, taking in the white and gray fabric crusted with red splotches that hangs off her body like curtains.

She frowns. "Do you not... wear clothes where you are from?"

"Why would we hide our forms as you do now? Are you embarrassed of your body?"

"No!" She objects like I've insulted her. "I have curves in all the right places." She sticks her hands on her hips to highlight this fact.

"How could anyone tell with those rags hanging off your bones?"

"Well, these aren't *nice* clothes and–you know what? We're not having this conversation." She throws her hands up and walks past me deeper into the room, which appears to be her home.

Nothing about it is remarkable. The area is drenched in yellow light, artificial even to my eyes so unaccustomed to this realm. Her shelves are bursting with books. A sad looking lounge is pushed to the wall. A strip of beads hangs on the wall, vibrant red and blue beads catching my eyes even from afar.

Minerva–Minnie–fucking Hells what does she want me to call her again? She's focusing on the center of the room, Looking down at the floor with furrowed brows as if the planks of wood are speaking to her. I approach a wall ornament, noting the center beads are the pure white of dried bone and in a shape like mouths with little teeth. I reach to touch, the little-mouths looking smooth, but Minnie pipes up.

"Do not touch that!" In a flash she's standing beside me. I don't know how her little legs carry her across the room so fast. "That's a family heirloom."

Unlike clothes or nakedness, heirlooms are something I'm familiar with. Devils often own heirlooms of immense power, be they the pinned wings of a fallen fae emperor, glasses that once belonged to an angel, or, in my case, texts detailing the mortal realm. What sort of power these beads hold, I have no idea, but I would rather not be hexed, so I pull my hand away.

"Thank you," she says, sounding exhausted. As if reading my, mind she breathes, "I need sleep."

"Show me your quarters."

She snorts, insulting me. "Yeah right."

I raise a brow. "If your bed was large enough to hold Alex, then it should be large enough to accommodate me."

Minnie rubs her temples. "Alexander was my boyfriend, so, yes, he got to sleep in my bed. You're a devil I accidentally summoned into my apartment."

"No one *accidentally* summons a devil. No matter how much they protest."

Minnie groans, rolling her eyes and throwing her head back. She walks past me back into the room with the mirror, turning quickly on her heels to glare at me.

"Nope. No entry." She crosses one arm over the other, blocking me. "Unlike you, I don't prance around naked."

"Prance?"

She shuts the door in my face.

"I *do not* prance," I grumble.

Though she's obtuse and haughty, she did bring me here. I may have doubted it upon seeing her, but it was a foolish thought to maintain. She summoned me for petty revenge. I won't give it to her, but I will make the best of my time here, the plane I could only read about... until now.

Ironically, I go to her bookshelves, studying the spines. Many titles mention Dukes, Lords, and Rogues, and I consider that perhaps we have a shared interest in history. The books lack the thick binding I'm accustomed to, the spines showing their use with wrinkles and tears at the edges.

Beside the bookshelf, I spot several portraits. One is of Minnie, sitting next to an old man in a chair; the pair share the same eye shape, round and inviting, but the old man's eyes are a warm brown, unlike her vibrant green eyes. Then there's one of Minnie as a young girl, embracing another girl much larger in size and statue. Their smiles are wide and exuberant. I can almost hear their girlish laughter through the frame. Another portrait shows a woman holding a baby, and I at first think it's Minnie holding her own child. Upon closer inspection, I see the woman, too, has warm brown eyes while the baby's eyes are green. This is Minnie as a babe, then, and the woman must be her abandoned Mother.

Curious.

I turn in place, taking in the rest of the room and spotting an open door. Inside there is another bookshelf sitting at the base of the bed. I step into her room and am greeted by more well loved books. Their titles are less grand, and I take notice of several recurring names: Jenkins, Riley, and Larsen. There's another book on her bedside table–whatever she's reading now.

While inspecting the book, I find her bedside table drawer is ajar. I open it further, expecting more books. Instead, I find an array of paddles. I grab the one on top, made of a pale wood with hearts carved into it. There are others made of leather and even a flogger.

Curious still.

The rough sound of a clearing throat pulls my attention away from the drawer. Minnie stands in the doorway, wearing nothing but a sheet wrapped around her torso with her hands on her hips. The longer we look at each other, the deeper her brows furrow.

I grin and slip the wooden paddle back inside the drawer. "Quite the collection you have."

She says nothing, marching over and shoving the drawer close, almost snagging the tip of my fingers.

"I was referring to your books," I assure her.

Her dusty clay lips are thin, and she points back into the living room. I could snap at her–quite literally try and bite her finger–but I oblige her silent request with a smirk.

As I leave I ask, "Are you being silent because I said no to our contract?"

Her lack of a reply confirms my assumption.

Back in the larger room, I fall onto the lounge. Minnie looks at me, distraught, so I ask, "What could I have possibly done to upset you now?"

She buries her face in her palms. "There is a naked man on my couch..." She disappears into her bedroom, then appears with a pile of cloth. "Here, so you don't have to... touch the cushions." She offers me the stack, raising a brow when I do not take it from her. "Can you just lay a sheet down? Won't you get cold lying there?"

Her anger has bubbled away. Which is disappointing. She's cute when she's angry.

She sets the pile on the ground and grabs one off the top, a thin but large piece of fabric. "Lay this one down and then the rest will keep you warm for tonight."

She hands me the sheet. Again, I do not take it. The little pout I'm already fond of appears.

"Freeze then," she spits before tossing the sheet at me.

"My servants prepare my bed."

"I'll remember that next time I summon a devil."

She goes to shut the door, but I leap forward and manage to catch the door's edge before she can shut me out.

I consider my words carefully. "I require... aid with my hair."

I will admit, in this instance, my vanity is stronger than my ego. The coils of Minnie's curls that hang around her face in an aura are too defined to be left unattended.

She snorts. "What, do your attendants tie your bonnet each night? Massage your scalp with coconut oil?"

"Of course. Well, I don't know what a coconut is but... yes."

She shuts the door in my face. But a moment later, it opens, Minnie now holding a shiny bundle of purple fabric with a floral design. She hands it to me, and I take it, discovering the fabric is a round shape with long ties around the back.

"Don't tell me you need help tying it," she complains.

"I am sure I can manage."

I tilt my head forward and gather my curls, making sure every strand makes it inside the soft circle before tying a knot at the base of my head.

"You're not tall enough to tie it anyway," I tease.

I lift my head, running my fingers along the smooth edges of fabric, ensuring it's tight enough so as not to slip off in the night.

"Purple suits you." With that she shuts the door again.

This time I know she won't be coming back.

CHAPTER FOUR

MINNIE

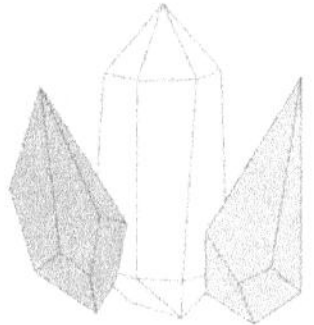

I BARELY SLEPT THAT NIGHT. How COULD I WHEN A DEVIL was sleeping no more than ten feet away from me on my couch. Sure, he hadn't been violent. My patience was more in danger than my life. But he was a threat, one I had let into my home and was now stuck with 'til I could figure out a contract. Even when the deal was made, I wasn't sure if Rosier would just... pop back into hell. Or was I going to have to design another circle to send him back home?

"Great job, Minnie," I mutter to myself throughout the night, hoping Rosier's hearing isn't good enough to hear me talk to myself.

My alarm blares, and the sun pours into my bedroom. The first thing I do is open my bedroom door enough to peek at the couch. Rosier is fast asleep and still very naked, having not bothered to cover himself with one of the thicker blankets I'd left him. Though he had bothered to cover the couch with a sheet as I requested. Maybe I'd gotten lucky and summoned a polite devil.

Then I remember catching him snooping around my

bedside table. Born in Hell or born on Earth, you just don't look through a woman's bedside drawers.

I slip past him, careful to step over the floorboards I know creak; devils might be light sleepers for all I know. Luckily, I make it to the kitchen without incident to start my coffee, then dip into the bathroom. Slipping off my bonnet, I run my fingers through my curls before grabbing some mouse. After pulling and scrunching each ringlet, I pin my front curls back with barrettes, two on each side, then turn my head back and forth to make sure each barrette is level with the opposing one. By the time I'm done putting on makeup, my coffee is finished brewing, and I pour myself half a mug so I have something to sip on while getting dressed.

I look over my shoulder at the back of the couch. I've only made enough coffee for myself–which is a lot, but that's because the coffee at work might as well be mud, and I always bring a big thermos from home to drink throughout the day. I shake my head, reminding myself coffee probably isn't even a thing in Hell. What had he said yesterday? *I don't know what a coconut is.* Here I thought Hell would be a tropical sort of environment, hot with humidity so thick you'd have to push aside clouds. It was either that or fire and brimstone.

Holding the mug with both hands I tiptoe behind the couch and lean over to get a proper look at Rosier. The bonnet I'd let him borrow is still affixed to his head. His arm covers his eyes, his torso stretched to show off his ribs and the contours of his abdomen. With the knowledge he won't catch me looking, I gaze at his naked form. Save for the hair on his head and his brows, he's completely hairless.

I drink my coffee, chastising myself for getting ideas. It would be a very bad idea to develop a crush on a devil. I told Amber yesterday I wasn't ready to date again. Though at that time I was still feeling a touch bad for ending things with Alexander so suddenly. Not anymore. Not after last night.

If I stand here gawking, my resolve will wear away in no time. I go and pick out an outfit. As I flip through my closet, I giggle, recalling Rosier's confusion about clothing. I guess devils walk around naked. Maybe it was super hot down there like I'd assumed, or maybe modesty isn't a value for devils. I really don't know much about the Hells–or any of the other planes, for that matter–just the basics.

There are several planes that surround the Mortal Plane: the Heavens, the Hells, the Fae Realm, the Demon Plane, and then the Veil, which covers all realms but is untouchable to those who have not passed on. It is said that witches used to cross into other realms all the time. But the fairy circles have all been destroyed, heavenly entities seem to have lost all interest in the mortal realm, and summoning devils had become rather taboo.

Can't imagine why. Maybe because it meant summoning a very naked squatter to come live in your apartment. I don't remember that scene in *Doctor Faustus*.

I grab a brown argyle skirt and its matching jacket, then a white turtleneck and a pair of thick black tights. I wear the same loafers to work every day, the ones with a tall heel so I don't look like someone got the dates mixed-up for Take Your Kid to Work Day. At least with the shoes, I stand at 5'6", *above* average height.

I examine myself in my wardrobe mirror, then check the time. Another ten minutes before I have to leave to catch my bus. Stepping back into the living room, Rosier groans, coming to life.

"Good morning," I say before taking another sip of coffee.

"Fuck you," Rosier grumbles.

I snort. "Not a morning person, huh?"

Rosier sniffs the air. "What is that?"

"Coffee..." I would offer him some, but he wasn't wrong last night, I'm not exactly happy he rejected my revenge proposal. "I can make you some... if you agree to my contract."

Rosier's eyes narrow. "You think bribery will sway me?"

"Worth a shot," I mutter before walking back to the fridge to fix up a quick breakfast, my usual yogurt, berries, and granola.

It doesn't take long for Rosier to lumber over, still very naked and still wearing my purple bonnet. He looks at my bowl, then back at me, a spoonful already in my mouth.

"This is yogurt. Do you guys have yogurt in Hell?" When he shakes his head, I explain, "It's kinda like cheese. You guys *have* to have cheese in Hell."

"Agricultural pursuits are not possible in the Hells. Nor do we eat through our mouths," he adds as I chew my granola slowly. "The endless suffering of the Hells sustains us. Here, vice is our source of energy." His brows furrow, as dark as his hair but comically straight, like they've been drawn on with a marker. "Shouldn't you know these things, little witch?"

"Bite me."

"Kill me, then." He gestures down at his bare chest. "Shouldn't be too hard even for a little thing like you."

Maybe he's messing with me, but I do wonder if devils can really die. The Veil is said to touch all realms, accept spirits of all sorts. Yet I can't imagine fairies or devils dying the same as humans. You can't exactly just clap and believe to bring back a dead family member. If only...

"I would rather not murder someone. That's taboo you know. Shouldn't a devil know that?"

Rosier scoffs. "Humans think fucking is taboo. Are you going to tell me everyone is celibate?"

He has a point—not a great one, but it's something.

"Killing you also wouldn't be a great idea since I still need a contract."

Rosier rests his chin in his hands, his fingers covering his mouth as he mutters, "So irritating."

"You'll have to speak up." I shove the last of my food in my mouth and bring the bowl to the sink to wash later. "I don't get why you're acting like this. I thought devils wanted contracts."

"How would you like to have some bitching, sniveling weakling tied to your soul–always in your periphery for the rest of time?"

I glance over my shoulder, and somehow his eyes are even more molten than before. I've assumed the lack of contracts between mortals and devils came from our end, but maybe it's the devils who have decided we're not worth the trouble.

"As interesting as that question is," I say, ", I have to get going, and I need you to stay put."

"You dragged me here and now you're leaving me?" His hand is now balled into a fist, pressed against his cheek.

"Yes, okay, I'm sorry, but I can't just call off. You can..."

I look around my apartment, cursing myself for not buying a TV or some other mindless thing. I go to my bookshelf and try to find something that won't give Rosier too many ideas. As if my collection isn't almost exclusively gothic stories of women being ravished by rogues and gentlemen. Maybe if I give him one of the gentleman books, he'll learn some manners.

I grab one of my nice-guy gentlemanly Regency books and bring it to him. "Here, educate yourself." To my surprise he takes the book, studying its cover of a bosomy woman sprawled against a stern looking man. "Or... read any of the other books I have. I'll be back as soon as I can."

Hopefully with a plan on how to fix this mess I've made. I might have to beg Amber to help me or find someone who can send him back. I'm already in way over my head, and if anyone is going to help me get through this, it's her. Hopefully she won't be too upset.

I go to leave my apartment only for the door to slam shut, a tan hand looming over me. I look over my shoulder to see Rosier, glaring at me with narrow eyes, like I'm a bug he's considering squishing but hasn't decided yet. Goose pimples cover my skin, but I ignore them, lifting my chin and keeping my lips tight.

"Are you done now?" I grab his wrist and pull it from the door.

As I exit my apartment, a warm voice greets me. "Hey, Minerva."

I shut the door lightning quick, afraid my neighbor, Kas, might sneak a peek inside. "H-Hi," I say to him, smiling wider than I normally do each morning.

Kas stands outside his door dressed the way I always imagine him, which is to say, very fashionable. He wears a turquoise sweater that complements the warm tone of his acorn skin. A nice pair of shoes poke out under his dark blue bell bottoms. As always, his medium length black hair and short beard are perfectly styled. I have no idea what Kas even does for work, but whatever it is, he looks good doing it.

"Heard your lover's quarrel last night."

My face drops and heats up. "Oh, God..."

Kas laughs. "Did you throw his clothes out the window afterwards?"

"No, but I should have." I mutter, and Kas laughs some more.

He leans down to whisper. "But what about the *other* guy you had over?" He wiggles his brows.

"Oh good, you heard that part, too?" I roll my eyes, now really wishing I had tossed all of Alexander's stuff out the window. Or maybe taken a swipe at his long legs when I had the chance.

"I'm not judging," Kas promises, "but I want to know if he's cute."

"I guess? Cute maybe isn't the word I'd use to describe him."

Oh my god, what am I saying? Why didn't I deny that I had a guy over? I should call Alexander hysterical, he's probably saying the same thing about me to his friends.

"He's a one night thing," I say.

"You never struck me as a one night stand kind of woman."

I raise a brow. "What gave you that impression?"

He's right, though. Maybe it's all the romance books or maybe it's due to the fact that I was likely the result of a hookup, but I can't get into sleeping with someone and never seeing them again. Or seeing them again and having it be awkward. I never kiss on the first date, and I never bring anyone home till the third. That's just how I operate.

"Maybe it's the prep school look."

"People on *Gossip Girl* hookup all the time," I inform Kas.

"Really?"

I nod. "It's, like, half the show."

"Huh. Maybe I should watch it. Anyway, is not-cute-but-sexy still in your apartment?"

"I never said he was sexy. Are you going for sloppy seconds?" I tease. "Because he's all yours."

I suddenly remember Rosier is a devil and not just some guy I met at a bar. It's easy to forget, probably because he's so appealing as a human. That had to be intentional, the forms of devils being appealing once they were on Earth. To lure people into debauchery or whatever.

"Not sure he's your type, though," I say, trying to dissuade Kas. "He's, uh... short."

Kas lifts a brow. "Sounds like he's not *your* type. If that Alex guy had anything going for him, it was height. And I like short kings."

"I'll give you his number after work."

I would *not* be doing that. Even if Rosier did have a cell phone. But I need to go catch my bus, so I wave goodbye to Kas and hurry out of my apartment complex.

———

I REALLY HOPED once I was in the office I'd be able to focus on anything other than the devil in my apartment. But my mind still swirls with images of the summoning circle and Rosier. I open up the editor on my computer in the hopes that familiar lines of Python will pull me out of my thoughts, but the code keeps shifting behind my eyes, turning into archaic symbols imbued with magic.

I don't regret my decision to go into computer science, even if I always preferred history, even if being the only woman in the room sucks. But now I work in cyber security for a manufacturing company and make enough to pay rent and Grandpa's nursing home and have enough left over for food. Okay, *sometimes* I go over budget—but only when shoes are on sale. And I had savings from living in my childhood home and commuting all throughout school. I'm set, really.

So why do I feel nothing?

I have the job, the money, maybe I don't get the respect, but I'm pretty low in the hierarchy corporation-wise. That's supposed to change the longer I'm with the company... so I've been told. I've tried to make every "right" decision. Minus the blaring misstep in my apartment.

Lunch comes around and I pull out my phone to text Amber.

> Hey I summoned a devil and he's sitting naked in my apartment. what do I do???

I delete the message and try again.

> Are you free this afternoon? I have something I need to show you.

Meet at your place or mine?

> Mine please! Around 5:30?

I've got a secret so keep this hush hush plz

Bet. Can this be a dinner date too?

> You know it, sugar

I thought you said you weren't dating again, sly.

A grin pulls at my lips, and I forget how pissed Amber is going to be when she finds out what I have to show her. I'll have to splurge on dinner.

CHAPTER FIVE

ROSIER

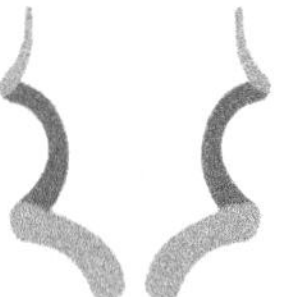

Minnie's raunchy read was disappointingly short, a mere 500 pages. It's fitting that such a tiny book, only the size of my hand, is filled with so much vigor, much like Minnie herself. The tomes of Hell are bigger than my head and twice as long. Devils of a solid mind could memorize those tomes, walk around as living knowledge to dispense to whatever Lord they aligned themselves with. Reciting tomes from memory was never my purpose, but I enjoy reading well enough.

I set the book down on the kitchen counter and contemplate grabbing another book off Minnie's shelf. None of her books appear especially long, but the vastness of her collection would take me a few days to get through, assuming I did nothing but read. Maybe I'd get to finish her whole library.

Dragged out of Hell to read a horny witch's hoard of smut. Riveting. The Archdevils would flock to me to hear the tale.

I walk to the window and find the world outside illuminated. People are walking about, and the buildings are made of stone, not so different from the towers of Hell. There are little green bulbs growing on scraggly, finger-like appendages right outside her window. Trees, I think they're called. Childish as it is, I want to look at them closer. I'd read about plants, living but not sentient beings that provide food to the other planes. No such thing grows in Hell. Nothing survives in the clay ground which we used to create brick and mortar for our castles, where lesser devils and damned souls toil.

It's tempting to open the window and reach out to grab a branch, to touch those green buds for myself. Then I remember I don't have wings to catch me if I fall. Hadn't Minnie mentioned if I went outside without clothes I'd be attacked? Mortals are known to be the violent sort–violent, vengeful, greedy, emotional, soft bellied beings but powerful in their own right.

I move away from the window and into Minnie's bedroom. There is a window in her room as well, the edge decorated with crystals: calcite, pink quartz, citrine, malachite, and topaz. They remind me of home. *Don't be so fucking soft*–nothing of this plane can compare to the Hells.

I find a closet, clothing hanging from the ceiling, some of the pieces similar to what Minnie wore this morning. I would never tell her, but she looked nice this morning. I like her better in clothing that clings to her body, giving me a taste of her thighs and ass. My cock twitches as I remember the array of paddles she keeps in this room as well, recalling the face she'd made when she caught me snooping. I consider how nice her thighs would look quivering, red with lashes.

Focus. This plane is getting to me. If I wanted a sopping cunt mewling over my cock, I could get that in the Hells, call on some lusting succubus to ride me in exchange for a place in my palace court. I'm not a King of the Hells or an Archdevil, but being a Prince has its perks.

I shut the closet, accepting that nothing of Minnie's will fit me. She's cute when she's flustered, but I have a feeling if I rip any of her things, I could forget about lounging on her couch. As I'm about to go back to reading, I spot a plush robe hanging off the back of Minnie's bedroom door. Holding it up against my body, the hem of the robe brushes my knee. This will work.

I slip on the robe, the sleeves barely passing my elbows and the tie around my waist torture in its tightness. Now modest in my clothing, I walk to the exit and step into the hallway where Minnie had argued with Alex. I shut the door to Minnie's apartment and feel a pair of eyes on me. I turn, and a figure jumps as soon as we make eye contact.

"Wow," a man chimes. He has brown skin like Minnie's but darker and much more golden. His hair is a silky black that brushes his shoulders, like mine but not curly. "Sorry," he chuckles. "Minerva really undersold you." I raise a brow, which the man must catch because he laughs again. "Don't take it personally; I'm sure she just doesn't want to catch feelings." He approaches, a familiar energy radiating off him. My forehead twitches as my brow lifts higher.

"Unless you want to catch feelings?" he asks. "I guess you are hanging around her apartment and whatnot. I'm Kamsa, by the way."

He holds his hand out, wanting me to... what, slap it? I have a hunch. Something about this man. "Know your place," I command from my stomach.

Kamsa tenses, taken aback for a moment before there is recognition in his eyes. "Now do my eyes deceive me?" He bows his head. "I didn't expect to come across a *devil* on this plane. I shouldn't pry but–"

"Minnie summoned me," I explain to the fellow devil.

No, there are no other devils on this plane; he has to be a succubus. Neither mortal nor devil but a breeding of the two, one that can freely travel between the planes. Bouncing back and forth is rather impractical for succubi. Often they stay in the mortal plane where they can easily feed.

Kamsa tilts his head. "Minnie? Sweet little Minerva? I didn't even realize she was a witch."

"All mortals are the same," I grumble. "How would you notice?"

Kamsa doesn't object, instead he keeps looking me up and down. I clear my throat. "Apologies," he says with a cough. "It's just been a long time since I've spoken to a proper devil. And never wearing a fuzzy bathrobe."

"Clearly it's been some time since you've been with your own kin if you're apologizing." Such a practice wasn't so much taboo as it was unheard of. "Let me guess, this isn't respectable attire?" It was hypothetical; I've gathered, based on how Kamsa is dressed and from the breeze on my ass, that this clothing isn't really meant for the outside world.

"Respectable? Maybe not, but you do make it work. You and Minerva aren't exclusive are you?" His lips and brow quirk in a way that makes me laugh.

"Lustful little succubus aren't you?"

Kamsa grins. "I won't deny it. I lack any shame. But..." He inches closer to me. "I am happy to be of your service. Be that service my body or..."

I cross my arms, recalling how I'd worked myself up back in Minnie's room. Using Kamsa as a fuck-toy feels like a waste. It's clear he's acclimated to this plane, something which I could benefit from.

"Tell me about the clothes on your back."

"WHAT DO you mean you two haven't slept together?" Kamsa, or Kas, as he prefers to be called, bemoans on the couch behind me.

As soon as I asked about clothes, Kas realized I had none, as if Minnie's robe didn't already give it away. He'd found some old clothes of his that covered me up the "acceptable amount," then brought me to a shop not too far from his lodgings.

An attendant measures my calves as I look back at Kas from one of the handful of mirrors surrounding me like acolytes. "I am not fueled by lust. Unlike you."

"You flatter me." Kas places a dainty hand over his chest. "But I don't get why she would bring you here other than a night of bliss. Or pain. I don't know what she's into."

I open my mouth to inform him pain is certainly something Minnie is interested in, then stop myself. I don't like the idea of Kas knowing that fact about Minnie. It could be that he's known her longer than I or it could be that I don't want him seducing her with the right combination of words. If there's one thing succubi are good at, it's stoking the fires of whatever sin they feed on. They whisper into the ears of warmongers or stroke the fragile egos of kings. I can see Kas promising Minerva he'd *be gentle unless she asked otherwise.*

"She summoned me to make a deal. Sign a contract."

"Ah." Kas nods. "That old song and dance. So what's the deal?"

"You think you're privy to my private affairs? I would never share the details of my contracts."

Looking through the mirror I see him raise a brow. I try to focus on myself, still becoming accustomed to this form. I was warned devils took on lesser forms when pulled into the mortal plane, but I didn't expect my form would be *so short.*

Kas keeps talking. "You *wouldn't* share, would you? Sounds like you've never made a pact with a mortal before."

I grind my teeth, feeling foolish for being so obvious.

Kas approaches me, clapping a golden hand onto my shoulder. "Isn't that sweet. Minerva will be your first!"

"I don't want a contract with her," I clarify. "Her demands are frivolous, and her voice is fucking annoying." Kas tilts his head as if he isn't convinced. "Power is something she lacks. She's a little stuck up witch. Why should I submit to her just because she summoned me here?"

"Tell you what. Fuck Minnie. I can gather my fellow succubi, and we can help you find the perfect candidate to sign a contract." The attendant from before walks back into the room with a rack full of clothes. I expect Kas to stall the conversation but he keeps going. "They'll know someone willing to give up their soul for the right price. Everyone has their price."

The attendant sets aside some clothes before turning to me. "Which would you like to try on first, sir?"

I look at the outfits, immediately drawn to one the exact shade of gray as burnt bone. I snap and point. "That one."

The clothing gives me a sharp, rectangular shape. A crisp white shirt that buttons all the way up to my collar suffocates me, and I'm wearing one too many layers. The attendant wraps another piece of fabric around my neck. My fists clench, and I want nothing more than to punch him as he ties the snake-like threads tight around my neck—some sort of mortal torture device.

"Hm, maybe without the red tie," Kas muses behind me. His hand rests atop his chin. "Too obvious, plus it clashes with your eyes."

"Get me out of this thing," I grumble. "I feel like I'm wearing an iron maiden."

Kas and the attendant look at each other, then the attendant looks at me. "Would you prefer I bring you something more business casual?"

"Yes," I bark, ready to try anything that isn't this heavy coat and cloth collar.

The attendant leaves, and Kas returns to my side. "We'll find you something, don't you worry."

"Why the fuck would I worry about that?"

"Come ooooon, isn't this fun? Aren't we building a beautiful friendship?"

I scoff. Since when do devils care about friends? "Let me guess, you would like to be something more than a lowly mortal-dwelling succubus?"

"Everyone wants to climb up the ladder."

I lift a brow.

"Mortal saying." He waves his hands dismissively. "I mean to say, of course I would want to become a fully fledged devil. It's in our nature to desire Kingship, to desire more. Don't tell me you are any different."

"I'm only a step below the Kings of Hell, remember that."

"Oh, I will." Kas grins. As the attendant returns with a stack of clothing in his arms, Kas adds, "I won't forget who's boss." Then he winks.

The attendant lifts up a shirt for me to look at, the fabric so thin that light filters through it. "Is this more what you would like, sir?"

I reach out and touch the colorful fabric, airy yet soft. Nowhere near as heavy or scratchy as the clothes I wear now.

"Finally."

CHAPTER SIX

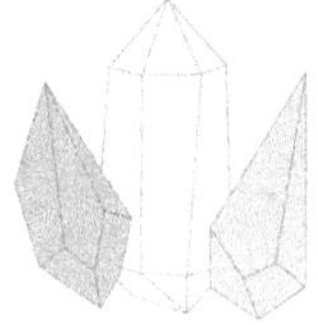

Amber's voice echoes through the stairwell. "I still can't believe how much you pay to live in this old place."

"It's not that crazy," I object. "And I like living in a historic building."

"No elevator is crazy. But anyway, what did you want to show me?" Amber asks, excitement in her voice.

"Um... why ruin the surprise?" I can hear the hesitation in my voice.

"You don't sound all that thrilled."

At least I'm setting expectations.

We make it to my door, and I drop my keys. With a huff I kneel down to pick them up, spending a little extra time down near the floor as I find the exact key I need. "Just remember, I'm showing this to you because I trust you more than anyone else on this Earth."

Amber tilts her head to the side, a few stray braids falling across her face. "Now you're making me nervous."

I open the door to my apartment and find... nothing. No one is on the couch or in the kitchen. The only sign that Rosier had been in the apartment is the bedsheet still laid out over the couch. I rush inside, figuring maybe he's snuck into my bedroom, either to nap on a proper bed or continue snooping through my drawers. Except he isn't in there, either.

"Huh," Amber remarks from the doorway. "So you did finally unpack. Is that the surprise?" She walks inside and sits down on the couch not even mentioning the bedsheet. "Well, your secret is safe with me."

"Wait, no, Amber–"

My dear friend is grinning ear to ear. "You don't have to be embarrassed. I know you want everyone to think you're perfect, but no one is going to judge you for taking three months to unpack."

"Uh, well, they shouldn't because how would they know that unless someone kept blabbing about my hovel to every-one?" I narrow my eyes, though I shouldn't care if people know I'm bad at moving. But it still bothers me.

I go to check the bathroom. Empty as well, but my bonnet is resting in the sink, which I do not appreciate.

"If you had just accepted help with moving," Amber calls to me from the couch. "I know you don't like people going through your stuff, but I'm pretty sure I was with you at some point or another when you bought all the things in this apartment."

Amber is being so casual, blissfully unaware of the situa-tion. Everything from last night's summoning had been consumed, from the chalk to the offering of earrings. Hopefully Alexander doesn't want those back because he isn't getting them. I'm not even sure where things go when they're consumed by a spell. Maybe to the plane of the summoned creature or perhaps the Veil.

I walk back to the living room, standing right in the spot

where the circle once was, my carpet and coffee table still pushed against the wall.

Amber's face falls into one of concern. "Minnie? When you said you had a secret to tell me..." She stands up, almost in slow motion, and places her hands on my shoulders. "Are you... Minnie, are you dying?"

"What?" Where did that come from? I guess we're both being a little strange today. "No, I'm not dying. Not as far as I know. It's worse than that."

"Worse than my best friend dying?" Amber knits her brows, her nose scrunching. "Not possible."

"You say that now..." I reach over to my bookshelf where the wand I made the night before still sits. I hold it with both hands, one hand on the base and the other covering the wand's crystal tip. "Amber... I cast a spell last night." She nods. "And I summoned..." It feels like I'm talking with a mouth full of peanut butter, the words sticking in my mouth. "I summoned something."

Amber's brows go from a tight V to an astonished O. She bats her thick eyelashes as if blinking could reset her brain. Finally, she purses her two-toned lips before speaking. "What did you summon, and where is it?"

"I don't know where it is."

Something snaps behind Amber's eyes. She opens her mouth then shuts it, her teeth clicking. She closes her eyes. "Minerva..."

If I shut my eyes, I would think I'm talking to her Mom right now.

"It gets worse."

"You know I thought you might say that..." She takes another slow breath, eyes still closed. "But hell if I know how it could get any worse."

"Funny... you mentioned Hell."

Amber's eyes open. "Minerva Holiday Morris, did you summon a devil? Of all things?" I must make some sort of face to confirm her suspicions because she groans before sucking her teeth. "*Why?* Why a devil? You couldn't summon anything else? You've wanted a cat for years! Summon a fairy cat or something."

"Because I need help."

"Help with what? Moving in?"

"Okay, you are really hung up on me being slow to unpack," I point out.

Amber shakes her head and ignores my comment. "I don't understand why you can't ask for help. You have to be drastic. Is my help not good enough?"

"Maybe..." I mutter to myself, but of course she hears.

"Minnie, I don't want to say something I'll regret later."

"How mature of you," I respond in a voice much too dry to not come off as an insult.

Amber's jaw tightens but then she takes a slow breath in from her nose. "Just... tell me. What's going on that made you think summoning a devil was..." She chews her lip a second before finishing with, "Appropriate."

"Because..." My voice becomes a whisper without me even realizing. It's like there's a curse on my tongue that prevents me from speaking on the matter, but I persist. "I know who my Father is."

I expect shock, some outcry of surprise, but Amber looks at me with what I hope isn't pity. She chews her lip again, but before I can ask, she gives me the answer I'm looking for. "When did you find out about Arthur le Fay?"

My eyes go wide. "When did *you* find out about Arthur le Fay? How long have you known he was my Father?"

"Only a month or so. The coven has a connection with this

couple in the city that helps out wayward supernaturals. One of them is a le Fay. He's concerned about you."

I immediately know who she's talking about because it's the very same person who informed me of the truth. His business card reads Lancelot le Fay. I had no interest in keeping the card or ever being in contact with him, but I remember that much. Now I find out he's asking around about me.

"What did you tell him?"

"Nothing," Amber assures me. "To be honest, we haven't even met, but I've spoken with his sponsor, and he says the guy isn't connected with the family at all anymore. But he knows how they operate. If you actually want some kind of closure, he's your man."

My nails dig into my palms. I should have reached out. No–I had no reason to trust him. Not then and not now. But Amber says he's safe, and I do trust her, not to mention being the next Supreme, she has even less reason to trust a le Fay.

"I don't want closure," I choke. "I want revenge."

"For what?"

"He wasn't around, Amber!"

"le Fay?" She shakes her head. "Yeah, he was too busy playing Scarface. Too busy using magic for selfish needs that put *all* witches in danger. All he wants is immortality. It's not about the money or instilling fear–well, that's gotta help his insane ego, but the point is, the guy uses blood magic, so he won't turn into some crusty, Merlin-lookin'-ass witch. Seriously, Minnie, isn't it best you weren't raised by him?"

She's missing the point. Arthur le Fay slept with my Mom, *cheated* on the Mother of his children, and left her like she was a rental. It had always bothered me that some man came into my Mom's life and left. For better or for worse I didn't care. If anyone deserved to be loved, it was Mom.

Now I find out he's got magic that could have saved her.

Blood magic. I would've given up my morals so she could've had a few more years. He needs to apologize. He needs to own up to what he did–what he didn't do.

My reply must not come fast enough because Amber speaks up. "Let's focus on the devil issue. We need to send him back to Hell."

"I agree." At least we're on the same page there. "How do we do that?"

"I... don't know."

I frown.

"Hey, you're the one who cast the spell."

She's right. It was such a silly thing to overlook, focusing on summoning without asking the all important question of how to send something *back*.

Amber rubs the back of her neck. "I'll reach out to the coven and see–"

"Don't tell them–"

Amber cuts me off, her voice sounding hurt. "I'm not trying to get you in trouble, Minnie. I'm just going to see if anyone knows how to send an entity back to its original plane. Though, it would help if I knew exactly what spell you used."

"I still remember the circle," I assure her. "I can draw it."

Amber scrunches her lips in thought. Leaving any trace of magic craft is a gamble, but so long as the page is destroyed promptly, it should work out fine. I can see in Amber's eyes she's thinking the same.

I rip a piece of paper from a notebook and grab a pencil and sketch out the summoning circle. Keeping my wrist steady I turn the paper to start the initial circle.

Amber chuckles, shaking her head a little. "Really gotta make sure that circle is perfect, huh?"

"I can't take complete credit for this spell, but I won't have it looking sloppy." I start drawing the symbols.

"Never sloppy. Always near perfect." I hand her the paper, and she looks at it, squinting. "Yup. Way too complicated for me." She folds it up and slips it in her pocket.

"I'll find him," I assure her. "He's not very pleasant, so I won't subject you to him."

"Pleasant and devil don't really seem like they'd go together." Amber pulls me into a hug. "I'm glad you told me."

My cheek rests against her shoulder. "I wish I'd told you sooner."

If I told Amber from the start, there wouldn't be a devil on the loose right now causing who knows what sort of havoc.

She releases me from the hug and walks to the front door. Her hand is on the doorknob. "I wish you had, too."

As she leaves, I remember I promised her dinner, but she's gone before I can remind her.

CHAPTER SEVEN

ROSIER

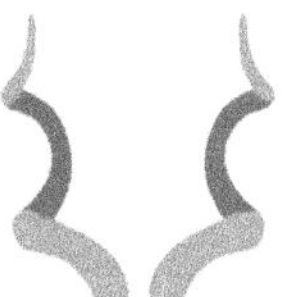

"I can't believe you didn't buy *one* suit," Kas whines. A bag hangs from his wrist.

"I'd rather fall into the most frigid pit of Hell than wear that monkey suit," I retort.

Kas continues to moan. "Also hate that you've picked up that colloquialism."

Another man in the shop had called the heavy clothing a monkey suit. The phrase makes Kas' face scrunch as if in pain, which I quite like.

The clothing I purchased is much lighter–linen, the attendants called it–that hangs loosely from my legs and torso. Vibrant colors are ample in the Hells, but plants not at all. I chose clothes with bold colors and designs featuring flowers and plants. The shirts are a nice mix of familiar and new.

"You look like you're going on vacation," Kas scoffs.

"Perhaps I am..."

Without a contract I can do as I please. Explore the mortal plane without answering the whims of a mortal. I could see the ruins of cities, touch the salt of the ocean shore, find out what the fuck a coconut is. More than that, I could be the first devil to really *live* amongst mortals. Then I'll return to Hell, and the Kings and Archdevils will flock to me, a herald of the moral plane.

There's a shrill sound down an alleyway as we walk past.

Kas keeps talking. "Well, as I promised, I'll find you some other mortal to make a contract with. Maybe even several!"

The high pitch sound rings out again, and I stop walking.

"Trust me," Kas insists. "You'll get contracts."

I'm much too interested in the sound to listen to Kas babble on. I walk down the alleyway.

"Rosier? Um, Prince?" Kas calls my name, not yet following.

The sound becomes louder and cries again and again. Stepping past a foul smelling metal box, I find the source of the noise, a creature about the size of an imp, curled up in a ball and yelping. Long white whiskers sprout along its nose, standing out against the creature's fur, which is the color of darkness. Green eyes, even more vibrant than Minnie's but with slits for pupils, look up at me.

I bend down to pick it up, and the creature hisses.

"Rosier!" Kas shouts, finally following me into the alley.

I reach for the creature again, this time grabbing it by the scruff of its neck, like one would a newborn hellhound.

"What are you–ew," Kas deadpans. "Dumpster cat."

"*This* is a cat?"

Kas furrows his brows, still looking at the creature like it might suddenly catch fire and burn us both. "Um, yeah, it's a stray cat."

"I've read about cats..."

I cup the cat's underside, still holding onto its scruff, and find a crooked tail. Cats are notable witch familiars, known to be fierce but poised. The cat shows me its fangs. I can see the fierceness plainly, though I fail to see the elegance that makes these creatures gods in some mortals' eyes.

"You don't think this one belongs to a witch do you?"

"I think it's pretty safe to say if it's eating trash, it doesn't belong to anyone. Including you."

Kas reaches forward, and I bring the cat close to my chest. I shoot him a glare and he shivers, his nature being to submit to my whims.

"Our building doesn't allow pets!" he says, as if that means anything to me.

Now resting against my chest, the cat starts to growl. No, not a growl. It's more inviting, but it does make the creature's whole body vibrate. The animal nudges its cheek into my chest, looking content with its shut eyes. Still holding the creature, I start to walk out of the alleyway. Kas mumbles, but he follows without another word.

As we approach the apartment, I'm met with a familiar head of curls. "You!" Minnie exclaims as soon as we make eye contact. That beguiling pout appears on her lips, and she marches up to me. "Do *not* run off like that!" She huffs. "I've been running up and down the building looking for you."

Her cheeks do look a little flushed, making the specks of brown across her nose and cheeks more noticeable.

There's a pause before she crosses her arms over her chest. "Well?"

"Well, what?"

She frowns. "Well... anything, *Rosie!*"

Kas snickers, then clears his throat. "Hate to ruin this cute little spat," he says as he steps between us, "but it's my fault. I offered to take him clothes shopping."

"I can see that." Minnie looks me up and down. "You look like you're going to the beach."

"I'm not sure I like your custom of wearing clothes," I confess.

The cat in my arms lets out a little scream. I scratch at it chin with my pointer finger, and Minnie's expression softens.

"Is that..." She reaches for the cat, scratching between its ears. The creature starts to rumble against my chest again.

"It's a dumpster cat, Minerva," Kas interjects. I glare at him. Despite this, he carries on, only looking at Minnie. "It's a trash cat from the garbage."

"Don't be mean to him!" Minnie covers the creature's ears. "Her? Does it have a name?"

Kas groans. "You can't be serious..."

We ignore Kas. "I haven't chosen a name yet. Maybe..." I think about the creature's eyes. "Leaf?" Kas groans louder. "Kamsa says pets aren't allowed in the building."

"Oh, right..." Minnie replies, though she's still pawing at the cat. "Well, the landlord doesn't come by that often. Though hiding the cat stuff will be a pain."

"Do you two hear yourselves?" Kas asks, and finally, he seems to gather Minnie's attention. "I never thought of you as impulsive, Minerva."

"*Impulsive?*" She repeats the word back to him like it's an insult. "Says the guy who bought some random man a bunch of clothes."

Kas places a hand on his chest, his voice dramatic and breathy. "I did that out of the goodness of my heart. Or... maybe it was the *devil* in me that did it." He winks.

Minnie looks back and forth between us, her eyes narrowing. "Did you two make some sort of contract?"

"Not necessary," I tell her. "Kas will do what I say regardless."

"Um, rude, and not wholly true. You can't bully me into everything." He scoffs before muttering, "Just most things."

Minnie and I look at each other as I say, "Kas, go buy this creature everything it needs to thrive in Minerva's apartment."

"Are you *fucking* serious?"

I don't bother to turn and meet Kas' gaze, only looking at my new companions: Minnie and Leaf. "Now."

Kas aggressively hands off the bag to Minerva. "Fine! *Fine!* Whatever you say *Rosie.*"

It's only when I hear the name on Kas' tongue that I realize how much I hate it. "Do not–"

But he's already waking away.

"HOLD STILL." I have Leaf by the scruff in Minnie's sink, the creature writhing and crying out like I'm torturing him. My fingers are covered in bubbles as I scratch under his chin. The water in the sink reminds me of the rivers of Hell it's so murky.

Minnie stands next to me holding a cloth, her lips taut with concern. "Be careful."

As she says it, Leaf claws at my knuckle. Past the froth of soap, I can't tell if he's broken the skin, but the burning feeling tells me it's not pretty. I give the beast one last rinse before handing him to Minnie, who wraps him in the cloth, still crying. Washing off my own hands, I see the cut plainly now, an inch long gash between the ridges of my knuckles. I touch it, and it stings like acid.

"I've always wanted a cat," Minnie admits.

All I can see is Leaf's wide green eyes in a black void. He's no longer struggling, and I'm not sure if he's capable of movement.

"My Gramps hated them," she continues. "Said they brought nothing but death and destruction." Minnie purses her lips, something clearly on her mind since we met her outside.

Yet she hadn't said anything beyond cooing over Leaf. "You like cats?"

"I've only ever read about them as witches' familiars. Our histories aren't so interested in the fauna and flora of the mortal realm. Though, seeing it in person, I wish that were different."

Minnie's brows raise, and she cocks her head. "That's a very sensitive sentiment. Are you sure you're a devil?" Her voice is so soft, like the strumming of a harp. I'm used to that question being asked in rasping, judgmental tones.

"You're the one who summoned me," I remind her for the second night in a row.

Minnie makes a *tsk* sound and mutters, "Not my brightest idea..."

She starts chewing at her bottom lip. I could ask her what was on her mind. But despite her earlier comment, I am in fact infernal, and torture, no matter how small or internal, will always be amusing. Minnie's self-inflicted turmoil, her chewed lip and distant gaze, is a joy to watch.

She sets Leaf down and frees him but continues to rub his body with the cloth. "So this contract... Explain to me what you get out of it?"

There it is. "If you sign a contract with me, your mortal soul belongs to me."

"That's all, huh? So you're like a soul lawyer? Making sure I get my dues in exchange for my soul?"

Leaf nudges her hand.

"That implies our contracts are fair and just," I say.

Minnie blinks.

Leaf comes to me, rubbing my legs. I chuckle and reach down to run my hand along his back. "Tell me, what is a fair trade for someone's soul?" I pause. "Make a deal with me, and when you die, you won't pass to the Veil. Your soul will remain in Hell with me for an eternity, until I eventually retire to the Veil myself."

"I didn't realize devils die."

"All things die, Minerva. The Veil awaits us all. Unless you somehow fail to cross over and become a demon." I pick up Leaf ,who makes a little *murp* sound but does not otherwise struggle. "But then even demons can be banished–exorcized, I think you mortals call it."

Minnie shakes her head before joining me on the floor. "I don't care if my soul is damned to Hell," she says, ignorant of what that entails. "Maybe I should, but I don't." Her head tilts. "I mean, Hell isn't that bad, right?"

"For me? Or for you? The torturer and the tortured."

I hold Leaf in my arms like a little babe, which he does not appreciate, quickly flipping over in my arms and falling back to the floor. He struts over to Minnie's lap.

"You'd let me suffer in Hell?" she asks as Leaf places his paws on her stomach and nudges her chest, his cheek rubbing against her breasts. Minnie scratches his head, encouraging him. "Well?" she pushes.

My jaw is tight. "Hell is not a paradise..."

I'm fixated on Leaf, who tries successfully to climb Minnie's chest. Minnie squeaks as he does so. He starts to lick her cheek with that scratchy tongue of his, and Minnie giggles.

"You will suffer," I tell her gravely, but she is too enamored with Leaf to care.

"Wow," Minnie deadpans. "You *are* sensitive. Why do you care what happens to my soul?"

"I care about Leaf's shits more than I care about your soul," I assure her. "An eternity from now, I don't want to listen to you bitch and whine about our deal despite me warning you. Eternity is a lot longer than your mortal life."

"I know what an eternity is," she bites back.

"I know that's not true." I point to her. "Mortal." Then back at me. "Eternal."

"If we're all going to die, what does it matter?"

"I just said I don't need to hear you bitch and moan–"

"Alright!" She throws her hands up, dropping Leaf, who darts around the living room like he's frightened. "I get it! I mean nothing to you, and I'm annoying. Happy?"

Leaf runs back into the kitchen and latches onto my leg, clawing and biting at it. "Why the fuck would I be happy?"

Minnie storms off and I follow her, Leaf still managing to cling to my leg as I walk, only for Minnie to step into her bedroom and slam the door in my face. Again, Leaf bounces around, frightened by the noise. Though the way he bounces onto the couch, looking around the room with bulging green eyes like he's about to be ambushed, only to leap again and run about, makes me wonder if this is his nature.

CHAPTER EIGHT

MINNIE

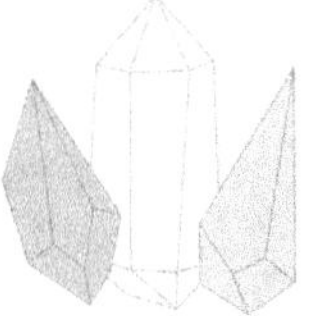

Unlike the night before, I managed to sleep. A sleep so solid, I almost missed my alarm, because of course, everything has to go wrong for me this week. I grab a random outfit, trying to get out the door as quickly as possible, and wonder what will be the resolution to this mess I've made.

Would Rosier refuse to make a contract with me and go back to Hell like nothing had happened? If he did, would Amber forgive me? I say "forgive," but nothing I've done has affected her personally. All my mistakes are only biting *me* in the butt.

Dressed in a dark blue jumpsuit, I leave my bedroom. Rosier is still asleep with Leaf curled up on his stomach. I pause, recognizing then that I've let a devil adopt a random cat. I've summoned myself the worst roommate imaginable, though so far the cat is the best part of this mess.

I decide I'll raid the cereal bar at work for breakfast. I brush my teeth and pull my curls up to the top of my head, smoothing out the edges with gel. With one last look in the mirror, I huff and go to leave.

Only to find Rosier awake and sitting at the kitchen counter.

"I'm leaving," I tell him as I grab my tote bag.

"You sound ecstatic."

"Catching on to human emotions I see." I start for the door, but Rosier gets up and manages to slam the door shut with his hand. Again.

Looking up at him, I pretend like I have the components available to make his big handsome head explode. As if I even know what I would need for a spell like that. Rosier tries to match my expression. I move to grab his wrist like the day before, but he grabs me instead, pinning me against the door. I keep my hardened expression despite feeling blood rush to my face.

"Your clothing is atrocious. Covering your body up in shame every damned day."

"And what of it?" I glare. "*Prince?*"

He falters, and I manage to slip one hand out of his grasp, enough to end this little game of his. He huffs and releases my other wrist before pushing himself off the door.

"If I come home, and your cat has peed on *anything*," I warn, "I'm kicking you both out to the dumpsters."

I flee before he can respond.

Kamsa catches me in the hallway. "Minerva–"

I groan without thinking, Kamsa giving me a little *are-you-serious* head tilt. "Sorry, sorry... What is it?"

"I wanted to apologize."

"Really?"

"No," he admits. "But you look like you need someone to say sorry about something."

How am I meant to respond to that? I settle on a deadpan, "Thanks. I gotta get to work. We can talk, if you want to talk, later, okay?"

He nods and lets me go on my way, which is a much kinder gesture than his weird not-apology.

Sitting on the bus, I pull out my e-reader like I do every commute. I resisted getting one of these for the longest time. I've always preferred physical books: the feeling of paper, getting to see my collection on the shelf, drawing little hearts next to my favorite passages. I thought I could handle reading my books in public; it's not like I'm the only woman in the world who reads romance. But one day in grad school, when I was commuting to campus, this guy would not leave me alone. He kept asking about my cowboy romance and if I liked riding cowgirl. Original.

After that, I decided it was less of a headache to buy books digitally and keep my taste a secret. I still buy physical books, of course. Nothing will beat holding a well loved book. But I can read a lot more stuff when I'm not so concerned with space on my bookshelf. Plus my e-reader always tells me what else the author has written. I could literally read forever with this thing, and if it weren't for my job, I probably would read romances from dusk till dawn, day after day, year after year.

Everything always works out in romance novels. The miscommunications are neatly tied up, or in the end, the leads speak their feelings plainly. There's a nice manor for them to retire to instead of a one bedroom apartment. Even if I was in a romance book right now, I'd probably be one of the sniveling ladies who sits about waiting for someone to fix them. I never understood the appeal of such a heroine 'til now.

Who doesn't want to be fixed? Just a little...

At least at work I can be busy: check emails, grab bad coffee, check more emails, wish the coffee tasted better. I know there's money in this company, so why is the coffee both too bitter and too watered down? As I shuffle into a conference room holding a styrofoam cup, I tell myself I'll use my lunch break to go out, buy an overpriced latte and a new book for the bus ride home.

Do I deserve it? I opt not to answer my own question.

One of my coworkers attempts small talk. "Any plans this weekend, Minerva?"

I lean back in my chair. *Hoping to kick out a devil; you know, the usual.* "Me and whatever book I decide to pick up."

"Oh, how exciting!"

He's not trying to be patronizing, I remind myself. I sip at my coffee, hoping I'll choke on it and get sent home.

"I'm going to this gala hosted by the le Fays."

So much for *hoping* I'd choke. As soon as that name comes out his mouth, I inadvertently gasp, the lukewarm coffee filling my windpipe. I cough, and everyone in the room looks at me like I'm doing a magic trick.

Someone pats me on the back. "I'm fine," I gag. "Just–down the wrong pipe." I swallow nothing, trying to push down the tightness in my throat. "You were saying?" I ask, my voice straining.

"It's this art gala being hosted by Guine le Fay. She throws one every year to raise money for some of the city's galleries and museums."

"Big philanthropist?" I ask, hoping he doesn't notice me scowling.

"Very much so. I wouldn't be surprised if MOCAD names a gallery after her–or at least a plaque."

An art gallery funded by literal blood money.

I fail to pay attention in the meeting. I don't think about what coffee shop or bookstore I'll hit up for lunch. Over and over my mind taunts: *Guine le Fay, philanthropist; Guine le Fay, kindly philanthropist...* Which turns into: *Arthur le Fay funds the arts in blood; Arthur le Fay funds the arts in fucking blood.*

When the meeting ends, I'm the first out of the room. I grab my tote bag from my desk and decide to take an early lunch. I open up my phone, my mind too hazy with hate to remember what options are even in the area. There's a text from Amber.

> Hey could you stop by the shop today?
> Whenever you're free.

> I'm free now.

> Oh shit, really? Aren't you at work?

> Not anymore I'm not.

I grab the bus that will take me to Lucky Witch and try mindlessly scrolling on my phone. But I keep opening up my text conversations with Amber, wishing she'd stuck around yesterday, stayed for dinner or helped me find Rosier. She would have gotten a kick out of Leaf. Or maybe she would have rolled her eyes and called me impulsive like Kamsa. But at least she would have been there.

At the shop, I take a second to appreciate the sound of the silver bell tied to the door. Silver is a protective metal, especially against other supernaturals. Maybe I should buy a little silver bell for Leaf and see how it would affect Rosier.

I take a deep breath, smelling sandalwood and agarwood burning. "I'm here," I announce.

Amber, standing behind the counter, quirks her brow. "Do we need to make this quick?"

"Nope. I don't think I'm going back to work today."

"You've never played hooky a day in your life. Not in high school, not in middle school..."

"Well, that changes today." I set my tote bag down on the floor under the front counter. "So, what did you find out?"

"It's been less than twenty-four hours, so jack shit." She

plays with one of her pastel braids, running her fingers along it as if trying to smooth it down. She's not looking at me.

"Well, you found something out, right?"

"I think it's time I tell you the truth, even if that's not what your Mom wanted."

The sweet smell and comforting familiarity of the shop is gone, dwarfed by this secret I didn't know about 'til this moment. Something my Mom didn't want me to know... Something *other* than who my Father is.

"Minnie, your family is cursed."

It feels like Amber is opening a trap door underneath me.

"That's... that's why there's no one around to teach you magic. Your family is cursed to die young."

When big announcements like that are made, everyone pretends like the world stops, like the universe is kind enough to give you a second to breathe. A moment to process. In reality, after dropping a bomb like that, the world begins to move very, very fast.

"Who cursed us?" I demand.

"It was centuries ago, Minnie. Anyone who would know is dead, so I can't help you there."

"Bullshit." I slam my hands on the counter, "Your mom must know something!"

"I've asked. Your Grandmother and mine tried to find a way to break it, but they couldn't. Without knowing who cast it or why it makes it near impossible to change anything."

No. It hit me then how futile hope is. *No, no, no.* My Mom died in her late thirties. Same as my Grandmother. As far as I know, I have no other family on my maternal side. No other witches to mentor me. Because they're all gone. Dead before even reaching middle age.

And *I'm* not going to reach middle age, either. I'm going to die, like everyone does–like all things do, according to Rosier.

But I'll die young. I'll die in less than ten years. If I had a child, I wouldn't ever see them become an adult. I could never have some fancy title at my job because I would never be able to get the years under my belt. What if I died before Gramps? It was unlikely, but not impossible. I'd already abandoned him once, and I'm doomed to abandon him again.

"Minnie, Minnie!" Amber speaks my name, trying to shake me out of my thoughts. She comes out from behind the counter and starts rubbing my back in circles. "Take breaths with me, okay?" She takes a long, deep inhale and a slow exhale.

I follow her lead, opening my mouth to take a heavy breath, my stomach and chest expanding. I exhale, then begin again, 'til I can finally speak. "This is too much..."

"I know," Amber agrees.. "I know it's a lot, and I'm sorry. Your Mom–"

I shake my head violently, not ready to think about Mom's involvement in all of this. If she knew, and she didn't tell me... or was it better if she didn't know? Did she even remember the family curse while she was dying?

My body moves faster than my thoughts as I finally manage to snatch my bag off the floor. I don't know if Amber is following me, but I don't want her to. I want her to watch me walk out the door, just like she did yesterday.

The bell on the door chimes as I push through the exit, rushing past another person trying to enter the store. As I stomp down the street I can hear my name in the distance.

"Minerva? Minerva!"

My short legs can only carry me so quickly down the street. Meanwhile, my vision becomes blurry as hot tears fill my eyes. I finally give in and duck into an alleyway, breaking into a sob the second I'm out of view of the sidewalk.

The tears come and then the snot. No amount of sniffling or blinking slows their crawl down my cheeks and lips. Using the back of my hand, I tried to wipe away the evidence, all while gasping for air, sounding like a bullfrog croaking.

Again, I hear my name at the mouth of the alleyway.

"Go away!" I sound like a teenager locked away in her room.

"Minerva, I... Hey I'm sorry." The voice isn't familiar to me. "I didn't think seeing me would upset you so much."

I turn, the sight of blond hair and green eyes shocking the sadness right out of me–Lancelot. The man who revealed my parentage. My half-brother. Besides our green eyes, we look nothing alike, him with dirty blonde hair perfectly styled to look a touch messy and pale skin free of freckles or any other blemishes. The only feature of his I could really call ugly is his brows, which are a shade darker than his hair and as thick as my thumb. He wears an oversized blue coat, and the fabric makes me think it's expensive.

"I know I'm the last person you want to see right now–"

I cut him off. "This isn't about you." A weak sniffle makes me pause. "If you wanted to catch me all worked up over you and your family, you should have found me earlier."

"Well I'm glad it's not me making you cry." He takes a step towards me.

I lash out. "My family is cursed, and I'm going to die young. I just found out. Still glad?"

"O-oh." Lancelot is so taken aback, I might as well have slapped him. "I'm... Shit, I'm so sorry, Minerva." He runs his fingers through his hair. "I came to the shop so we could talk."

"We don't have anything to talk about."

I start to walk back to the sidewalk, this alleyway no longer my private crying quarters. Lancelot doesn't stop me but he does follow me up the street.

"Okay, okay, so maybe *we* don't have anything to talk about, but I want to talk to you."

I lock my eyes on the horizon. "Sounds like a you problem."

"Yeah what else is new," he scoffs. "Can I at least give you my number? If you ever want to talk?"

"Talk about what, exactly?" I have no idea why he wants to act like we mean anything to each other.

"Magic? Books? How much we hate our dad."

That gets me to stop walking. "*Our* dad? I don't know him."

"And I wish I didn't know him. See?" An over the top smile spreads across his face. "We're already bonding." His expression settles into something less clownish. "I think, when you're ready, we could actually talk about a lot of things. But I'm not going to force you."

The revelation that my life will be cut short due to no fault of my own had completely blasted away my anger towards the le Fays, but the rubble remains. I sigh, crossing my arms over my chest. "It was really messed up for you to just show up at my house."

"The first time? Or the second time?"

"Give me your number." Lancelot perks up like I've offered him a little treat. I hand him my phone and let him type in his number. Holding my phone, I notice the name he's listed his number under. "Lance?"

"What? You think I want to be called Lance-a-fucking-lot?"

I snort. "It's pretty corny."

"It's terrible. Better than being named after dad, but..."

The mention of Arthur le Fay takes the wind out of our sails. Not to mention I'm still cursed. Which I will absolutely wallow about for at least the rest of the day. I still owe myself a new book. Maybe I'll get a nice pastry, too.

"I'll text you," I tell Lance. I'm not sure if I mean it, but he nods. "I need some time."

"We've got time."

"*You've* got time," I correct him. "Me? I've got half a life to live. So I'm going to be selfish with that time."

A half smile pulls at Lance's lips, and with that, he turns around and leaves.

Lancelot le Fay. What an absolutely atrocious name.

CHAPTER NINE

ROSIER

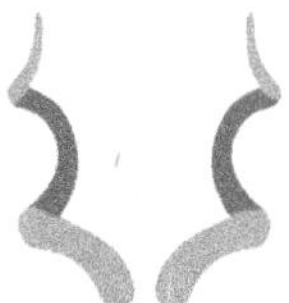

READING IS A LOT HARDER WITH A LITTLE HELLCAT ALWAYS biting at my fingers. I'm about a hundred pages into another one of Minnie's books when Leaf decides to bite my hand. It doesn't hurt, at first, then it starts to feel like dirks being shoved between my knuckle bones.

"Enough," I say, grabbing him by the scruff. He lets out a little *murp* as I place him back down on the floor... only for him to hop right back onto my chest and attempt to bite my wrist. "Quit it, foul beast!"

There's a knock at the door, followed by Kas' voice. "Rosie!" he sings. "I hear you in there. Come out, come out."

Two obnoxious little creatures. Must be a special kind of morning.

I get up off the couch and go to the door. Kas is standing there with a smirk. "I have something—okay, wow, you're still naked."

"Do I need to be dressed when in my own home?"

"No, no." He shakes his head. "Sorry, it's been a while since I've spent time with devils. I sort of forgot the customs."

I raise a brow but motion with my head for Kas to come inside. He follows, Leaf running up to greet him with a battle cry.

"Explain to me how you can forget customs." I start to riffle through the bags of clothes Kas bought me yesterday, trying to find the undergarments that are supposed to be put on first.

"Well, I wasn't born in Hells, you know. Most succubi aren't. And to be honest, I've spent very little time in the Hells. I prefer this plane."

"Of course you do; there's more energy to feed off of. But don't you have some sort of master?" Besides me, of course.

Kas snorts. "No. I'm sure you'll be surprised to hear devils don't really care much about their half-breed offspring."

In fact, I know it all too well, but still, I push back. "That's not entirely true. I've met succubi in Hell who are part of their parents' entourages."

"Good for them, but most of us are nurtured by humans." Kas walks over to the couch and sits down, noticing the book I'd been reading. "*Highlander Heroine?* You like white guys in kilts?"

"It's Minnie's book."

"Oh, she definitely likes white guys, so that makes sense."

My lips contort as I recall that Alex person. Minnie's ex-something. It shouldn't bother me that she's had lovers–I've had plenty. Then again, lover means something different in the Hells than it does here. No one ever declares their love for one another where I'm from; they only declare unions to strengthen their titles and expand their lands. I don't believe devils can feel love. We can't feel empathy or pity. That's what puts us above humans, what separates us from the weeping compassion of the angels.

Regardless, I want Alex's head on a fucking pike.

Not that I'll ever see him again. Minnie seems pretty happy

with him staying the fuck away, and I'm glad to see him gone. Which is troubling because why do I care?

After I dress myself, I try to pull Kas' attention from the book he's skimming. "Now that I look like a court jester, what did you want to talk to me about?"

Kas is muttering about the lack of illustrations.

"Kas," I hiss.

He stands immediately, his cool demeanor slipping. "S-sorry." He clears his throat. "I was just looking for the good stuff." He tosses the book aside before turning around on the couch to look at me. "I have some people I want you to meet."

KAS BRINGS me to a brick building with the words *Industry Lounge* written in a pink tubing across the top. Inside the building, the brick motif continues, but the ceiling is covered with overlapping draping fabric, creating an interesting sort of tapestry. The place is pretty open, with a bar on one side and couch-like seating on the other. But what catches my attention is the circle of chairs and their occupants in the center of the room.

I frown and look at Kas. "Is this meeting about me?"

He reaches up and claps a hand onto my shoulder. "Rosier, these are some of the other succubi I know." Everyone lifts their heads at that, except for a white girl with long, inky black hair, who doesn't look up from her phone. "Everyone, this is Rosier, a *Prince* of the Hells."

"He doesn't look so tough," a person with knotted hair breathes, unimpressed. A succubus wearing a monkey-suit like the one I tried on yesterday rolls his eyes.

"Where is Seira?" Kas asked.

Monkey-suit chuckles, "She's busy. Got some vampire

wrapped around her little finger. Apparently he's on the council and everything."

"Jeeeealooous," the girl with the phone drones. She drops the phone in a plush looking purse before reaching in and grabbing another, different phone. She taps at the screen and continues to bitch. "I don't get why an envy succubus wants a sugar daddy."

"I'd like a sugar daddy," the person with ratty hair and a stained outfit chimes in. "Less work you know. They give you food, give you clothes; they give and give, and you don't have to do shit."

"Open your legs," Kas shrugs. "But I see that as a bonus."

I pinch the bridge of my nose, my face scrunching. "Hate to stop this *illuminating* conversation, but what is going on?"

"I just thought," Kas says, "since you're a hellish hot shot, we could help you, help us."

"Spread the wealth," the girl with the phone says, still not looking up.

"Explain this to me plainly," I command. "Quickly."

The room goes quiet.

"Let me say it another way then." My voice rumbles. "Why would I waste my time with a bunch of lowly succubi? None of you look all that impressive. Most of you look worse than the cat I pulled out of the garbage yesterday. One of you didn't even bother to show up!"

"Why don't we start with introductions," Kas interjects. "I'm Kamsa, a succubus of lust."

"This is asinine." My words stop nothing.

"Tim Leeds," the man in a suit says. "My vice is pride." His skin tone reminds me of Minnie, though his hair is black and cropped short.

They skip over the individual who might as well have crawled out of the same dumpster as Leaf.

With a sigh, the girl with the phone finally drops the object in her purse and introduces herself. "Chanel Hugo, and I'm a greed succubus or whatever."

"Let me guess," I turn to the person who still hasn't spoken, who looked the least put together. "You're apathy? The often forgotten vice?"

They yawned, "Yeah, name's Moniz."

"I don't care."

I turn to leave, but Kas blocks my exit. "Hey, hey, hey—remember who bought the clothes on your back."

"If you want them back..." I tug at one of the buttons on my shirt, but don't move to take the garment fully off. "I'm trying to understand your plan here. I show you lot some *charity*." I look back over my shoulder. "And what? I get a bunch of deadbeat succubi at my beck and call?" I need to remind them where they stand. Literally. "Stand up!" I order all of them, and they do so like soldiers.

"The fuck!" Chanel shrieks, her purse falling from her lap and spilling onto the floor. Moniz gets up but flops back down into the chair almost immediately. I guess I can't command them out of their nature.

I turn back to Kas, crossing my arms over my chest . He lifts a finger, as if telling me to stop. "If you would let me explain. We know all the big sinners of the city. *I* figured—" Kas seems really proud of this plan I haven't agreed to yet. "—that we could introduce you to these people and *you* could make contracts with them. Really it's much more of a win for you than for us."

"But," Tim presses, "we do expect you to remember who made your connections. Give us a little credit. Maybe a place to stay if we ever want to visit Hell."

I'd rather have Leaf claw my eyes out than admit it aloud, but it's not a terrible idea. Had I any interest in making contracts, it would be an efficient way to collect as many souls as possible while on borrowed time. Minnie has already threatened to send me back–and she's both smart enough and stubborn enough to do so in time.

"I'm not going to make a deal with just anyone," I caution the group. "After all, their souls will forever be intertwined with mine. I've already declined one contract."

Kas lifts a brow. "I thought that whole denying Minerva's contract thing was foreplay?"

"Whose Minerva?" Chanel and Moniz chime, though Chanel, clearly, sounds much more interested than Moniz.

"I don't have to explain anything to you," I remind Kas.

"You don't," he agrees. "I'm just going to make assumptions, then. Like that you don't want poor Minerva's mortal soul being trapped in Hell."

The other succubi all *oooh* at different frequencies, like an infernal choir.

I've let this scummy little succubus get too comfortable with me. My father said this would happen, that even a pinch of mercy would be my downfall. This is hardly the audience to bring forth my ruin, but I still can't have them seeing me as one of them.

"Bite your tongues." The song is cut short. "Bite harder. Till you bleed." My focus now is on Kas, his mouth thin and his expression uncomfortable.

"I will deny any contracts I please. I won't be goaded by a bunch of low ranking succubi." I leave.

Tim manages to speak past his tongue. "Tho thath it?"

Kas follows me, making an array of noises with his closed mouth.

I groan, "Speak."

He opens his mouth and sounds more ridiculous than usual. "Well that was shit."

"A misstep on your part. Go jerk off and cry about it."

"Why won't you sign a contract with Minerva? Truly?"

I start walking faster, but Kas manages to keep up with my stride, the whole time staring at me like an eerie portrait.

"I told you. She bores me. She wants revenge." I scoff. "No other caveats, just revenge against a man she's never even met."

Kas' head tilts thoughtfully. "Here I thought you were some young gung ho Prince." I almost inform him that I have no idea what he's talking about. Instead I let him keep talking. "But you're pretty passive."

I grab him by his collar so he stops walking, then box him up against a nearby wall.

"Listen—if you can stop those prancing thoughts of yours and fucking listen." I lean down, dropping my voice to a hissing whisper. "Do not mistake my approach for kindness. Unlike you, I'm not only fueled by lust—trying to crawl back into the cunt that bore me. I don't need to take and take until taking loses all meaning. My pride can't be bruised with one act of denial. There is no room in my plans for other's ire, and I will not laze about waiting for opportunities to come. I am a Prince, and I am all of the best of sin. I will take what *I want* and make it *mine* on my own terms. You lot are fodder. Half of what I am, quite literally."

I start to walk away, Kas sputtering behind me.

As I step out the door, I call over my shoulder, "Let's go. Leaf needs company."

CHAPTER TEN

MINNIE

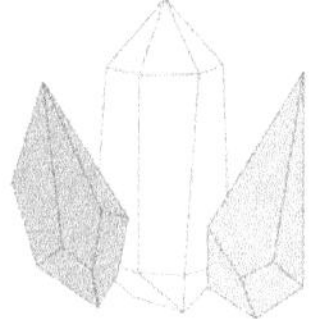

As the bus takes me further and further away from Lucky Witch, I feel more and more helpless. Cursed by long dead witches, Amber and I at odds, my half-brother so desperate for a relationship I can't comprehend him wanting, and a devil who refuses to make a deal with me. Sure, Rosier is here because I summoned him, and Lance seems nice enough, but I'm not sure what to even do with a brother. I shouldn't be too upset with Amber. Of course, she knows things I don't; it comes with the territory of being the daughter of the Supreme. And I can't fault her for following my dead mom's wishes. Maybe, if we could stop storming off on each other, we could solve the curse together.

The bus stops a few blocks from my apartment, and I hop out. I wonder if Rosier is still sitting around naked. He better be. Well, the naked part I could go without, even if he's nice to look at. But if I get back to the apartment and he's gone again, I don't know what I'll do. Chain him to the couch or something, but I picture him turning that into a sex thing. He was pretty keen to sleep with me that first night.

As I fiddle with my keys I keep considering Rosier wrapped in chains, trapped on his knees with his hands behind his back, looking up at me with rage and desire. I drop my keys for the second day in a row and roll my head back to huff.

As I step into my apartment, a chirping meow greets me. Leaf struts over, his tail twitching happily. "Well if you're looking for attention, then Rosie probably isn't here."

I frown, and Leaf meows again. I can't be mad at him. I get down on my knees and scratch between his ears. Sure he's a dumpster cat, but he's *my* dumpster cat. Er, Rosier's dumpster cat... our dumpster cat.

There's no point in trying to hunt Rosier down when he could literally be anywhere–especially when he's got Kas. Plus, it's nice to pretend like Rosier isn't my responsibility, my mistake. I grab a random book off my shelf and settle on the couch. Leaf joins me, climbing right into my lap and curling up into a perfect little black ball. It's hard to focus on my book when he's being so cute.

I'm not nervous about anything till the sun is gone, and in an instant, the wall I put up in my attempt to be unbothered comes tumbling down. "Screw this–" I grumble and get up off the couch, ready to go out into the night and find a certain devil. But as soon as my hand is on the door, Leaf starts howling. "Oh, right, dinner."

Right as I turn, the door to my apartment opens and hits me in the butt, causing me to fall forward. Leaf bolts, running back to the couch. I look over my shoulder to find, who else but Rosier. Perfect timing.

I stand up, balling my fists. "What did I tell you about leaving the apartment?"

Rosier cocks a brow. "And what have I told you since I arrived?" He leans down so we're at eye level. "You. Don't.

Control. Me." He says it with such gravitas, my whole body shivers.

"Well, I can send you back to Hell–sooner rather than later."

He snorts. "Here I thought you didn't know how. Otherwise..." He steps closer so his lips are in my ear and says in a husky voice, "You would have done it already."

"You're going back." I walk away, as if I have anywhere to go. I settle onto the couch, and Leaf hops up, rubbing his head against my knee.

"You're not going to send me back," Rosier objects. "You still haven't made a contract."

I run my hand along Leaf's silky black back. "You denied my contract." I shrug over exaggeratedly. "Oh well. Guess you'll have to wait for another witch to summon you."

Rosier flops down on the couch with such force it scares Leaf, who bolts into the bedroom. "Giving up already? I thought you were a smart girl, Minnie. Simply come up with a better contract. I'm surprised you haven't already."

"I've been busy." There is no way I'm telling him about the family curse or any of the other troubles my sperm donor has thrown my way. He would probably use it against me, as a way to tease me. "Besides, who says I have to sign a contract with *you?*"

"What." It's not a question. He seems offended.

I use the sweetest voice I can muster, the one I would use at clubs trying to get guys to buy my friend's shots—"*oh I don't drink thanks but my girlfriends do.*" "There are plenty of devils in Hell, Rosie. I'm sure one or more of them aren't so picky about revenge. I bet–"

My thought is cut off by Rosier grabbing my chin. He glares at me with molten gold eyes, staring down his long curved nose.

"You summoned *me* first. If you're going to sign a contract, it will be with me."

"Will it now?"

I try to pull away, but Rosier keeps my chin locked in his hand. He leans down, his eyes level with my eyebrows, his full lips almost touching the tip of my nose.

It's distracting to say the least but I'm quick to continue, "What are you going to do to me?"

"Right now? Or if you keep vexing me?" To my surprise his thumb finds my bottom lip. He hums to himself as he tilts my chin back so I'm looking up at the ceiling, my neck feeling very exposed. "If I mark up your neck, everyone will know you're mine."

"I'm not–" I manage to pull away this time. Rosier doesn't attempt to grab me again, the hand that was holding my chin now resting on the back of the couch. "I'm not yours–not yet."

"*Yet.*"

It occurs to me that he could also make a contract with anyone. I doubt a lot of people are summoning devils these days, but he's already on the Mortal Plane. I'm sure there's someone who would sell their soul for a bigger butt and lips. And plenty of people that would sell their soul for money. Maybe those things are all too boring for him.

"You want me," I say finally. Rosier stiffens. "But you can't have me. That must drive a Prince like you crazy. Has anyone ever told you no before?"

"I denied *your* contract," he reminds me.

"But you still want a contract," I shoot back. "Very intriguing..."

Rosier makes a face I can only describe as a pout. "I ought to spank you."

"You wish." It's my turn to lean into him. I get on my knees in an attempt to look taller than him, but at most we're eye level. "You've been wanting me to sleep with you since the first night you got here. Now you're talking about spanking me when you know–"

I've put myself in a corner.

"When I know what, Minnie?" An unsurprisingly devilish smile pulls at his lips. "That you get off on that? Sweet little witch like you with a drawer full of whips and paddles."

"I don't have whips–don't be dramatic."

"You want to see something dramatic?" His arm wraps around my waist and pulls me forward, but instead of sitting up in his lap, he lays me across his legs. It's a familiar position, one I usually have to beg guys to put me in. I brace myself for impact but Rosier's hand runs along my spine. The anticipation kills me, and my bottom lip quivers.

He leans down, his curls brushing my cheeks and neck. "That. That is dramatic. Action is dramatic. Not your nipping words raging in my ear like an insolent imp."

"You haven't actually hit me." I point out, my voice distant even in my own ears.

The hand stroking my back reaches my butt and palms it. Rosier hums with content. "Why would I give you exactly what you want?"

"Because you want it, too." I bite my lip, expecting, hoping that will be enough for him to slap my rear.

Instead, his voice rumbles, "Stand up. Take off your clothes."

I'm tempted to tell him no–just to see what he does. I sit back on my heels and start unbuttoning the buttons of my jumpsuit.

Rosier grabs my wrist. "Stand up. Give me a show."

Is he serious? It's a jumpsuit; how am I supposed to make that sexy? But I go stand in front of him. He leans into the couch, his arms outstretched, then spreads his legs. He looks at me like I'm the only other thing in the room. I pull at my buttons, practically tearing them off.

"Slower," he growls.

I mutter, "Usually people charge for this sort of stuff."

Most of the buttons on the top of my jumpsuit are already undone, so I start sliding down the long sleeves one at a time, letting them hang off my shoulders. My cleavage is exposed, and I know Rosier can see the edges of my worn pink bra. I trace a finger from my collarbone down my sternum, brushing my fingertips along my breasts. Rosier hums with approval.

I pull more fabric down away from my chest, waiting for Rosier to do... something. Say something gross or start touching himself. Instead he watches me, and in turn, I can't stop watching him. The top of the jumpsuit hangs around my waist.

"Turn around." He lifts a finger and makes a little twirling motion.

I hate doing as he says, but I know I have a great butt–and I know my panties are actually cute today, pastel purple with lace at the edges that hugs my curves. I turn around and slip my thumbs into the waistband of the jumpsuit, swaying my hips as I slowly push the clothing down my body. When half my rear is exposed, I stop pulling at the fabric but keep moving my hips.

Rosier grumbles before that gravely voice of his gives me another command. "Keep going. I want to see those thighs."

All this just to see me in a pair of panties and an old bra that doesn't do my chest any favors.

My butt is completely exposed, and I bend over, sliding the pants down my legs. I take the opportunity to look past my legs back at Rosier, his hands still resting on the couch and his gaze firmly on my ass. Finally, I've completely stripped and I turn back around to face him.

I'm about to walk to him when Rosier tells me, "Wait." I

knit my brows in confusion and he explains, "I've never seen you like this. I want to appreciate it."

I stand there, not sure what else to do.

After a few moments of looking me over, Rosier nods, then pats his thighs. "Come here. You know what to do."

"Do *you* know what to do?" I retort. But I return to the couch and lay across his thighs like before.

Rosier immediately palms my ass again, his other hand holding my chin so I'm forced to look forward.

"I know how to make devils submit, but you are a bit more of a challenge."

A firm hand spanks me, and I make a sound like a squeak toy. Rosier's hand rests on my ass, his fingers giving my cheek a good squeeze. Then he spanks my other cheek, and I manage to stay quiet.

"Interesting..." he mutters to himself. His hand leaves my ass. "You're going to keep count of every time I spank you, understand?"

"Yes," I respond, my voice breather then I intend. I must sound so desperate—and maybe I am.

"Hmm... I'm not sure I trust you to actually listen. Stubborn little thing." I grit my teeth, wishing he would start already, as he says, "Repeat back to me, what is it you're supposed to do?"

"Count off every time you spank me," I tell him, finding it impossible to hide the frustration in my voice.

"Good girl." With that he brings his hand right down on my ass, hard. My whole body jerks on impact, and Rosier holds my chin tighter.

I gasp and almost forget what I'm supposed to do. "One!" I say much too loudly.

Rosier doesn't seem to mind because he spanks me again, right on the same spot, leaving a stinging feeling.

"Two."

He keeps going, the sharp sound of flesh hitting flesh echoing in my apartment.

Finally I count off, "Ten."

He chuckles, rubbing my stinging flesh. "There. Isn't it so much easier when you comply?" He squeezes my chin. "But we're not done."

Good, I want to say, but he spanks my other cheek, and all I can say is, "One."

The whole reason I have a *"drawer full of whips and paddles"* is because no one ever does it right. At least no guy I've ever dated. Every time I've looked at my butt after a spanking session, I've found nothing, not even a hint of purple.

I don't think that's going to be a problem this time around.

"Nine..." I bite down on my lip with the final impact. "Ten." I breathe.

Rosier draws little circles with his finger on my upper thigh, giving me a chance to decompress.

"Hmmm... I think you need a little more discipline. Again."

He wastes no time giving me another spank and I count off —"One!" Then he spanks me again, all too quickly, and my voice falters. I pant and gasp, and Rosier clicks his tongue as his palm rubs against my sensitive bottom.

"The cracks are starting to appear... Again."

This time I manage to speak with confidence despite my cheeks burning. "One..." His harsh smack makes my whole body shake. Again. "Two." On it goes 'til, finally, "Nine..." One final, harsh smack against my stinging rear. "Ten."

Suddenly, Rosier grabs the waistband of my panties and pulls them so the fabric slides against my folds. His fingers dance along my thighs and rear but never touch me where I want it most. And he knows it.

"You really do love punishment, I can see it..." He chuckles.

"Little masochistic witch. Little sopping cunt." He sits me up so I'm straddling his lap, then he shifts his leg so I'm resting on one thigh. "Why don't you finish yourself off on my knee."

Again, he's not phrasing it as a question. Though, it's not a command either; I know what a command sounds like on his tongue. He leaves room for me to say no–and when I don't respond immediately, he reaches up to brush some curls behind my ear.

"Or if you've already had your fill..."

I say nothing, instead taking hold of his shoulders. I start to rut my hips against his thigh, the friction to die for. I hum, keeping my lips and eyes shut tight.

That's when Rosier purrs, "Look at me."

I shut my eyes even tighter.

Rosier grabs my chin and repeats, putting emphasis on every word, "Look. At. Me."

My eyes flutter open, and Rosier releases my face to grab my hips, forcing me to grind faster and harder against his thigh. I can't hold back my pleasure, gasps accentuated by little cries. I make sure to keep my focus on Rosier, hypnotized by his eyes, by his blinding white grin, by the way his curls frame his face.

My panties are completely soaked. Before I know it I'm on the edge, gripping his shoulders like they'll keep me from falling. My breath hitches, and an embarrassingly high pitched whine leaves my lips as my body flushes with warmth.

Rosier strokes my arm. "There. Feeling better?"

"I..." I wish I could snap at him with some witty retort, but my brain is much too fuzzy for that right now. Plus it would be a lie. I do feel better, even if I am in the same bad situation. "I feel good," I admit. "Um, one second..."

I slide off his thigh, and he doesn't stop me.

I go to my bedroom and shut the door before going to my full-length mirror. I turn around, arching my neck over my shoulder. My rear is the perfect shade of purple and red, clearly irritated. I run a hand along my curves, skin still hot, feeling little welts bubble against my skin. I breathe, elated and excited in a way I haven't been for so long. I know I enjoy this but it always felt shameful.

That's not a problem this time.

CHAPTER ELEVEN

MINNIE

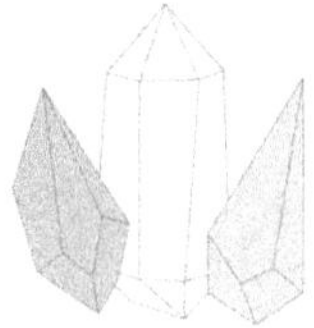

Not wanting Rosier to get any ideas about what I'm doing, I grab one of my oversized tee-shirts and slip it on before returning to the living room. As soon as I open the door, Leaf runs out from underneath my bed and into Rosier's lap. He starts attacking the thigh I just humped.

"Hey!" Rosier scolds while my other cheeks grow red hot. He grabs Leaf by the scruff and drops him on the floor. Leaf hops right back up, entertained by this new game.

I force myself to laugh, and Rosier turns to me. He looks so... unfazed as if we'd just been sitting and chatting instead of him swatting my ass.

"It's getting late..." I swallow, but it doesn't help my next words sound any more confident. "Goodnight!"

I shut the door much too hard.

As I lay in bed, there's a hollow feeling in my stomach. I know I don't want to be alone, but my only option is the big devil sleeping on my couch. Or Leaf, but I don't think he's really the type to cuddle, what with how he bounces off the walls like he's made of rubber. My hand reaches out and touches the pillow next to me. I can't think of the last time someone has made me finish and they haven't slept over. Actually I don't think it's ever happened. I'm too much a sap to let people leave after sex.

I sit up in bed, feeling childish as I call out. "Rosie?"

"Don't call me that infantile name," he demands through the door. "What could you possibly want?"

"Can you come in?"

There is a moment of silence. "You're allowing me entry into your chambers now?"

"Yes," I tell him. The door starts to open and I add a caveat, "But you're not allowed to go through my stuff."

This doesn't stop Rosier from opening the door and taking a single step inside.

He's naked again, wearing my floral bonnet. He crosses his arms over his broad tan chest and looks at me, expectantly. I swallow a lump in my throat and find it hard to meet his eyes. I start fiddling with one of my sheets.

"Can you... Do you want to sleep in my bed tonight?"

The mattress shifts as Rosier climbs onto the edge, but he doesn't crawl close enough to lay beside me. His eyes narrow, like an animal stalking its prey. "What brought this on?"

"I don't usually... have sex with people randomly."

"You count that as sex?"

"Oh, come on," I groan. "I think me riding your leg counts for something.

He chuckles, "If you say so, Minnie."

Finally he crawls forward and lays down beside me. I don't hesitate to rest my head on his chest. He's warm, his heartbeat louder than I expected. The hollow feeling is gone, replaced with a security like I've been wrapped in a dozen blankets.

"You really mean it." Rosier mutters. "You get very attached to your companions, don't you?"

"You say that like it's a bad thing." I yawn, his body making a nice pillow. I try to forget that he's completely exposed. Though it doesn't bother me all that much. "Don't feel too flattered. It's probably subdrop."

"Explain."

"Our not-sex was an emotional high, so now I'm at an emotional low. I think. It's been a few years since my girlfriend explained all this to me."

He nods, "So men really can't punish you correctly, can they?"

Despite myself, I snort.

"You said you don't normally do this." He looks at me with genuine curiosity. "Explain that too."

I look up at him. "I'm sort of a two date minimum kind of girl." Rosier raises a brow. Obviously he doesn't know what I'm talking about. "Before I have sex with someone. It's a two date minimum."

"I've been here two days," he points out. "Three, really."

"No, uh, a date is like a dinner or going to an event with someone. A way to test out the relationship, make sure you like each other."

Rosier's eyes light up, and he seems to understand. "Like courting in those books of yours."

I nod. "Yes exactly." I guess it's my turn to ask a question. "Do they have courtship in the Hells?"

"A version of it. For political reasons."

"Is that how your parents did it?" His muscles tense. "Sorry." I would have reacted the same if he asked about my parents. "I shouldn't... it's not my place to ask."

"My Mother made a pact with my Father when she was alive," he explains. I tilt my head to the side, the similarities not lost on me. "When she did finally pass, my Father chose her as his consort."

"Did... she have a say in it?"

"Minnie." Rosier looks at me with a blank expression. "The whole point of the contract is so devils have souls in Hell they can command. Choice isn't an option. We can command lesser devils, too, but there is a certain power associated with controlling the souls of mortals."

Social capital? I guess if Rosier is a Prince, there has to be some sort of court, and I've read enough Tudor era romances to know how that goes.

"Being the consort to a Prince of hell doesn't sound that bad," I say with a shrug.

Rosier snorts. "You would think that. I've noticed some patterns in your reading." I shoot him a frown, making it clear I don't appreciate the comment but he continues, "It's far from a love story. My Father chose my Mother, she bore me, and I grew up surrounded by devils of my caliber. When my Father passed, my Mother passed on with him."

"How long ago was that?"

"You mortals are so obsessed with time. I don't even know how to explain it, but it was not that long ago that they passed, along with all the other souls my Father reaped–thousands of years worth."

All things die, Minnie, his voice echoes in my mind.

"You've got me beat," I tell him. "I never knew my dad. Probably a good thing."

He lets out a snort. "I doubt your Father was worse than mine." Before I can explain the mortal intricacies of crime lords, Rosier reminds me of an obvious detail. "Prince of Hell and whatnot."

That *is* pretty bad. Or pretty good? "You turned out alright?" I offer.

"Alright?" He knits his brows, a hint of sneer on his lips.

I can't help but laugh. "You don't seem that bad for a devil. Not that I've met a lot of devils."

"Your neighbor is literally a succubus."

My face scrunches. "Okay... but I didn't know that. And succubi are different from devils, right?"

Rosier nods. "They're born of a union between a devil and a human. Witches, usually, for obvious reasons." He smirks, squeezing my thigh under the covers. I bite my lip, trying not to read too much into his touch, but he notices. "What are you thinking about?"

I'm quick to make up something. "If your Father took all his souls with him when he passed then, who do you have under your control?"

Rosier clears his throat. "If you ever actually come up with an interesting contract, then you will be my first soul."

I blink, then grin. "I'll be your *first?* How cute." I giggle. "I'm honored."

Rosier's lips are tight. "That's *only* if you come up with an agreeable contract. Otherwise, there are plenty of other humans who would be willing to make a deal with me."

"But how many of them will be interesting enough?" I retort, my grin still plastered across my lips. He says nothing. I pester him further, fluttering my eyelashes. "Who else could possibly be as clever as me?"

His body shifts below me before he wraps his arms around me. "Go to sleep, Minnie." He rests his chin atop my head, and he whispers, "I'm not accustomed to this being held like this."

I shiver, not sure where the rush comes from. Maybe it's the simple fact that he's a devil, that he's not of this world.

This tenderness is as temporary as it is intoxicating.

I close my eyes, my cheek pressed to his chest.

Again, he says to me, "Sleep, Minnie."

It's a command I happily follow.

CHAPTER TWELVE

MINNIE

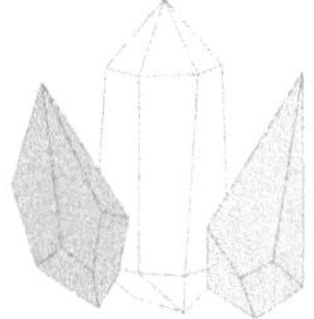

I wake up before my alarm to send an email telling the office I won't be in. I've got enough sick days saved up that it shouldn't be an issue, and if it is, then I guess my lifelong fear that a day off would ruin my life wasn't unfounded. Email sent, I shut off my alarms and flop back into bed.

I wrap Rosier's arm around myself like a blanket. To my surprise, his arm pulls me closer to him, like I'm his favorite plushie. I have to stifle a laugh at the image of him holding some big fluffy pink teddy bear.

When I open my eyes again my phone is ringing. Rosier and I blink away sleep, but Leaf seems to think the sound is some sort of doomsday alarm because I can hear him running around.

"Make sure your cat doesn't destroy my apartment..." I mutter as I tap Rosier's shoulder. He rolls out of bed, muttering Leaf's name over and over while I pick up the phone. "Hello?"

"Hey." I recognize Amber's voice immediately. "Are you at work? You don't sound great."

I rub my eye with my palm. "I'm home, and I just woke up."

"Wow. Proud of you. Last time you took a day off you were vomiting."

"You know, I probably still could have made it into work if Gramps hadn't insisted I stay home." I'm only half joking.

"Can I come over?" Amber asks.

Neither of us say anything for a few moments. Rosier walks back into the room holding Leaf and scratching between his ears.

"I know I'm probably the last person you want to talk to right now," Amber admits. "Keeping that secret killed me inside..."

"Do you feel better now that the cat's out of the bag?"

Rosier lifts a brow and then holds out Leaf, his little black legs sticking straight in the air, and I have to stifle my laugh.

"Not at all," Amber says glumly.

"You can come over," I yawn.

"Are you going to be awake when I get there?"

I smile. "If you promise to bring me coffee, I probably will be."

Rosier inches closer to me, clearly interested in the conversation.

"Deal. I'll be by with coffee in like half an hour," Amber promises.

Rosier speaks up. "You humans and time. How can an hour be halved?"

That confirms that he can hear Amber's side of the conversation, which wakes me up like being drenched in cold water. Not that anything has been said he doesn't already know, but it's one thing when he has his nose in my business versus everyone else's.

"See you soon." I feel bad hanging up on her so suddenly,

but I don't want her saying something without realizing a literal devil is listening in. I frown at Rosier. "Okay, eavesdropping is not okay. I'm going to assume you didn't mean to–"

"That's a very naive thing for you to assume."

"You are such a spoiled brat."

"Do I need to spank you a second time?"

I ignore him.

AMBER KNOCKS AT MY DOOR, and instead of opening it up wide enough for her to enter, I slip out and meet her in the hallway.

"Hi." I give her a smile.

"Uh..." She looks past me at my apartment door, two coffees in her hand. "Hi? Sorry are we–"

"I have someone over, remember?"

Amber's eyes go wide. She leans over to whisper in my ear. "Is he in there?"

Rosier's voice calls through the door. "Yes."

I spin around and open my door a crack. Rosier's golden eyes peer at me from the entryway. He hasn't bothered to put on clothes, but I'm not even fazed by that anymore.

"Stop. Eavesdropping!" I scold. "It's rude! And if you keep it up, you'll be living with Kas for the rest of eternity."

His eyes narrow. "I'm getting the feeling you don't want me to meet your friend."

"I don't."

I can feel Amber looking over my shoulder. "Yeah, hi, the friend here. I'm really just here for Minnie. And I'm not really friendly with devils. Sorry."

"Don't apologize," I tell her, already starting to shut the door. "He never does."

Rosier grabs the door and opens it wide, exposing himself to the entire hallway.

Amber hides her eyes behind the cups of coffee. "Oh shit–okay, wow. I did *not* want to see devil dick."

Rosier and I glare at each other, my jaw tight. "Put on clothes."

"Are you coming in?" he asks.

"Not when you're naked, we're not."

He huffs, then walks away.

I take Amber's arm and guide her into the apartment, still shielding her eyes. "I'm sorry about him."

"Don't apologize," she says, finally lowering the coffee cups to look at me. "Like you said, he never does."

We both laugh, and I regret not telling Amber about Rosier sooner. Maybe if she had been involved with this mess from the start, things would have gone a lot smoother.

She sets down our coffees, and I'm quick to drink mine. Rosier saunters back into the kitchen, buttoning up his shirt.

Amber ignores him. "Minnie, listen, I know everything right now is... messy. But I want to help–if you'll let me."

The steam from my coffee warms my downturned lips. "You think I wouldn't let you help?" I mean, I need it–clearly–but I'm curious why she thinks I'm so against it.

"You never accept help," she points out. "None of the Morrises do. Remember when your Gramps almost broke a hip because he wouldn't let me help him carry something?"

"You'll have to be a bit more specific," I admit.

"Exactly my point." A soft smile appears on Amber's face. "There's a lot of stuff that needs fixing. Not just the devil in your apartment."

Rosier makes a dramatic *harumph*.

I hold my coffee in both hands. "I know he has to go. I *want* him to go since he's such a pain."

Rosier mutters, "Ironic you mention pain after last night."

I speak up, so Amber can't ask what that's all about. "But maybe he can solve our little curse problem? That's one of the things that needs fixing, right?"

I can already tell Amber isn't going for it, her lips in a hard line. "Making a deal with a devil isn't beating the curse; it's just replacing one curse with a different curse."

"Not to be cheeky," I say with a shrug, "but devil you know versus devil you don't?"

She doesn't look amused. "To be honest, Minnie, I think there's a baseline problem we have to solve first."

There's a knock at my door, probably Kas. Rosier must assume the same because he goes to open it. I can't see the entryway, but I recognize the voice.

"Oh–uh, sorry, I might have the wrong apartment."

It's Lance. *Why is it Lance?* I abandon my coffee to go investigate.

"I'm looking for a Minerva–" Lance sees me and his eyes, so similar to mine, go wide. "Minerva, hi." He smiles and glances up at Rosier. "Who's your friend?"

"A devil from Hell I summoned to get revenge on Arthur le Fay," I deadpan.

Lance manages to maintain his smile while also looking completely panicked. "That's... wow, that's, uh–"

"You don't have to say anything."

"No, listen, that's really, uh, impressive..." His eyes look past me. "Amber!" He says her name the same way someone might say "my hero!" Lance gestures to Rosier with his thumb. "You didn't mention my sister was proficient in summoning."

"I am *not* your sister," I correct him before turning my ire on Amber. "And you told him? What's he even doing here?"

"He literally just said I didn't tell him." Amber crosses her arms over her chest, looking like the spitting image of her Mom.

"And I invited him." I open my mouth, but she cuts me off. "I know you don't want to talk to him, but he knows the le Fays. There's no one else that can answer the questions you have, the fears we both share."

I purse my lips. I'm not interested in a brother... but I am interested in our Father and what he could possibly want with me. I huff and look back at Lance. "Come on in."

Lance looks at Rosier before taking one tiny step inside my apartment, walking like a newborn deer. We all settle on the couch except Rosier, who stands over us with his arms crossed. Everyone is looking at me.

"So... am I paranoid or is Arthur le Fay after me?" I ask.

"If he were after you, it would probably be too late," Lance admits. "But, no, you're not paranoid. I think he might be considering–" He lifts his hands and makes air quotes. "–making you part of the family."

"And what does *that* mean? I'm guessing I'm not joining the trust fund."

Lance's eyes fall to his lap. "I left the family because of the rituals. Blood magic rituals."

"You don't have to give us any details," Amber assures him.

"Um, yes, he does," I object. "Is he going to kill me?"

Lance picks at his nails. "Eventually. Probably."

"But why now?"

Considering I'm going to die in the next decade anyway, I'm not so fazed by the idea of being slaughtered on some stone tablet with a magic knife. It's one memorable way to go out, better than languishing for months with an illness.

But my question still stands. "Why is he so interested in me now?"

"I don't know. You're not even usually the kind of person he targets." I must make a face because he elaborates, "My father is obsessed with latent witches. He thinks they hold a certain kind of power."

It clicks in my head like the last piece of a puzzle–or it all comes crashing down, like Lance pulled the last load bearing brick out from the foundation. My Mom never had magic despite her Mother. Gramps is human and Grandma was a witch, so my Mom was... human, if a human is a witch without magic. Point is, Arthur le Fay sought out my mom thinking she was a latent witch.

I think aloud, "He was going to kill her..."

Rosier chuckles. "And he fucked her instead."

I glare at him, and in my periphery I can see Amber doing the same. Lance looks bewildered.

"So offended over the truth." Rosier shakes his head. "Minnie wouldn't be here otherwise."

Though I know digging deeper will only make my blood pressure rise, I look back at Lance. "So your dad kills latent witches for immortality. Is that it?"

He blinks. "Um... more or less, yeah. But he's not immortal. The rituals keep him young, but he's just delaying the inevitable."

"All things die," I recite. Lance nods. "Well, that settles it." I look at Rosier with defiance. "I want to ruin that man's life, and I'm willing to sell my soul for it."

Amber grabs my arm. "Minnie, seriously? That's what you got from this conversation?"

"Yes, seriously! Amber, he *used* my mom. And he has enough power he could have saved her if he wanted to." I turn to Lance. "Right?"

Lance's eyes dart back and forth between me and Amber. "I-I guess? Probably?"

"Minnie..." Amber's hand slides down my shoulder to take my hand. "Think about this." Her eyes glisten like stones at the edge of a lake. "When you die and you're dragged to Hell, you'll regret not moving onto the Veil. That's where your Mom is waiting. That's where your Grandpa will go when it's his time. Your Grandma, all your ancestors–you're giving that all up. For what? Revenge?"

"Don't listen to them," Rosier purrs. He has an appropriately devilish smile on his face. "If you don't at least try to ruin this man, then you're forgiving him for his transgressions against you. Against your own Mother."

"Stay out of this," Amber bites, her hold on my arm tightening.

"That's rich coming from you." I snap at Rosier. "You didn't agree to my revenge proposal before, so what's changed?"

Rosier reaches down and grabs my wrist, pulling me up from the couch. Amber still has my other hand, making this tug-of-war rather literal. Rosier holds my chin between his thumb and forefinger. "We could do more than revenge, Minnie."

"Piss off!" Amber stands up from the couch, her stiletto nails digging into my skin. "You can spout all the shit you want–say it in Latin, even–but you're taking advantage of Minnie."

Rosier leans down, resting his chin on my shoulder and pressing his cheek to my neck. He still holds my face between his fingers, my mouth covered by his shoulder. "I can offer her things you can't." He hisses in my ear like a snake, though he's talking to Amber. "Beyond revenge, power you can't imagine, let alone create for yourself. Because I'm a Prince of Hell, and you are a single line of history. Unremarkable, you two are."

I lift my head so I'm not suffocating against his shoulder. "And you're a pain is what you are."

His head turns, and he nips my ear. Even worse, I make a

little yelping sound–right in front of Amber and my half-brother. I crane my head to try and get a look at Amber.

Her top lip twitches in a snarl before she shakes her head like she's shaking off her rage. "You're incapable of understanding. I love Minnie; she's like my sister. Love, family, loyalty–devils don't have those things, do they?" Her eyes burn as she steps closer, the two of them like stone bookends and me a flimsy paperback.

I try to wriggle out of Rosier's grip. "Let's just all stop–" I manage to break free. "And consider, oh, I don't know, what *I* want to do for a second?"

Amber's expression doesn't soften. Rosier scoffs.

"Amber," I say tentatively, "if Rosier can do things we can't–"

"You're seriously considering this shit? Still?"

"Between the curse and my dad coming after me, yeah, I am." I furrow my brows. "Don't tell me you wouldn't do the same–"

"I wouldn't."

"Because you don't have to! You have *everything*: your parents, your magic, the coven at your back. All I've got is him." I gesture to Rosier. Past Amber, Lance's mouth hangs open. "What would you do, Lance?"

His mouth shuts like a trap, and he clears his throat. "I don't want anything. I just want peace and quiet."

A dismissive sound hums at the back of my throat.

Lance frowns. "You know, I'm the only one sitting here who actually *lived* with the le Fays. Out of my brother and my sister, I was the only one who got out. Even *my* Mother sticks around. Just putting that out there."

"See?" Amber gestures back at Lance. "Your brother–"

"He's *not* my brother."

Lance's frown is even heavier now.

Amber lets out a humorless laugh. "But you'll act like this revenge plot is a family affair. Some melodrama like in all your corny books."

"Enough!" I shout and forget that there's anyone else in the room but the two of us. "Amber, you need to decide right now if you're going to be my friend or the Supreme. I need my friend to tell me the truth and support me–I need her to see things from my side."

"And I need you to stop letting your daddy issues make decisions!"

"*Oh!*" I shake my head. "You *had* to bring up daddy issues, didn't you? Real original."

"Doesn't need to be creative when it's correct."

"Get out!" I shout at her before looking at Lance. "Get. Out!" I turn on my heel to look at Rosier. "All of you!"

The room is painfully silent. Everyone is staring at me like I'm the main event of some circus performance. "Minnie, please." Amber's tone is so cool, it makes me want to scream again. "I want to help you. I'm sorry if it doesn't feel that way, but I swear I'm trying."

"And I'm just trying to help myself," I bite back. "I'm sorry you can't see it."

Without another word, she starts heading for the door.

Lance is back to looking like a newborn deer, his green eyes darting around the room. "I'm... sorry." He gets up. "Really, I am."

He follows Amber, and they leave together. The door shuts, and I'm left alone with Rosier.

But not for long.

I speak through my teeth. "Get out."

"You can do better than that." He chuckles. Without words he insults me, that laugh of his worse than any taunting. "All that rage? Let me see it."

I turn that insult into a boon. "You want so, so much and are never satisfied. Is that all you are? A big, needy child who has to keep pushing to get enough attention or you'll wither away?" I push my pointer finger into his sternum. "You say you can do all these things for me, but I haven't seen any proof. You're all talk. And I'm sick of the sound of your voice. Go play across the hall with Kas! Go play with yourself! I don't care, just get *out!*"

I can't tell if he's impressed or hurt, his face not portraying any real emotion. But he has to feel *something*. He can deny mortal emotions all he wants, but I've seen his jealousy, seen his indulgence. He feels rage and pain as I do.

He heads to the door, and I follow him, watching him cross the hall to knock on Kas' door. Finally I slam the door, locking it, the act itself more comforting than any actual security.

Leaf is at my feet now, rubbing his cheek against my calf. "You, you can stay." I pick him up, and he starts purring. "In fact, you're not allowed to leave. Ever."

CHAPTER THIRTEEN

ROSIER

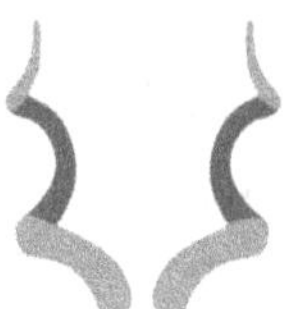

As I knock at Kas' door, I hear Amber and Lance talking in the stairwell, failing to be very quiet.

"It's my fault..." Lance practically whimpers.

"Hey, none of that, Minnie wouldn't accept you blaming yourself for her choices."

Kas opens the door. "Did Minnie kick you–hey, where are you going?" I walk to the stairwell, finding Amber and Lance on the landing below.

"She's gotta be having an existential crisis," Amber remarks. "Which, fair. She's had a lot to reckon with."

I stand in the very entrance of the stairwell, unable to see Amber or Lance. Perfect.

Lance still sounds miserable. "Like finding out she has a half-sibling and a terrible dad kind of reckoning?"

"I should have told her about the curse sooner," Amber laments. "Even if her Mom wanted different..." There's a pause, and I assume Lance makes a face that compels her to continue. "Minnie, and all the women in her bloodline before her, are cursed to die young. Pretty shitty deaths, too."

"Minnie's Mom…"

"Cancer. The kind that starts in the lungs and claws its way up to the brain. Makena… she was stubborn like Minnie, kept fighting despite the diagnosis, despite the curse. But it got bad."

I purse my lips. Makena, Minnie's Mother, sounds tragic. The sort of tale mortals lose their minds over. Write poetry and songs about. I don't really care; I'm incapable of feeling pity, especially for a woman I've never met. But Minnie bears the same curse. Someday the curse will take hold and ruin her as it has for generations.

Amber hisses to Lance, "But you didn't hear that from me."

"Poor Minnie… I thought my Mom's co-dependency was bad…"

"I don't know if I would say they were co-dependent, but toward the end, Minnie took everything very personally. Like when her Mom didn't recognize her and threw a book at her. Makena was confused obviously, but the few times Minnie has talked about it, it's like she forgets the woman had brain cancer."

"Grief is complicated."

"I know…"

I speak up finally. "You humans and your platitudes." I step into the stairwell proper and look down, finding Amber and Lance have made it to the very bottom.

Amber crosses her arms. "Oh, so now the devil is going to lecture us?"

"You two should be so lucky to hear me speak."

Kas joins me in the stairwell. "Rosier! If you're going to stay over, can you let me know? I was going to have some friends over tonight–though I guess you could always join in." He rests his arms on the railing, looking right at Amber and giving her a crooked smile. "Forgot my manners. You can join, too."

"Wow…" Amber draws out the word with a dry tone. She

puts a hand on her hip and looks up at Kas, matching his smile. "I don't think your friends could handle me."

"You're probably right," he purrs. "Hey, Lance!" He waves.

Lance, his face flush, manages a little wave. "H-hey, Kas."

"That invitation extends to you, too." He winks.

"I-I have a-a boyfriend," he stutters. "A boyfriend who would *not* like this conversation."

It's hard to believe that man is related to Minnie at all. I see it in their eyes, in the round tips of their noses and their square jaws, but Lance reminds me of a damned soul, while Minnie is so much more.

It would be easy to blame Lance's skittish nature on his Father—so I do. And it makes me wonder what a man like Arthur le Fay would do to a woman like Minnie. No, not a woman, to a child—to the smiling little Minnie I saw in the photos on her bookshelf.

"Hey, Devil-Man," Amber calls from below, somehow noticing I'm lost in thought from the depths of the stairwell.

I narrow my eyes at her, now concerned she's more powerful than she seems. I'm winning Minnie over to my side, and within time, I know she'll keep me here. But that matters not if Amber is the stronger witch of the two.

She continues, "I meant what I said back there. Minnie means the world to me. Hurt her, and you won't have to worry about being sent back to Hell."

I raise a brow.

"Because I'll chain you to this plane 'til you wither away. Lock you in some church basement where all you'll feel is light and love and emotional mush 'til you starve."

Kas and I glance at each other, both a bit shaken by her threat. "You sound rather eager," I say, feigning nonchalance, "but I don't need to be teased. Come back with those chains, and I'll take you seriously." I smirk. "I'll even get on my knees if you'd like. Make Minnie jealous."

Amber doesn't offer a response, instead storming out of the building.

Lance hesitates. "Tell Minnie I'm sorry. I shouldn't have come. I didn't mean to upset her."

"I don't pass on messages. Especially sentimental ones." I push off the railing and head back to Kas' apartment.

Lying on Kas' couch, I reflect on Minnie's curse, her relationship with Amber, the mild figure of Lance, and, of course. Arthur le Fay. Holding a vendetta against a man I've never met is foolish, but for the le Fay's patriarch, I'll make an exception. What a pleasure it will be to watch him fall from the pedestal he's placed himself on. And he *will* fall. All things die. All things come to a crashing, burning end.

I can't stop thinking about Makena, wondering what the woman in the portrait would look like sickly and dying. How those brown eyes could turn hollow and distant but somehow still alive. I wonder, though I've seen it myself. My own Mother... nothing but a mortal soul chained to her master, my Father.

I try to recall if she ever held me the way Makena held Minerva in that portrait. I know when she looked at me, there was no spark behind her eyes that would convey attachment. As if a wandering soul could feel anything beyond emptiness, a painful yearning for a body, for life, for free will. Yet she held my hand. I know this to be true. On more than one occasion, she led me through the halls of our home.

My Father's home. She had no claim to his lands or titles. She barely had a claim to me: the younger Rosier, the Princes' heir. The spare. I have to chuckle, even now. For so long, I was an afterthought... until it was too late. One moment my Father held a kingdom in his hands, and the next, it was gone.

And now, it's mine: every mining cavern, every corridor, every grain of sand–it's mine, because I was smart enough not to get caught up in grudges. I refused to partake in a silly war game. Instead I sat at home, looking upon my Father's empty throne, knowing well enough then that it would be mine.

I sat on that throne as I watched her fade away, like a statue of sand, bit by bit carried away on the winds. My Mother's face was never something I found all that remarkable until it was gone. When I shut my eyes, when I focus, I can see it: her curved nose, her full lips, her curly black hair. As I lay with my eyes shut, I realize I don't remember her at all. I only remember the things she left me.

This mortal form of mine, short and useless, is her living memory.

Perhaps I can do something with it while I have it.

Minnie is a force to be reckoned with. Even when she's not upset, not bubbling over with rage, there's a crackling energy around her. I thought it was a matter of her being a witch, but having now been in a room with two other witches, I can confirm that her energy is unique. And I know now that she's going to get her revenge with or without me.

I should stick around for the show.

CHAPTER FOURTEEN

MINNIE

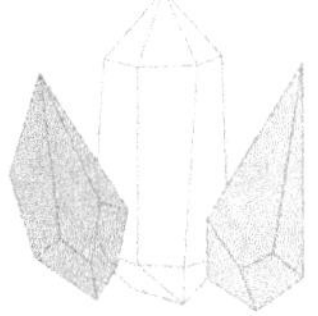

I'M ABOUT HALFWAY THROUGH MY SECOND BOOK ON MY E-reader when I finally feel some sense of peace. Sitting alone with a cat next to my knee and a nice cup of coffee fixes most things, I think. Not that anything is fixed. Not that anything *needs* to be fixed. Amber and I just have different ideas about how to handle things.

I finish up my now lukewarm cup of coffee. Home brewed. The two cups of coffee Amber brought us are abandoned on my kitchen counter. Amber said I'll regret not passing onto the Veil... as if any of us know what the Veil even entails. It's easy to imagine a paradise, some sort of heaven. Likely, it's more like Amber said, a place to reunite with one's ancestors. I guess it would be nice to commiserate about dying young together, but that's making a lot of assumptions. As nice as it would be to see my Mom again, I would rather she still be here and now.

Leaf stretches, yawing to show off his pink tongue.

"How are you tired?" I ask. "You've been napping all day."

Leaf blinks slowly.

"You're missing out on a great book." I show him the screen. "Secret relationship, a family fortune, a masquerade ball..."

Leaf looks at me with blank, green eyes.

Sighing, I say, "You think we should let Rosie back into the apartment?"

Leaf hops off the couch and starts walking towards the front door.

"I'm not happy with him, but we're not exactly fluffy and domestic. Minus adopting you, I guess that is pretty soft, right?"

Leaf meows a sound like sandpaper against a chalkboard as if to say, "I'm a cat remember?"

"Maybe I'll just go talk to him," I decide.

In a few steps, I'm at Kas' door. I knock, and half a second later, he's in front of me, dressed in a loose fitting tunic.

"Ugh, finally," he says.

He moves aside, and I see deeper into his apartment. It's not so different from my own, minus the decorations: gold statues of figures with multiple arms doing yoga, thick curtains over the windows, and plush black leather furniture. Though one the couches looks more like an art installation than a couch...

Rosier lays on one of the couches like a corpse, flat on his back with his face blank.

"He's been moping for hours," Kas complains.

Rosier's rumbling voice assures me he's not actually dead on that couch. "I am *not* moping."

Kas rolls his eyes.

"I'm bored," Rosier insists. "You bore me."

Kas covers his heart with his hand and makes a mock offended sound. "Wow. I'm going to have to remember to cry about that later." He steps into his apartment, and I follow, the sweet smell of jasmine and lilies hitting my nose. "If you two could work things out so I don't have to cancel on my guests tonight..." He meanders into his kitchen, perhaps to give us some sense of privacy.

I walk to Rosier and sit on the edge of the couch near his head. Minus his eyes, he doesn't move a muscle, like laying here for a few hours has turned him to stone. I realize then that I'm not sure what to say to him.

I finally settle on, "Leaf misses you."

"Did he tell you that?" Rosier asks.

"He did, actually."

Both of us let our guard down for a moment, smiles appearing then disappearing like a specter.

"So," I begin, "I have an idea–"

He lets out a dramatic moan and covers his eyes with his forearm. "Minnie, the contract–"

"It's not about contracts," I explain. "Revenge or not, I want to confront my Father."

Rosier snorts, but there's a hint of a smirk on his lips. "Why?"

"I want him to apologize for everything he did to my Mom. Everything he didn't do for us. He's a powerful witch trying to become immortal. Surely he could have given my Mom a potion or charm–something to slow the curse, or something to make her passing on less... terrible. And on top of that I'll have a devil at my beck and call."

"Except I'm not at your beck and call."

"Not yet."

Rosier slides his arm off his eyes and looks... amused?

Kas calls to us from the kitchen. "Count yourself lucky, Rosie. At least Minnie isn't asking you to start a war or something."

I stand up and make my way over to the kitchen island. "What do you think, Kas?"

"Mmm, a dangerous question, Minnie. I have many, many correct opinions."

I lean across the island resting my chin in my hand. "Confronting my Father with a devil at my side is intimidating, right? Even if we haven't made a contract."

"Who says you two haven't signed a contract?" I'm ready to explain when he winks. "Never show your hand, Minnie dear. There's no way to tell whether you have or have not signed a deal with a devil."

"Don't give her ideas!" Rosier shouts, but Kas already has a scheming smile on his face.

"Besides, it's not the deal itself that's scary. It's the possibility of that deal."

"So... I should make my Father believe I've made a deal, but not imply anything specific?" I ask.

"That's what I would do." He crosses his arms over his chest and shrugs. "But what do I know? I'm just a couple thousand-year-old succubus. Seen empires rise and fall and all that."

I quirk a brow. "Were you involved in any falling of empires perchance?"

Kas grins, but I don't inquire further. After all, he did just tell me the less someone knows, the more intimidating you come off.

I purse my lips. "You wouldn't happen to know how I could get tickets to the Institute of Art Gala this weekend do you?"

"Tim can weasel his way into anything. Including three gala tickets." When I cock my head, not sure why I would need three tickets, Kas explains, "I refuse to miss a scheme."

The more I think about it, the less I mind it. Rosier and I together, we're a couple, but with Kas, we're sort of a posse, a little more intimidating and a little more organized. "I've still got my graduation dress." I think aloud, trying to plan.

"What's your size?" Kas asks,

"Um, it depends. I'm short and wide on the bottom but not wide at all at the top."

"It would be cutting it close trying to get a dress altered by Friday," he mutters while nibbling at his thumb. "Not to mention, I'm going to be tearing my hair out getting a certain devil in a suit."

Rosier is still laying on the couch. "Why do I have to wear a suit?"

Kas knits his thick brows. "It's black tie. They literally won't let you in if you don't have a cumberbund on."

"A *what?*"

I butt in. "Don't worry about it. I'm sure you can handle one night of wearing a tux. You survived Hell all these years."

"Hell isn't really hellish when it's your home, Minnie. You keep forgetting this." Even standing in the kitchen, I can see him roll his eyes on the couch.

"If Hell on Earth is wearing a suit, then maybe you'll develop some empathy for your subjects." I walk over and take his hand, attempting to pull him up from the couch. "Come on." He doesn't budge. "Am I going to have to command you to get up?"

His voice is sly. "Maybe..."

"Don't be a brat."

"Coming from you?"

I catch sight of Kas at the island, his chin in his hands, watching us like we're on stage. He notices me staring and squeaks. "Oh, ignore me, keep doing whatever this is. Foreplay or something."

That gets Rosier to sit up so he can glare at Kas.

Kas is wrong, we're not flirting. But he's not completely off base regarding our relationship. Though, I'm not sure there is a word for the set up Rosier and I have. If someone asked if I wanted to sleep with him, it would be an easy no, but that would conveniently leave out last night. We're like magnets, sometimes polarized against each other and other times drawn to one another. I guess we don't need to label it. I'm going to have an eternity in Hell with him to figure out what it is we are to each other.

With Roiser sitting up, I take the opportunity to drag him to his feet, this time he obliges. "Kas, maybe we can schedule a dress fitting tomorrow? Once I'm done with work?"

Kas nods. "I'll make some calls, if I can't get anyone to see us, then my gal Chanel can. I'll text you the address."

"Thank you."

"It's nice to be appreciated," he says with a wink and a smile.

CHAPTER FIFTEEN

MINNIE

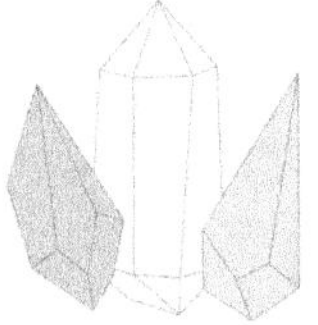

We return to my apartment, Leaf practically screaming as soon as we walk in.

"Quiet, hellbeast," Rosier remarks.

"I know we're late with your dinner." As I walk into the kitchen, Leaf is at my heels. I grab a can of wet food, noticing Rosier eyeing my e-book on the coffee table.

He picks it up and starts skimming. "Did you get to the ball yet?"

"Um, no. Spoilers! She just got her mask for the ball."

I plop the tuna-adjacent sludge on a little plate for Leaf, who is singing the worst belting style ballad I've ever heard. He finally stops once there's food in his mouth. "How did you know about that?"

"You have this book on your shelf, too."

Guilty as charged. I don't even need to confirm his claim; the amount of times I've bought a book twice is too many to count.

"And I read it," Rosier explains then snorts. "Obviously."

He's mentioned this before, sorta. Comparing dating to

courting, calling out my questionable attachment to gothic rakes. But I didn't think he'd paid so much attention that he could recognize a book from a single page.

Curious, I go to my bookshelf and grab a random book. "What happens in this one?"

Rosier looks at the book thoughtfully. "That's the one where she's been in love with the local Earl all her life, but a Viscount comes in to try and seduce her. Actually, *every* man in that novel tries to seduce her. But she settles on the Viscount."

He's right, but my curiosity isn't satiated. I grab another book, this time settling on a more pointed question. "What was your favorite scene in this book?"

"How do you even know I've read that one? You have about a hundred novels." There's a pause. "But to answer your question, my favorite scene is the kidnapping scene. Where the Lord and his companion steal the heroine in the night. I find it funny he'd go through all that trouble."

I blink, knowing exactly what scene he's talking about. It's one thing to recite the plot of something, it's another thing to have an opinion on it. I grab another book. "And this one? Assuming you've read it."

"I have. And it's the fellatio scene."

I snort, covering my mouth, hoping to stifle my laughter but failing miserably. Roiser makes a face, and I laugh more.

"You can't judge that!" Rosier protests. "All these books end in raunchy sex anyway."

"No, no." I wave my hand, still smiling with laughter. "I mean, yes, you're right, I just can't believe you call it 'fellatio.'"

"What would you call it?"

"Um, a blowjob? Giving head? A sloppy toppy?"

Rosier smirks. "That's the most crude string of words I've come out of your mouth. You curse like you live in a nunnery."

I lift my chin. "Thank you." I know I should change the

subject away from sex, but his choice of vocabulary has me curious. "What would you call what we did last night? You said it wasn't really sex." I disagree. but we don't have time to get into all that.

"You submitted to me," he replies, taking the book from me and eyeing it like he's started reading it again.

"That's pretty vague," I point out.

"I had you over my knee, and you did everything I said." His golden eyes glance over the edge of the book. "I could have told you to do anything, and you would have done it. Like the good girl you are."

A shiver runs down my spine, but I shake my head. "I'm not used to guys being into that, alright?"

"Into what? Making you submit? I find that–" He stops his thought. "Well, you *are* stubborn. I guess mortal men can't handle putting you in your place."

"In my place?" I step towards him. The glossy illustrated cover still hides half his face, but I can tell by the lines around his eyes that he's smiling to himself. "Nice try." I lean back on my heels. "You're not going to get me worked up tonight."

"You say that as if it takes effort."

I roll my eyes, snatching the book away. "I'm going to lay in bed and read." I start to walk away but hear him follow me. I glance over my shoulder. "I told you I'm not in the mood."

"So we can't be close to each other?"

"You're confusing. You call yourself a devil, but you're trying to cuddle with me."

"I said nothing about cuddling."

I get into bed, laying against the headboard and cracking open the book with the fellatio scene. I deserve a good reread. "If you want to lay next to me, fine." I should tell him to mope on the couch, but I don't.

He gets into bed on the opposite side. I feel his eyes on me and look up from the words to catch him with his face propped up on his elbow, watching. I return my attention to the page, but he's already caught me looking–at least, I assume that's what brought on his low rumbling chuckle.

Rosier shifts next to me, laying flatter on the mattress. His hand slides onto my lower stomach, and he grabs my hip, but there's still space between us. I nibble at the inside of my lip, not sure if I can really call this cuddling.

"You can pick something to read if you want," I say with my attention still on the page.

"I've had my fill of your epic tales. I'd much rather watch you." I try to immerse myself in the book and ignore my own rogue in my bed, but I can't because he says, "Or you could read aloud."

"This isn't a storytime corner," I tell him. "And *you* should read to *me*–here." I hand him the book, expecting him to swat it away, but instead he takes it from me with a cocksure smirk.

"'His hand groped the swell of her breasts.'" His rumbling voice makes for the perfect narration. He'd make a killing doing audiobooks, assuming that's not beneath him. "'Lilac, innocent as a lamb, gasped in horror, yet her body lifted to meet his touch...'"

He keeps going, and I watch and listen. Something about hearing him articulate these words creates a whole new narrative in my head. He's a rake, of course, the sort that shows up to the London Season with a reputation and a long list of broken hearts. He probably keeps his long curls free flowing when he can, another clear indication of his wild nature.

But who am I in this little scenario? I'm old enough to know that all these historical romances are fantasies. I know I can be the daughter of the Count or a Princess. But I'm fatherless, which is a scandal. But why do the men get to have all the fun? Every good heroine should have a scandal.

Rosier's voice pulls me from my thoughts. "'I want you.'" I blink and then remember the book in his hands. "'I crave you, Lilac, like your namesake craves the sun.'" Rosier pauses, looking at the pages with a confused brow. "What's a lilac?"

"It's a purple flower. Small petals, but they grow in bundles from large bushes."

"Ah." He nods, then starts reading again.

I inch towards him, trying to be subtle before I give up on that and slide under his arm to rest against his chest.

Rosier says nothing, still reading aloud like he's a living breathing audiobook. "'No one has ever held me like this. I fear my heart may tear out of my chest and run off—run off with you.'"

His fingers trail along the waistband of my pants. But it could be an absentminded touch. His eyes are still fixed on the page. "'I must be careful not to finish this, Lilac. Not till we're wed. Yet she desired him wholly, forgetting all about her station and the world around her...'"

Every good heroine should have a scandal.

I take Rosier's hand and guide it under my waistband. I look at his face to see if there's any reaction. His teeth drag along his full bottom lip, hesitating a moment before continuing to read aloud. But then his hand slips farther down my pants and starts to stroke along the satin of my panties. I close my eyes and let myself listen to him. Feel him.

His tone becomes throatier as he reads. "'His heart began to hammer as, for the first time, Lilac reached for him.'"

Rosier presses his fingers against my bud, and my breath catches in my throat. I'm torn between tearing off my clothes, removing the barrier between us, and the sense of security that comes with being clothed. But I give in and slide my pants and panties down in one swift motion.

Rosier doesn't waste any time dipping his fingers between

my folds, only his fingertips inside me. "'In the light of the grove, Lilac's rich caramel curls bounced as she took more and more of her lover in her mouth, an act she had only heard of in hushed whispers from the scullery maids.'"

He pulls out, his wet fingers continuing to lightly stroke my folds as he reads aloud his favorite scene. I don't remember it being so filthy, and perhaps the words themselves aren't any more graphic than the rest of the novel. But that's part of the appeal, the heightened and sometimes too flowery language to describe giving head of all things.

Rosier's fingers finally slide deep inside me as he grabs my waist and pulls me flush against his body. "I crave your mouth," he growls in my ear. "I crave the pink of your lips."

I can't recall if that's part of the book, or if he's actually talking to me.

Thankfully, I hear the book flop against the mattress, and Rosier's now free hand starts roaming up my breast. His fingers curl inside me, and I can't stop myself from whimpering.

"There, relax for me." His lips are still pressed against my ear. He starts to pump his fingers, and I go stiff. Rosier hums against my skin as he slows down, but presses deeper inside me. "So, you like it slow?"

"Yes," I breathe in spite of myself.

"Slow and deep..." He thinks aloud as he does just that. His long fingers reach inside me, moving oh so slowly in and out of my pussy. His thumb swipes along my clit, and I bite my bottom lip. Rosier has to notice because he doesn't let up, his thumb swaying back and forth like a pendulum.

"Fuck—" I whimper.

"I love it when you curse," he murmurs. "Angels be damned—you sound better than any fucking hymn."

He dives down into my neck, teeth grazing my skin. I

inhale a shaky breath as his lips wrap around my skin. I grab the back of his head and yank him back.

"No," I huff. "I can't have you giving me hickies."

Rosier hums, his eyes closed. I jerk my hand back, and his hum turns into a whimper. *Oh...* I'll have to remember that. But for now I release his curls, bringing my hand from the back of his head to his lips, covering his mouth with my palm.

"No biting. Or sucking. Else this ends right here."

He nods, and I pull my hand away, his own fingers still inside me. He starts moving them again, slowly, his thumb pressing against my clit. As we start up again, I'm back to whimpering, saving my little breathy *fucks* and *pleases* for when his fingertips brush along the sensitive spot inside me. Then he curls his fingers and massages that spot exclusively, making me shake from my thighs to my lips.

"Rosie..." I whimper. "Don't stop."

"Never," he promises me. "I'm not *that* cruel."

He starts grunting like it's his cock pumping inside me instead of his fingers. My voice is trapped in my throat while my mouth hangs wide open. I want to hold out but I can't, my whole body going taut before a wave of warmth washes over me. I think we're done, but Rosier pulls back his fingers then brings them to my lips.

He doesn't have to say anything. I suck on them dutifully, tasting myself. His molten gold eyes look down at me with reverence, like I'm a work of art, like I'm the first woman he's ever seen.

"Good little witch."

He shoves his fingers deeper in my mouth, his knuckle brushes my top teeth, and I almost gag. His fingers are so far back down my throat. I shamelessly bring my knees together and rub my thighs, the space between my legs still slick and warm. Rosier drags his fingers out of my mouth, and I make sure my lips are firm around them, his fingertips exiting with a sharp pop.

I catch my breath despite only lying there and taking his fingers. Rosier's curls obscure half his face, and I reach up to push the looping strands behind his ear. He really is the perfect rake, dark and tan with striking features. Though I've never seen any leading man on book covers with his bent nose or bold chin. It makes him feel more real… less like a fantasy.

Still catching my breath, I manage to form words. "Do… you want me?" Rosier tilts his head, and I recognize my words don't make a lot of sense. "Fellatio?" I offer, the word still sounding silly to me.

"I am more than satisfied." My eyes trail down to his crotch, but he lifts my chin to look at his face. "You deserve rest after today. Tiny witch, all worn out."

I snort. "What does any of that have to do with me being small? Plenty of short people are filled with rage."

"But none of them are so intoxicating while doing so." Rosier wraps his arms around my waist. "Sleep, Minnie."

I'm getting used to his commands.

CHAPTER SIXTEEN

MINNIE

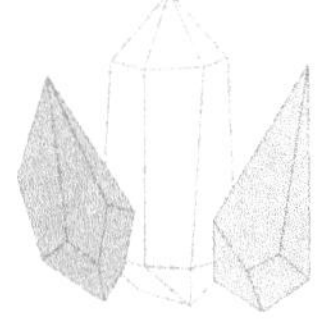

My alarm blares, and I sit up in bed, still naked from the waist down. Classy.

Rosier is still laying next to me, his hand draped over my hips and the book beside him. He stirs, his face a mess of wrinkles and lines.

"Shut up..." he grumbles to someone. Better not be me.

I turn off my alarm and hop out of bed, afraid to look at my hair. I slip on some shorts before peeking in the bathroom mirror. I'm due for a wash anyway, but the back of my head is sure to be a tangled mess. I huff as I fluff up my curls with wet fingers.

My phone buzzes on the counter with a text from Kas.

I managed to get us a fitting. Chanel will be there, and Tim will drop by the tickets while we're there as well.

You're amazing.

I know 😊

I'll send a car to pick you up after work.

As I leave the bathroom, I'm hit with the familiar smell of coffee. I blink, seeing Rosier standing by the coffee pot. "When did you learn to make coffee?"

He snorts. "Is pouring dirt into a cup that difficult? It's rather straightforward."

Kind of hard to argue with that. Coffee, water, press button, wait. Maybe I don't give him enough credit. He reads, he can follow directions–when he wants to. He's useful, and I'd rather eat wet coffee grounds than admit it out loud.

Oh, he's also good with his hands, can't forget that.

I rush back into the bedroom to get dressed: a simple women's suit and white turtleneck. I return to the kitchen, and Rosier hands me a cup of coffee. I know I'm setting myself up for failure by trying it black, but I'm curious. One sip, and I'm assaulted with a bitter, acidic taste.

"Wow that's strong," I choke.

Rosier makes a face, I can't tell if he's offended or embarrassed. Either way, I grab a handful of sugar packets, ripping them all open at once and pouring them into my coffee. As I drink it with a piece of toast, I feel Rosier's eyes on the back of my neck.

"What?" I ask, putting my hands on my hips and mirroring his grumpy face.

"I can't taste your neck when you're wearing that ugly thing." I realize he's talking about the turtleneck. "You keep covering yourself—it's maddening."

I roll my eyes. "I think you'll survive."

Then he's next to me, wrapping an arm around my waist, "I could taste you somewhere else." He palms at the front of my pants, and it takes me a second to realize he wants *me* for breakfast.

"You'll survive," I remind him, peeling his arm away from my waist.

I grab a to-go mug and transfer the strong brew, not wanting to waste his work.

I'm ready to head out, the door halfway open when Rosier slams his hand above my head, effectively shutting the door. My good mood is gone, and I glare at him.

"Are we going to keep doing this?"

"Is this not our goodbye?" His rumbling voice is like an earthquake, making me shiver. He brings his face to my neck despite the turtleneck, the tip of his nose trailing along my jaw. His lips find my ear, "Stay with me."

I'll admit, staying here and letting him eat me out on the kitchen counter is way more appealing than sitting at my desk all morning. But I manage to open the door enough to slide out into the hallway and think I'm finally free, just for him to slap my ass as I'm walking out the door. I seriously hope the sound of the door slamming covers my surprised squeak.

Once I'm alone in the hallway, I mutter, "Perv."

But I smile to myself as I walk to the bus stop.

I'M at the office before everyone else and start to catch up on yesterday's work. It's like there was a company-wide announcement that I was out of commission because I have twice as many emails as usual. Hopefully, it will make the day go by quickly. I'm looking forward to trying on dresses and seeing Rosier pout in his tux. I wonder if Kas will make him wear a bowtie or something to make us match.

Despite all the emails, by the afternoon, I'm left bored with nothing to do. The phone at my desk starts to ring, and I jump like it's transmuted into a snake. I thought that thing was just for decoration. I pick up the receiver with no idea who could be on the other line.

"H-hello?" I ask nervously.

"Minerva Morris, floor fifteen?"

"Y-yeah..."

"Car downstairs for you."

I blink, realizing this must be the front office for the building and the car must've been sent by Kas. "Th-thanks." I hang up, not sure why I'm so embarrassed. People probably order taxis all the time, and that's all this really is anyway.

At least, that's what I think 'til I get downstairs and actually see the thing. It's a proper black cab, tinted windows and everything. The driver stands outside wearing a suit and tie, opening up the passenger door when I get close. I give him a nod, feeling my cheeks grow hot. Luxury sounds great, but this is a bit much for a dress fitting.

It's a quick drive to the shop. I try to be quick and open the door before the driver can, but it's like he can teleport.

The passenger door opens, and I finally find my words. "Thank you."

I take about two steps inside when another man, also dressed in a full suit, meets me. "How can I help you today, madame?"

Where does Kas find these people? "I'm meeting a friend here. Kamsa?"

"Right this way."

He leads me to the back, opening up a door that leads to a big room with a raised, circular stage surrounded by mirrors. There's a couch and a coffee table set up behind it, and a side room with a drawn curtain. Kas and Rosier are sitting on the couch while a woman with black hair all the way down to her butt examines a rack with a dozen dresses on it.

Kas stands up, "Minnie! How was the drive?"

"You have a driver?"

"Of course, I've had one for decades. Not always that one, of course, but I never got into the habit of driving myself."

I look past him at Rosier, who's sitting with his legs wide on the couch, wearing his normal, loose fitting clothes. "Did I miss the tux fitting?"

Rosier pipes up, "I'm not putting it back on."

"Awww," Kas and I bemoan together.

Kas looks at him with knit brows "You won't even put it back on for Minnie?"

I shake my head. "I'll see it during the gala. It's fine. By the way do we have the tickets–"

The door bursts open, and a very frustrated man walks past me and right to Kas. "Here." He shoves an envelope at Kas' chest. I can tell he wants to leave, but I step in front of him, blocking his path.

"Hi, I'm guessing those are the gala tickets?"

The man lifts his brows but still manages to look angry. "They are. I'm guessing you're the reason Kas came crying to me last night about those tickets?"

I give him a smile. "Guilty as charged." His jaw tightens.

Kas waves the tickets. "Thanks for these, Timmy-dear. Maybe next year we can go all four of us?"

"Bite me." He marches off.

Both Rosier and I look at Kas, who calls after his friend, "Come by my place if you want a proper bite, dear!"

"I thought you said he was your friend?" I ask.

"He is. He just gets bitter sometimes. Part of his nature." I tilt my head, and Kas continues with a flourish of his hand, "He was good friends with Alexander the Great; I was good friends with the Pauravas. Ancient history, but he still gets worked up about it."

"You're soooo old Kas," the woman with black hair drones. "And what do you have to show for it?"

To my surprise, Rosier comes to his defense. "Says the bitch begging for scraps."

Harsh.

"As if!" She plants her hands on her hips. "I don't beg."

"Right." The smirk across Rosier's face tells me he's not going to let up. "You're here out of the goodness of your greedy little heart. How does altruism feel? Or should I call it what it is —ass kissing?" The woman makes an offended noise, but Rosier's not done yet. "Kas does a much better job than you do."

"You could say kissing ass is in my nature." Kas grins.

The girl with black hair doesn't look any more amused.

"Anyway..." I walk over to the array of dresses, grabbing a black one just so we can get the fitting started and move on from this devil dick measuring contest. I look at the woman. "Will you... sorry, what's your name? Are you able to help me with the zipper"

"It's Chanel, and that's *actually* why I'm here." She glares at Rosier, who is ignoring her, looking rather bored with his knuckle pressed against his cheek. Chanel takes my wrists and pulls me into the changing room, drawing the curtain with a huff. "Ugh, those two are so fucking annoying. Kas really found his match made in Hell with that one."

"You're talking about Rosier?"

"Yeah." She rolls her eyes. "That one."

She holds out a hand, and it takes me a second to realize she's asking for the dress. I hand it off to her before undressing.

"Are all Princes like him?" I ask.

"Like Rosier? I wouldn't know. I've only been to Hell once, and I certainly haven't spoken to any devils with actual rank. You're going to have to take your bra off."

"Right..." I completely strip the upper half of my body while Chanel preps the dress. "Succubi can go to Hell whenever they want, right?"

"Yeah, we can jump between Hell and Earth. Beings of two worlds or whatever." She talks like she's telling me her commute. "But Hell is a shitty place." She looks at me in the mirror. "Revolutionary, right? Bet you wouldn't have ever guessed." She pools the dress on the floor so it's easy for me to step into it.

"I guess, but it's hard to picture."

Chanel pulls the dress over my body and starts securing it in the back. It's a scoop neck dress with a mermaid silhouette covered in black sequins.

"It can't just be fire and brimstone," I say.

Chanel responds by opening up the dressing room and motioning me to step out onto the little stage. I follow her silent directions, and I'm greeted with a dozen versions of myself from different angles. I run my hands over the rough sequins. The top is loose, and I can definitely see parts of my chest that should be covered. There are also sections where there's more fabric than needed, creating pockets.

"It... sure is sparkly."

Rosier snorts.

"Those sequins are hand stitched," Chanel sneers.

Which is an impressive detail, but it's still a bit too much, not to mention uncomfortable against my bare arms.

"I'm not sure I want to go with black," I think aloud. The color reminds me of a funeral, and I'm trying *not* to die so soon.

Chanel complains, "Then why'd you pick black?"

"Could you keep your fat tongue in your mouth?" Rosier bites. I turn to him, finding both Kas and Chanel are looking at him a little bewildered. Rosier's ire is focused on Chanel. "If we wanted to hear how expensive your dress collection is, we would have asked. Minnie is classy, not coveting." His smoldering eyes shift to me. I frown, not really a fan of how he's talking to Chanel. "Purple might look nice on her... a lilac color..."

"I like purple," I hesitantly agree.

Not because I don't think lilac would look nice but because I don't want to encourage him. There's a shifting of hangers. Through the mirror, I look back at Rosier, who focuses on me. Or, I should say, on my ass. His eyes are narrow like he's glaring, but the curl of his lips is unmistakable. You let a guy touch you once...

Okay, twice.

Chanel walks back over, holding a pastel purple dress with a slit that reaches up to the hip. The fabric is silky and catches the dozen lights surrounding the mirror.

I smile. "That's perfect."

I take Chanel's arm and lead her into the dressing room. As soon as we're inside, I notice she's staring at my hand wrapped around her arm.

"Sorry," I say softly before shutting the curtain on my own. Chanel hangs up the dress and starts undressing me. "So... when you went to Hell–"

"Why do you care?" She helps me slide out of the dress. I open my mouth to explain, but Chanel is faster. "I don't know what it's like for damned souls." She slides the purple dress over my head. I realize there are a row of cloth buttons in the back. Chanel starts buttoning me, leaning in close to whisper in my ear, "But if you're curious for the reasons I think you're curious, I wouldn't worry. You're not going to languish in the bottom tiers. Clearly Rosier has plans for you."

I try to catch her gaze in the mirror, but she's quick to return her attention to the buttons. I wonder how she sees me, fraternizing with devils. A debaucherous mortal? A power hungry witch? It occurs to me that Chanel's Mother or Father or whichever might have made a deal with a devil as well.

I turn to look at her, so many questions in my mind, but I ask the least obvious one. "How old are you?"

"Young. I was born in 1789. Aquarius." Still looking at me, she reaches back and opens up the curtain.

Rosier and Kas both turn their heads to look at me. "Now that's a dress!" Kas hoots.

"Right?" Chanel speaks in a tense vocal fry. She leads me to the mirrors. "She looks wicked sexy. We'll have to hem the bottom, but other than that, it fits great."

Up on the little stage, the bottom of the dress pools around my feet, but the single shoulder halter is much better suited for my body. There are large gold safety pins that accent at the hip and front of the dress. I can't help but pop my knee, showing off the dress' slit. Chanel claps, and I smile over at her.

Rosier barks, "Leave us."

Both Chanel and Kas practically run out of the room.

I look at Rosier with a frown. "What's that about?"

He approaches the stage but doesn't step onto it. With his height, he doesn't really have to. He holds my hips, looking at me through the mirror.

He leans in and kisses where my neck meets my collarbone. "I like you with your hair up," he growls against my skin. "Easy access. None of that walled-off shit you wear every damn day."

I chew the inside of my lip. I'm not confused by his coming onto me; that's been the only consistent thing in this relationship so far. I don't get how he can be so cruel to everyone and so gentle with me. I reach over and touch the back of his head, encouraging him to keep kissing me. Rosier's lips move up my neck, then my jawline.

"Why are you doing this?"

"I want you," he says, obviously.

"So fuck me, then?"

Rosier lifts his head, and I can see his bewildered expression in the mirror. "I forget you know that word."

I roll my eyes.

One of his hands reaches to cup my ass, sliding along the smooth fabric. "I think I'd rather fuck you in my true form."

My brows knit. I know werewolves and vampires have monstrous forms, but I never really thought about Kas or Rosier looking any different than they normally do. "What do you normally look like?"

"If I have to wait, then so do you." He kisses my shoulder.

I shake my head. "You're being weird."

"I want to have you all to myself. Take you when you're truly mine. Body and soul..." His hand trails up my thigh, his fingers threatening to slip under the fabric of the dress. "Body, soul, and cunt." No longer teasing, looking through the mirror as his hand disappears underneath the silky fabric. "I haven't gotten to taste you yet..." His voice sounds almost lamenting.

He delicately traces his fingers along my panties, then grabs my breast, pawing at me. I let out a surprise whimper, still focusing on the mirror in front of me. Rosier's golden eyes are like a lion's, staring at the mirror, staring at me. His thumb and forefinger pinch my nipple through the dress, and I let out a choked gasp. I watch Rosier's hands, watch my mouth hang open in ecstasy.

"That's it," he speaks into my collar, his voice gravelly. "Now you see what I see. You're all hot and bothered, your body begging for me."

I reach back and grab his thighs, pressing our bodies closer together. "You think... I've never done this before?" Rosier's fingers push my panties aside. "Watched myself?" He brushes my folds, already wet.

"You're full of surprises," he chuckles. "Such a filthy little witch, trying so hard to be seen as pure." He shoves two fingers inside me. I wince, and he coos in my ear, "Shhh." He curls his fingers, thumb brushing over my clit as he nibbles at my ear. His fingers pull out of me and out from under the dress. Still watching the mirror, he brings his fingers to his lips and sucks like I did last night. He moans like I'm on my knees gagging on him. "You're to die for, Minnie."

The door opens, and I cover myself despite still being fully clothed. Kas has one foot in the dressing room. "Not to interrupt, but we kinda only have the fitting room for a few–"

"Get out." Rosier growls, his words vibrating against my shoulder.

"Right, yup, leaving now. Just maybe we could grab–"

Rosier turns and marches over to him. He grabs him by his shirt collar and pins him to the closest wall. "Always so chatty, Kamsa. Why don't you shove some dick in that hole the way you were born to?"

I hop off the stage, almost tripping over my dress. "Stop! Let him go!" I step in between him and Kas, glaring at him with my fists balled at my side. "I said let him go!" Finally, Rosier lets go of Kas' collar with a grumble. I cross my arms over my chest. "That was rude. And cruel! Kas is helping us. Helping *me*. We wouldn't have been able to get those tickets without him."

Rosier crosses his arms, mirroring me. "I would have found a way."

I snort. "Yeah right." His eyes narrow. "You didn't even have clothes before Kas helped you out. You have no right to treat him this way."

Rosier raises his voice. "I have every right–"

"You know you're not even half as charming as you think you are. Jerk."

Kas steps in like a referee. "I adore a lover's spat, really, I do, but I'm fine." He fixes the top button of his shirt. "I kinda like being manhandled."

I scoff and start walking back to the dressing room, the chain above rattling as I throw the curtain shut. "Chanel! Can you please come help me!"

We get the dress and leave promptly.

CHAPTER SEVENTEEN

ROSIER

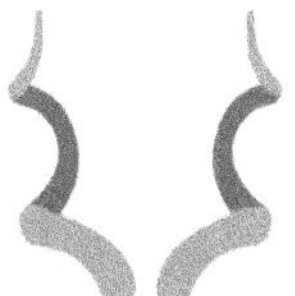

Jerk is far from the worst insult, yet it echoes in my head like the wail of a dying soul. *Jerk. Jerk. Jerk.* Minnie sits with her arms crossed, pouting out the car window. Kas sits between us, a neutral wall.

I lean over to whisper in his ear, "It didn't hurt when I grabbed you, did it?"

He looks at me with furrowed brows, his lips crooked. "Of course, it hurts. You're a lot stronger than me, you know."

Still looking out the window, Minnie pipes up, "Usually when someone hurts another person, they apologize.

I grit my teeth. If I remind her of my nature, she'll only pout further, kick me out again and again and again. I prefer her apartment, with her books and where Leaf can run around like a mad imp. I like sleeping in her bed. I like waking up beside her.

Kas touches Minnie's shoulder. "It's okay Minerva, honestly. It's not the first–"

Refusing to let Kas inform Minnie of the previous instances I've manhandled him, I cut in. "I'm sorry."

Both Kas and Minnie look at me with wide eyes. Then Minnie's eyes narrow, like she's expecting more. But what the fuck else is there to say?

"I... shouldn't have been so aggressive. You didn't deserve it..."

Kas' face softens.

"...in that moment," I finish. "You have an attitude that needs to be tethered."

Kas laughs. "It's a good thing I like hands on me. Just promise me you'll give me a kiss afterwards next time, yeah?"

I glance past him at Minnie, hoping she'll object. She looks at Kas. I want her to look at me. "Sure..."

Soon I find myself standing in the middle of the hallway between Kas and Minnie's apartments. Minnie opens up her door, and Leaf comes bolting, attaching himself to my leg. "Needy little thing," I scoop him up in my arms. As I scratch his chin, I face Minnie, waiting for her to say something.

Her cheeks are hollow and her lips puckered, clearly thinking. What I would give to hear her thoughts. "He's probably hungry." she says finally before waving me inside.

Kas pats me on the shoulder before he disappears into his own apartment.

Minnie opens up a can of food, and Leaf hops out of my arms to sit at her feet, his bent tail swishing back and forth.

"Cats are different than I imagined," I think aloud.

"What were you expecting?" She shakes the can over a small plate, the food slopping down. "Do you guys even have cats?"

"Our own version. They're much larger—more heads and tails."

Minnie sets down the plate, and Leaf starts feasting, snapping and slurping his food.

"Since cats are common witch familiars," I explain, "there

are quite a few documents in the library that detail them: sneaky, conniving creatures that strike fear into men."

"Must be a pretty old text," Minnie remarks as she leans against the counter. "Familiars and cats aren't really the same thing, anyhow. Familiars follow a witch's will. You can't command a cat to do anything."

I chuckle. "I've noticed."

"That's what I like about them," she says, and I quirk a brow. "They're independent, have an attitude about them." She bends down and pats Leaf's backside. "Plus they've got cute toe beans."

"Toe beans?"

Minnie picks up Leaf, who lets out a roaring meow, upset he's being pulled away from his dinner. Minnie lifts up one of his paws.

"Toe beans!"

She squeezes a little brown pad on the bottom of Leaf's paw. I fail to see what's so charming about them, unlike Minnie who has an amused smile as she paws at Leaf. She releases him, and he swiftly returns to his meal.

I clear my throat. "I'm glad you're no longer angry with me."

"Oh I am," she says with a casual air as she walks past me. "I don't like being associated with a brute."

"You were the one who summoned a devil. Did you expect me to be gentle? Charitable?"

"I expected you to make a contract with me. Didn't really think about your manners, or lack thereof." She goes to the couch and picks up a book left abandoned on the table.

I join her, though she doesn't look up from her page. "Perhaps... you could teach me manners." She tilts her head and rolls her eyes. "I'm serious! I can at least try. I haven't had much of a chance to act properly. In the Hells, we thrive on insults and threats. Cruelty is expected, revered. To show kindness is to show weakness."

"I'd like to see your weak side." She says it in a light and casual voice that makes me shiver.

I hold her wrist, careful not to grab it. "How? I don't know how," I admit.

"You did apologize to Kas... I guess for you, that's a pretty big step."

"Those words have never once left my lips."

"First time for everything." She shrugs and sets her book down."But you do know how to be kind. You're nice to me."

I blink, feeling like I've been tossed into the deepest, coldest pit in Hell. Tightening my hand around her wrist I pin her down on her back. Keeping one hand above her head, her free hand reaches up to touch my chest. Pressing right against my sternum, against my heart.

"Rude," she breathes like she's reached a mountain's peak.

"You like it," I growl. "You enjoy it so much, you mistake it for kindness."

She looks up at me with those big green eyes. I could only compare them to emeralds when we first met, the only shade of green I have ever known. Now I look at them and see the deep green of leaves, of budding flowers, of life. It's a good reminder of what she is–mortal. With limited time.

She pushes up on my chest and slides out from under me, sitting on the floor a moment before standing up, her hands on her hips. "I like manners," she scolds.

"I don't know what those are!"

Her eyes dance around in their sockets. "I'm sure you've seen devils beg for mercy. How about we start there?"

"Mercy? From you?"

Her head tilts, her big eyes looking almost innocent. "I could send you back. Kick you out. Run to Amber and have a whole witch coven on your tail." She bends at the hip so we're eye level. "Maybe I'll ignore you, since you're so desperate for attention."

"*I am not.*"

She snorts and shakes her head before standing upright again.

I stand to meet her. "Perhaps I have been too gentle with you," I reach for her chin. "What with your–"

She swats my hand away. "Beg," she bites. "Or you can kiss this plane goodbye. I'll get back at Arthur le Fay on my own. Just like how I summoned you on my own."

Know your place, the voice in my head prompts me, but I know if I say that to her, it could very well be the end of things. I'm not ready to go back to Hell–have no desire to be questioned about my time here, to dance around the fact that one witch with a vendetta I didn't fulfill was my arbiter.

So I lower myself to my knees, pressing my chin to my chest, averting my eyes. Once I am settled on the floor, I look up at her, looking for that little smile of hers. To my dismay, her lips are in a hard line, eyes dull and bored.

"To present myself like this before you is a great shame," I tell her.

"Are you going to cry about it?"

I scoff. "Devils don't cry."

"They aren't supposed to apologize either. Guess that makes you special." Her hand rests under my chin, lifting my head so my neck is completely exposed. "Do you want to be special, Prince?"

I swallow, Minnie no doubt seeing the stone in my throat bob nervously. "I want many things..." I admit. "I want power. I want every corner of the Hells to know my name. And I want my face between your thighs."

"I'll say it again." Her voice is a slow drawl. "Beg, Prince."

"Forgive me, Minnie." My voice strains. "I want to stay here—with you."

She starts playing with her curls, twisting strands around her fingers, paying more attention to her mindless act than to me. "Except you won't form a contract with me. You refuse me."

"I don't think you need me. You're powerful enough as is." She looks at me then, a coil of hair still wrapped tightly around her finger, and I tell her, "Anyone who can't see your power is a fool, lying to themselves for their own ego. You're smart, cunning, and ruthless when you desire it." I inch toward her, still on my knees. "You're intoxicating... and so beautiful."

She scoffs.

"I cannot even imagine a being that could rival you," I continue. "I want to watch your eyes roll back as I pleasure you. I want to feel the curves of your body."

"I've heard all this from guys who reek of cheap liquor at the club. Try again."

I bite my cheek before backtracking. "You're right. You could take care of Arthur le Fay by yourself. But I want to see you ruin him. What a pleasure it would be to watch him fall, as so many empires do. To stand beside you in the ashes. Please, Minnie." I bow my head, looking only at her feet. "Let me stay."

The room is still, like time has stopped. The torture ends when Minnie strokes my crown. "Could be better, but we'll work on it."

I glance up at her, my face still angled to the floor. "Let me offer you my body."

"What part of 'you wanting to sleep with me isn't all that flattering' don't you get?"

I clear my throat. "I know mortal men have never been able to satisfy you."

She furrows her brow and opens her mouth like she's about to object but doesn't speak. Her mouth closes and she purses her lips.

"Tell me your desires, Minnie. Let me be a conduit of your pleasure."

"What if I want to step on you?"

I bend forward, pressing my forehead against the floor. "Let me be the servant you summoned. Use me."

Silence. I can't see Minnie's face in this position. The anticipation is worse than any punishment she could deal me.

"You won't know what it is..." she begins, then trails off. I lift my head to look at her, and this somehow convinces her to keep going. "Pegging?"

"If that is your desire, I am open to learning."

She swallows, her cheeks turning red. "So... I have a toy, and I use it on you. I'd be the one fucking you."

The words on her tongue make my cock throb.

Her voice jumps an octave. "But we don't have to!"

"I want you to fuck me. I'm curious to feel how you'll use me." I struggle to fathom how this is such a big request. "Can I see the toy?"

She nods and rushes to her room. I follow her, standing in the doorway, awaiting instructions. She's halfway under the bed, only her legs poking out. "It's here somewhere–" I hear some shuffling. "Wait a second–"

I cover my mouth to hide my smirk and stifle a laugh. She's so eager, and I don't want her thinking I'm insulting her.

When she pops out from under the bed, there's a sparkle in her eyes I have never seen before. In her hands is a harness with a pink cock, five inches long with a curve. It's inoffensive, far from intimidating. Yet Minnie's voice seems unsure.

"Is this okay?"

"Of course. I'm surprised it's not bigger." I start to unbutton my shirt as I approach her. Her cheeks are somehow an even deeper shade of red, and it's spreading to the tip of her nose. "I promise you, I want this. Now, please." I dip a finger inside her tall, white collar shirt. "Take off this terrible thing."

We undress, tossing the constraining fabric to the floor. Seeing her bare breasts–small and pert, just like her–makes my erection stir. Once her pants are on the floor, I grab her hips and take one of her breasts into my mouth.

"You're distracting me," she murmurs.

I release her nipple and kiss the space between her breasts before looking up at her.

"I'm supposed to be the one in charge," she reminds me.

I pinch her nipple and her breath hitches.

"You're not even fully undressed," she scolds.

I pull down my pants and flop onto the bed, lounging with my hands behind my head. She rolls her eyes, but one corner of her lip is curled in a smile. She climbs onto the bed, straddling my legs and taking hold of the base of my cock. I exhale, a special spark ignited by her touch. But she doesn't move her hand.

"Are you going to touch me?"

"Are you going to let me work?" she shoots back with a tilt of her head.

Her expression is soft, but she still manages to make me feel bad for speaking out of turn. It makes my blood boil, not with rage but with white hot lust. I nod, keeping my mouth shut.

Minnie hums. "We talked about you learning manners." She releases my dick. "While I get ready, maybe think about your words a little more." She grabs the harness and toy, standing up on her knees. She pulls the straps from their buckles, wrapping the leather around her thick thighs and hips. She pulls the leather taut, her warm bronze skin spilling out over the straps. "Tell me again what you want." Her voice is low and still achingly gentle. "Maybe use some of those mortal words you never use."

"You want me to beg some more?"

A smile appears on her lips.

If I'm going to be bossed around by any mortal, it should be Minnie. Still I bite my tongue before forcing the words out my mouth. "I want you to touch me please."

"How do you want to be touched?"

"Please stroke my cock."

Her hand reaches forward and grabs my length, finally rubbing me up and down. I groan, my head rolling back onto the pillow. I'm not used to this body, but it feels surprisingly good. Minnie slides her thumb over the head, and I shudder. Something wet drips down my length and look back to see spit dripping from her lips down to the head of my cock.

She knows what she's doing. If I was in my true form, she might not. Perhaps I should warn her that I'm much bigger in reality, a different shape—but not now. Not when she's finally giving me the attention I've wanted since we met.

"Fuck, this feels so good, Minnie."

She giggles. "We're just getting started. I think you're nice and hard now." She sits back on her calves. "Grab the lube from the bedside table. It's in the top drawer."

"If I can find it underneath all your other toys," I taunt.

"Careful," she warns. "I might smack you with one of those toys."

I find a bottle in the corner of the drawer. "Is that a threat or a promise?" I ask as I hand her the lubricant.

She pours the lube right onto the toy before dripping some onto her finger tips. She reaches between my legs and circles my hole, making it nice and wet.

"You don't have to be so gentle," I say right before she slides a finger inside me. It's a nice feeling but hardly enough.

She slips another finger inside, starting to fill me the way I want.

Her fingers curl, massaging me, I take deep breaths, appreciating the sensation.

"Relax," she encourages. "I'm sure you want it rough, but why would I give you what you want right from the start?"

Her other hand reaches for my balls, massaging them in time with her curling fingers. My lips fall open and deep breaths turn to deep moans. I raise my head to look at her, smiling at me kindly while her eyes are devious, like she's a devil herself.

"Minnie, please, I want you to fuck me."

"And I will. When I decide you're ready." My head flops back onto the pillow and she laughs. "Such a spoiled brat."

I grit my teeth and mutter, "You're the brat."

She squeezes my balls, and my whole body goes stiff. She releases me, and I catch my breath, like I've survived an attempted assassination by suffocation. Then she slaps them, the stinging sensation making my head spin.

"I'm sorry," I gasp. "I'm sorry, please! I want you."

She pulls her fingers out, and I stifle a whimper. Her hands grab my thighs, opening them like a gate. I lift my head again so I can watch her press the toy against my hole.

"Keep your legs open," she commands.

Then she releases one of my thighs to grab the shaft of the toy to guide it inside me. The head slides in, then she pushes her hips forward, fitting perfectly between my thighs.

"You're so big Minnie," I gasp.

She laughs, her face still scarlet but nowhere near as widespread as before, the color resting on the rounds of her cheeks.

Once she's fully inside me, she begins rutting her hips. My lips are shut, trying to contain my moans. Then she grabs a handful of my curls and pulls my head back, my mouth opening for her. I moan and gasp, the sharp pain pairing perfectly with the pleasure between my legs.

"A girl could get used to this..." Her hips slow. "Keep your mouth open."

I do as she says, and she spits in it, a warm glob of her saliva pooling on my tongue. Always so attentive, her hips begin to buck faster and harder.

I swallow her gift to me before gasping, "I'm at your beck and call. I can be your toy."

"I don't want a toy," she tells me without hesitation. She grabs my thighs again, pushing them up so my knees are against my chest. "I want a man—one who will tell me how much he loves being under me." Her nails leave claw marks on my skin.

A growl leaves my lips. "I want your dick every day, Minnie." She bites her lip. "You're the only mortal I'll ever let fuck me—the only mortal I *want* to fuck me." With a wide grin, I sigh, "The only one who can satisfy me."

She releases my thighs, one hand now against my upper chest and the other returning to my cock.

As soon as she touches between my legs I lift my hips in need. "Yes! Yes, Minnie, please!"

She uses her hand on my chest as an anchor as she grinds against me. "It's adorable how you beg. I should keep you here just for that."

"Hells," I curse. "Keep me here, keep me in your bed."

"Only if you're good," she warns.

Her hand strokes me faster, and I know it's only a matter of time before I burst. My moans become more strained, more desperate. Minnie keeps fucking me with her toy and hand, a steady rhythm that reaches my heart, thudding in my ears. Finally, I grab the sheets, threatening to tear them as I finish, warm seed spreading across my chest.

Seeing this, Minnie gives me a few more deep thrusts, her

hand firmly holding the base of my cock. More thick ropes spill onto my body, till eventually it dwindles to little drops. Minnie releases my length, sliding out of me, and I catch my breath.

She flops down beside me, her breathing as heavy as mine. "How do you feel?"

"An odd question to ask." I need another moment to gather myself. "When I'm a feeble mess in front of you."

"That doesn't sound good, Rosier."

"I feel amazing," I assure her. She's laying on her side now, looking at me. "And you?"

"I feel... fucking powerful." Her face falls. "Is that wrong?" Her brows furrow further.

I reach to touch her cheek."Who taught you to relinquish control? That you should shun power?" It's my turn to knit my brows and frown. "I should murder this man."

Minnie shakes her head, "You'd have to murder a lot of people."

"Then so be it," I agree. "I am a devil, after all."

CHAPTER EIGHTEEN

ROSIER

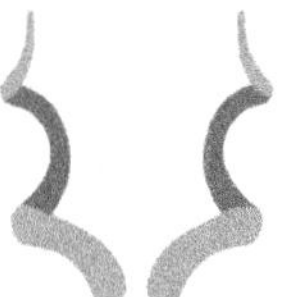

I FALL ASLEEP FASTER THAN I WOULD HAVE LIKED. BUT I fell asleep in her arms, sniffing her hair that smells of floral oils and her skin that smells like sunshine.

The morning sun hits my eyes, and I grumble as I cover my face with my arm. Last night took more out of me than I expected. It could be... what did Minnie call it, dropping? I try to ignore the sounds of footsteps and running water, yearning for a few more minutes of rest. Or a few hours.

"Rosie..." Minnie whispers, and I groan. "You don't have to get up, I'm going to work."

It takes a moment too long for me to comprehend what she's saying. By the time I realize she's leaving, that we haven't had our goodbye, I hear the front door shut and the pins click into place.

"Shit–" I toss the blanket aside and bolt for the door. "Minnie!" I step into the hallway, looking back and forth the corridor looking for her. She couldn't have gotten far with those tiny legs of hers. "Minerva?" I run down the hall to the stairwell, catching sight of a familiar head of curls at the bottom. "Minnie!"

She looks up at me, her eyes so big I can see the whites of them from up above. Her hair is high atop her head, showing off her round cheeks. She's wearing a skirt today, her plush thighs on full display. Her mouth opens, but a different voice calls from below.

"Put some fucking clothes on!" There's an older woman on the steps below, her face a mask of rage and disgust. Suddenly, I understand what it means to be naked. "Don't make me call someone!"

I take one last look at Minnie before rushing back to the apartment. I've left the door open, and Leaf is strutting up the hall. "No you don't–" I mutter as I scoop him up and lock us both back inside the apartment. I press myself against the door, holding Leaf to my chest.

He lets out his grating meow that lets me know he's hungry.

While Leaf eats, I put on some clothes, a bit shaken by the woman in the stairwell. Now dressed and with Minnie gone for the day, I stand in front of her bookshelf.

I'm a bit more specific about my preferences with her collection: no overly gentle, kind, sniveling men. They're rare– Minnie has a clear preference for the more crass gentlemen– but when they do appear, I want to throw the book out of the window. I also don't enjoy anything contemporary. Historical books have balls, duels, and complicated rules of courtship. Devils might not care so much about affairs of the heart, but the hierarchy that exists in these books, they would appreciate.

I also rather enjoy when the couples argue, when they toss each other aside in a fit of jealousy or because something has been left unsaid. It's like watching lower devils tear at each other, neither one achieving any sort of victory. But in the end, the couples succeed. Always.

Sometimes I learn something new about mortals from the pages, things about flora or how paints used to be mixed. I think I'm learning more about what mortals want as well. Why there even need to be so many books about love.

And, obviously, I like the fucking.

Before I can settle on a title, there is a knock at the door. "Rooooosie."

I'm going to kill that succubus.

I march to the door and open it right as Kas sings again, "Rooo–oh, there you are."

"I take back my apology from yesterday." I notice standing behind him is Tim, Chanel, and Moniz. I lift a brow. "The gala isn't till tomorrow."

"Exactly." Kas shows me a stack of papers he has in his hands. "And we need to prep. Without Minnie."

He pushes past me inside the apartment with his procession of succubi. My teeth grind against each other. He wants to scheme in Minnie's apartment without her. It's an obvious betrayal.

Maybe our little game of begging affected me more than I realize.

Kas spreads his stack of papers on the small table in front of the couch. Each one has a small portrait attached to the corner. I grab the first one, the image of a man with pale skin and eyes looking back at me.

"Richard is an odd one," Kas says, "but Tim has it on good authority that he would make a contract."

So that's what this is about. I drop the paper, letting it float to the ground. "I told you, I have no interest in making a contract with anyone."

Tim's face is a mess of wrinkles, and Chanel looks equally as pissed, while Moniz looks half dead.

Kas sits next to me on the couch. "Okay, so not Richard. In

fact, fuck Richard–he's a vampire anyhow and might not even be able to make a contract. How about–"

"What do you mean?" I'm not interested in whatever Richard wants, but the fact he wouldn't be able to make a deal at all is intriguing.

"I'll answer your question with another question; do vampires have souls?"

"Fuck if I know. I've never met a vampire." I recall the conversation back at Industry Lounge, the succubus Seira who has some vampire at her beck and call: a sugar daddy.

"Then they probably don't, so fuck you, Richard, and let's move on." Kas grabs another piece of paper from the stack. "So this woman is a real bitch and a half–"

"I'm not signing a contract," I tell him again.

Then I look at the group of succubi. Tim's arms are crossed over his chest, and Chanel's propped her hand on her hip. At this point, I think Moniz *is* dead with how the whites of their eyes are showing.

"If you lot think I'd spend eternity with some bitchy woman or soulless vampire, you all should concern yourselves with finding a brain instead of finding me a contract."

"Kas!" Tim whines, not unlike Minnie when I've properly vexed her. "What's this guy's deal? You keep telling us he's a Prince, but I'm starting to think he's a fraud."

I lean back into the couch, considering how to punish this insolent worm. "Eat cat shit." Tim goes stiff, baring his teeth before he starts to walk toward the box that Leaf relieves himself in. I raise my hand. "Stop." Tim stands in place, his body still straight like a rod. "As entertaining as that would be, the smell would be unbearable."

"You're kind of shit at this," Chanel speaks up. "You know that?"

My top lip curls, and I click my tongue. "Again with your heedless words. But I'll bite. What is it exactly that I'm shit at."

Moniz yawns. "Being a devil."

I bite my tongue, hard enough that even my mortal teeth could chop it right in two. I don't hold back for their sake. If anything, this is a punishment for myself. A lashing for being so... I'm not sure what. I don't refuse contracts out of kindness the way Minnie suggests. In a fitting selfishness, I do not want to prattle with mortal souls for eternity. Even if I were to torture them, to leave them at the bottom of some fiery pit in Hell, they would still be intertwined with my being. I would own them, yes–but the tether would drag me down as well.

To be soul-linked is a burden I do not want. How does that make me any less of a devil?

When I release my tongue, a metallic taste hangs in my mouth. "Bold words coming from someone who is only half a devil, who must draw on the power of others. Including mere mortals. What are any of you without humans, anyhow?"

Chanel makes a squeaking sound. "What are you without a contract?"

"Plenty more than you." I glare at her.

"Rosier..." Kas sounds hesitant. Good. He should be careful with his words now that Minnie isn't around to protect him. "I don't... get it. Why are you being so cagey?"

"Cagey?"

He furrows his brows. "I mean, why won't you sign a contract with *anyone?* You're the first devil to reach the mortal plane since...Honestly, probably since Chanel's mom, and that was back in the 1800s."

"You're assuming these people would even make a contract," I say... "That they would believe in such things."

Kas leans down and snatches the piece of paper off the floor. "Richard would believe it. He's old enough to remember a time when devils did come to the mortal plane to make deals. Unlike your generation."

"What?" I'm genuinely confused now. How could my age matter–as if I could even determine my age in any manner that makes sense on this plane.

Kas shrugs. "You're young. Had your title handed to you. Most devils of your rank had to work to become Princess. But it's more than that, you're... I hate to say it–"

"Then shut your fucking mouth." I grab the paper from his hand and rip it up. Then I gather the other papers and crush them in my hands like clay to be molded for a pot. "I don't need contracts. I don't need you all. I *need* nothing. I am–"

"Yeah, yeah, the best of sin, a Prince of the Hells, Minnie's favorite–whatever it is that makes your cock stand up so tall." Kas rises and starts to usher the others out of the apartment. "Have a good day, Prince."

I consider throwing something at him: a book, perhaps, or maybe the whole damn couch. But they're all out of the apartment before they can see just how badly they've wounded me. As embarrassing as that is to admit.

I could sign a contract with anyone. Richard or Minnie–anything with a soul is mine for the taking. I simply refuse them. That's not weakness, that's power. I'm denying them access to my power. Yet the longer I sit here, in this tiny apartment surrounded by romance books, sitting on a plush couch outside the room where Minnie and I have laid together, the less powerful I feel.

You will never be a proper Prince, a voice, not my own, tells me. *You will always be a half-breed, neither succubus nor devil, too far flung from mortality to be accepted by your Mother's kin.*

"That's not true..." I hardly realize I'm speaking.

Minnie accepts me. Not that it matters. She's nothing but a witch with the power and drive to summon the first devil in centuries. Hardly even that. She's only a moral with bright eyes and lips I will dream about. She burns like a flame. She's...

Soft hearted little shit.

I bury my face in my hands, hiding from the voice in my head. Leaf hops up and starts nudging my wrists before diving under my arms and settling on my lap. I pull my hands from my face. He looks so content with his eyes shut as he rolls onto his belly to stretch his legs. I rub his chest, making the mistake of petting his stomach and he pounces on my hand. I chuckle as his fangs dig into my knuckle.

Perhaps I am too soft... and compassionate. Maybe I am neither a devil nor a succubus. My Father wasn't the only one who procreated with the souls of the damned; there are others. Spares. Bodies to fill the space of our forefathers when they fall. We're devils so far as anyone can tell. No, we must be devils. How else would Kas and his cohort submit to me with such ease?

I am the best of sin. Could I not also be a spark of humanity?

ROSIER

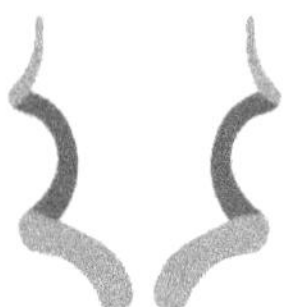

Hours pass, and Minnie opens the front door with a huff. She pulls out the loop that keeps her hair atop her head. "Oh, you're here."

"Is that surprising?"

"You tend to run off with Kas," she points out as she makes her way over to the couch.

She sits down beside me and rests her head on my shoulder. It's like she's cast a spell, shocking me with some sort of magic that makes my muscles go tense. Her big green eyes glance up at me, her cheek still pressed against my shoulder.

"What's up?" she asks.

Lying comes easy. "I'm bored," I grumble. "I've been cooped up in this place all day."

She sighs. "Well, I'm too tired to take you out anywhere." She sits up, and I want her to rest against me again. "Kind of ironic, a devil suffering on the mortal plane."

She scoops Leaf out of my lap and holds him to her chest. He lifts his head and licks her chin. I wonder if I shoved him aside so I could be the one lapping and nipping at her skin if she would throw a fit.

I consider another way to irritate her. "Kas has been trying to find me other mortals to sign a deal."

Minnie focuses on Leaf. "Except you're not interested in contracts, so he's wasting your time."

I lean forward, wrapping my arm around her without even realizing it. "If you could inform him of that fact."

"You want me to tell him it's because of your mommy issues?" She says it like it's obvious, as if I've asked her the color of the sky. "Or are we keeping that between us?"

Her statement isn't obvious at all. It's incorrect. My Mother isn't the reason–why would that ever be it? How could a woman I only knew from a distance be the catalyst for my angst?

"Takes mommy issues to know mommy issues," Minnie explains, like she's read my mind.

My shoulders slump, and my voice goes low. "You admit you have mommy issues?"

"You didn't hear that from me..." Her eyes float about the room, looking anywhere but right at me. "But... yeah, I kind of do."

"Mommy and daddy issues must be a winning combination."

Her expression darkens like I've insulted her–but in truth, it's a complement. Her angst, her rage, is beautiful. No one else sees how strong it makes her like I do.

"Wipe that face off," I command. "It's as you said, takes issues to know issues."

Leaf leaps from her arms, and she turns her body in my direction. "Are you saying you also have daddy issues?"

"No, the Prince of Hell was a lovely guardian. Always said

he was grateful to have a child. Applauded me for my studies. Praised me for every little thing I did."

She grimaces, thankfully catching my sarcasm. "I never thought about... you being a kid."

"A Princling," I correct.

"A child, Rosie. You were a child. It sounds like one without any real parents."

"I had servants," I tell her. "Is that different?"

"Parents aren't really servants. They do more than servants. They nurture you and teach you right and wrong. They hold you when you're scared." Her head tilts, and her voice becomes distant. "They bring you to the library and read to you, scold you out of love. They're your everything when you're little."

Her eyes sparkle like polished diamonds, only for the glimmer to fall from her eye in a single drop that takes me aback. I reach for her cheek, holding her face like she's a precious heirloom. Another stream descends down her cheek, and I swipe at it with my thumb, tracing along the little specks of brown that dot her cheeks and nose.

It's as if my touch awakens something in her because she pulls back, pawing at her eyes with her palm. "Ugh, God, this week is getting to me."

"Mommy issues," I point out. "You're thinking about her, aren't you"

"I always am." She chokes. "I hate crying in front of people."

"I don't see why..." The edges of her eyes are red and she inhales sharply through her nose. Yet I can't stop looking at her. I hold her face once more, this time cupping her cheeks in both hands. "Maybe you should cry more often."

More and more, her eyes sparkle, and droplets fall down her cheeks. Some, I push away, while others, I let round her chin and land in the space between us.

"I hate crying..." she repeats, voice wavering.

I don't know what to say, so I keep holding her face, keep catching warm drops of water on my fingertips until her eyes are clear again, and her breathing is normal.

To my delight, she smiles at me, leaning into my touch. "You're confusing."

I relax my hold on her cheeks. "You are an odd little thing, Minerva. Scared of all the wrong things."

"What do you mean?"

"You should be terrified of me."

A dry chuckle leaves her lips. "You're right. I should be. I should have been afraid of you from the start." She rests a hand atop mine, trapping me. "Even before I summoned you, I should have been frightened."

I huff and pat her cheek with my other hand. I've let her get too comfortable. But when I try to pull my hand away, she takes it in her own palm and brings it back to her cheek. Both her hands have mine now. Holding them against her like... like she needs me. Not my power or a contract but *me*.

Crush every ounce of kindness! My Father's voice irritates me like Leaf's tail under my nose in the dead of night. He's a damn hypocrite, acting like he didn't desire a mortal. As if his lust for my Mother didn't hide some fondness. Why else would he have chosen her if not in response to some *feeling*?

I lean down, and she closes her eyes. In anticipation of what, I'm not sure. "The gala is tomorrow."

Her eyes open like she's been shaken awake from a dream. "R-right." She clears her throat and shakes her head. "That's right, I have to go see Amber tomorrow."

"I thought you and Amber were finished?"

"We're best friends. It takes a little more than a man to tear us apart."

"I'm more than a man, Minnie."

She ignores me. "She's going to do my hair and then we have to get ready. You've got a whole suit to put on." At that she smiles.

"You know, I've heard this human phrase. Birthday suit–"

"Do *not*." She covers my mouth with her hand, and I smile against it. "What happened to manners?"

I hold her wrist and drag her hand away. "I may need another lesson before tomorrow." I release her wrist. My hand touches her knee and slides up her thigh, making it to the edge of her skirt before she takes my wrist in turn and tosses my hand aside.

"You're going to behave because if you don't, I can just have Kas be my date."

"I don't recall us agreeing to be each other's dates, Minnie." I place my hand on her knee once more, keeping it there. "And based on your books, we'll need a chaperone, I need to ask for your favor."

She giggles, her smile reaching her eyes. "Go ahead then, ask."

"Minerva..." I swallow. "Shit, what's your last name?"

She purses her lips, trying to subdue her laughter. "Morris."

"Minerva Morris, it would be my privilege to escort you–" I reach for her hand, holding it like it could crumble in my palm. "–to that stupid fucking gala." That laughter she's been trying to contain escapes, lines forming around her eyes and mouth. "Is that a yes?"

"Yes," she agrees. Her fingers wrap around my palm. "I would be delighted by your company. Though, I'm not sure the rest of the guests will agree."

I pull her to me, leaving no space between us.

"Rosier," she scolds. "I need sleep. Don't make me exile you to the couch tonight." I open my mouth, and she presses a finger to my lips. "I'm going to get ready for bed."

She hops up, and I watch her walk away, admiring how her thighs brush together in that skirt. Though, it only entertains me for so long before I'm thinking about the gala, about what will happen to us once Minnie is satisfied with her revenge.

Once she's settled in loose fitting clothing, she grabs a book and flops into bed. I do the same, shedding my clothes and laying beside her with a book. It's a familiar image, her head resting on my chest with my arm wrapped around her. I could grab her breast. Tug at her pants till she lets me touch her. Beg for her. This, simple as it is, satisfies me, however.

I can still smell her floral scent. Brush against her soft skin. Admire how her lip twitches with glee when she reads a line she likes or how her brows furrow when something has gone awry in her story.

Meanwhile in my own book I read, "*Clayton approached Judith, the young heiress shutting her eyes as if such blindness would allow for naivety. His lips met hers in a kiss–*"

A kiss.

"Minnie–" I begin, only to find her book resting on her chest and her eyes closed. Dreaming.

With a huff, I set my own book aside, then take hers and do the same, careful not to jostle her from sleep. I hold her to me, hot breath puffing against my neck. Even now she feels so remarkable to me.

If only I knew how to make her mine.

CHAPTER TWENTY

MINNIE

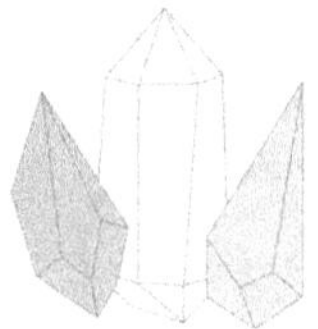

Rosier and I both groan when my alarm starts blaring. Most Saturdays I sleep in, but it's going to take Amber a few hours to get my hair in gala-ready shape. I actually remembered to wear my bonnet last night–not that it's my fault a certain someone's been distracting me recently.

I rub my eyes with my palms, my scalp already stinging as I think about the knots Amber's going to pick out of my hair. I shut off my alarm.

"Go back to sleep," I urge Rosier, but he lumbers up and out of bed.

"You need coffee," he grumbles as he leaves the room.

I'm not going to argue.

I toss on a pair of sweats and an old t-shirt, then grab as many of my favorite conditioners and hair accessories as possible and toss them into a tote bag. Rosier already has my coffee in a travel mug. It's sweet, but I'm still wary about the taste.

"I think Amber will have something for me there," I tell him.

He frowns.

As soon as I have my hand on the doorknob, Rosier is behind me with his hand on the door. I roll my head back and groan. "I thought we were done with this."

I know better than to turn and face him but I do it anyway. He still has that face, frowning like a child while his brows are knit in confusion.

"What is it?" I ask. "Struggling with an insult for my outfit?"

He's as still as a statue and then suddenly he's not. He leans down to kiss me. I could pull away; there's enough space between my back and the door, and he isn't holding my face. Or I could kiss him back, melding our soft lips and tasting him on my tongue. But I like what he's doing, holding my bottom lip between his, our noses pressed together.

He finally releases my lips, and I flutter my eyelashes, waiting for him to say something. I'm met with silence. Rosier's hand leaves the door and reaches for me, holding my chin and brushing my lips with his thumb. He shuts his gold eyes and moves in to kiss me again...

But I turn and open the door, no resistance this time, and practically run down the hall.

I don't stop rushing till I'm sitting on the bus. I touch my lips, still warm and tingling even though it's been at least five minutes since we kissed.

Our first kiss...

"I LOVE YOU, but you're a mess," Amber says about a half hour into doing my hair.

It's our usual set up: a few bags of snacks open on the floor where we sit facing her laptop playing a shonen anime. Since

Amber's better at hair, I always let her pick what we watch, even if I'd prefer a magical girl show. She hasn't ask why I need to be so dolled up, perhaps her last act of kindness.

"Have you considered a wig? Or I could grab the clippers."

"You really want me bald?" I snort.

"You'd look cute as a cue-ball." She ruffles the top of my head.

"That's all? Not revenge for..." My voice trails.

Despite everything, Amber agreed to do this for me. I asked for her support, for her to be my friend, and she's doing that.

She sighs and continues to section my hair. Over-the-top shouting and punching sounds fill the room while we sit in silence. I try to think of the right thing to say, the magic words that will fix things between us, put us right back to where we were a week ago, sitting in these exact spots, giggling over a magic circle.

In the end, it's Amber that breaks the silence. "You know I still care about you a lot." She takes a clip and pushes aside my combed out curls. "You've made some shit decisions this past week, but that doesn't change anything."

"Of course, it changes things. We can be at odds and still care about each other."

Amber wraps her arms around my shoulders, holding me like a little kid. In her eyes that must be what I am, a petulant child who keeps insisting she knows best.

"Amber–"

"Why aren't we enough, Minnie? The coven, my mom and I–"

"You *are* enough," I assure her. "You're just not what I need anymore."

She *tsks* and releases me from the hug, getting back to the task of my hair. I keep expecting her tug at the strands. It wouldn't be difficult to make me yelp in pain; I've always been tender-headed. But she keeps up her gentle touch like she always does.

"Maybe we're on different paths," I offer.

"We're not even in the same forest," she points out. "And it sucks."

"Being without you does suck. But Rosier..."

She bops me on my head with the flat side of her brush. "This is a boy-free zone."

"He's not what you think."

She hits me again with the brush, a little harder this time, a little more deserved. I think we're really done talking about boys, but she makes one last comment. "If you want to date a literal devil, don't come to me for approval. That's on you."

A new episode begins. The content might not be to my taste, but the opening is catchy.

Amber, once again, starts a much needed conversation. "You know, no matter what happens tomorrow or next week or next year, I'm always going to think about the days we would chase each other around the shop. I'll remember Mom finding us passed out on this floor with a dubious looking plant between us and laughing. At this point, I just hope you can do the same."

I break the cardinal rule of detangling and turn my head to face her. Amber clicks her tongue, but I persist. "I could never hate you, Amber. You've hurt me, but that's because... because you matter. Your opinions matter to me. If I could take you with me down this...whatever it is I'm going through... if you wanted to follow, I would let you."

Her face falls. "You know I can't, Minnie. I have responsibilities and loyalties to uphold. 'Til last week, I thought you wanted to help me with those things."

"Maybe the real issue is we both want things for each other?"

"Mmmm, *is* that the issue? Because I can think of a few other glaring issues." She shakes her head. "But I'll say your favorite words, Minnie: you're right. We don't *need* each other anymore."

I purse my lips. "Those *are* my favorite words, but right now they don't feel so great."

"Good." She turns my head so she can get back to work. "Pain means it mattered."

"You'll always matter to me."

Amber hums and snags a knot close to my scalp. I wince, and she giggles. "Means it mattered," she reminds me.

With my hair combed out, deep conditioner applied, and cap on, we take a tea break, the smell of mint wafting through the air.

"Could I borrow that practice ink?" I ask.

Amber eyes me warily. "I should say no."

"I want to figure out how to reverse the spell I initially cast."

Her brows jump, and she sets down her tea. "You're sending him back?"

"I have to have a spell before I can send him back." I sigh, melodramatically. "If only I had some of that nifty practice ink to see if my sigils are right..."

"Nifty? What kind of *Little House on the Prairie* smut are you reading?" Despite her teasing, Amber grabs the paper, ink, and glass pen.

My confidence wavers when the first circle I draw glows red. It might as well make a buzzer sound like on a gameshow. I snatch another piece of paper while the first one burns. Amber watches me, steam curling around her face.

"Maybe if I connect–" As soon as I connect the two sigils, it sets off the spell and the ink glows red once more. "Rude..."

Over and over, I draw and talk to myself—red, red, and more red.

"Your tea is cold," Amber points out. "And it's time for the wash."

"One more."

I set the pen down, stretching my fingers and taking a deep breath. The sigils are so clear in my head, but piecing them together is where the image fades. It occurs to me to work backwards, quite literally, from my initial spell. I pick up the pen and start with the final sigil needed for the summoning spell.

I have to pause and make adjustments as I go; some things aren't plugging in the way they did when they were in a different order. Amber's shoulder rubs against mine. Finally, I have the last sigil written and place my hand over the paper and chant.

It glows bright blue before immolating the paper.

BY THE TIME I'm back at my apartment, it's about four hours before the gala starts. Chanel is already at my apartment with a trolly of makeup, chatting about how being late is always in fashion. We're about to separate, Chanel and I in my apartment while Rosier and Kas go to his, when I grab Rosier's wrist.

"Do *not* throw a fit over the suit," I order him. "They literally won't let us in if you're not wearing every piece of the tux, okay?"

Rosier's nose crinkles as he snorts. "I won't throw a fit, as you put it."

Kas mouths a thank you to me before exiting.

Chanel swatches four different lipsticks before finding one that matches my natural color best. I can't help but eye the boxes upon boxes of makeup she's brought. "You're like a walking Sephora."

Chanel scoffs. "I'm an Estée Lauder, thank you very much." She says the brand with such a heavy French accent it could snap the Eiffel Tower in half.

Leaf at one point jumps onto the tower of makeup, and Chanel hisses at him like she's a cat herself. Which somehow works, and Leaf scurries off but stays close enough to watch.

With my makeup finished, Chanel buttons me into the dress, careful not to mess with my hair. After getting out every knot and doing some deep conditioning, my ringlets could make Archimedes blush. Amber slicked back the front sections to lay flat and placed two large gold hair clips perfectly parallel on each side.

I go to my jewelry box in search of more gold. I've got plenty of necklaces and rings, but in my heart, I've already decided what to wear. I take out the heart shaped door knocker earrings that were my Mom's and slip on a few gold bangles left by my Grandmother.

I step out of my bedroom holding my gold leather heels. I bought them as a statement piece, but they hardly stick out when I'm already dripping in opulence. Kas and Rosier are standing around, both of them dressed in their tuxes, both with purple pocket squares, though Rosier's is a deep royal purple while Kaz' is a vibrant orchid shade. I notice they both have lavender boutonnieres pinned to their suits as well.

Kas spots me first and grins. "I think we might have to play bodyguard because everyone is going to want a piece of you tonight."

Rosier looks at me, and his eyelashes flutter. Half his hair is pulled back in a bun, still allowing his curls to brush his shoulders while showing off his sharp jaw. He says nothing at first, and I wonder if he's holding back an insult. Instead...

"You look beautiful. As you always do."

An insult would have been easier to swallow. "Thank you." I reach up and touch the lavender sprig on his lapel. "Who decided on this?"

"Rosier, of all people, insisted." Kas rocks back on his heels. "He wanted lilacs, but they didn't have any, especially on such short notice. So, lavender it is."

Rosier and I catch each other's gaze but say nothing. I could ask why, but I already know the answer. He wants to see them for himself, the lilac flowers in our book.

Silence has been hanging between us for a bit too long, and unlike our usual staring contests, this time we have witnesses.

In an attempt to break the awkwardness, I sit down to slip on my shoes. "Do you think they'll be checking bags at the door?"

Kas snorts. "What, are you bringing a knife?"

"A wand would be a good idea."

I close the clasp on my shoe and go and grab the wand I used to summon Rosier. I hold it in my hand, thinking about how I could use it. Offensive magic is uncommon, and I certainly don't know any. I set the wand back down and go and grab some chalk instead, along with a few spare crystals.

Chanel makes a face. "You're going to keep a bunch of chalk in your purse? Ruin the lining?"

"We all have to make sacrifices." The tools roll off my hand into my open envelope style bag with a convenient strap on the wrist. Rosier then threads his arm through mine. "Do I look nice?"

"I already told you, you always look beautiful."

"I know, but I like hearing you say it," I smirk.

Chanel glares at him. "If you smudge her lipstick, I'm going to be livid."

CHAPTER TWENTY-ONE

MINNIE

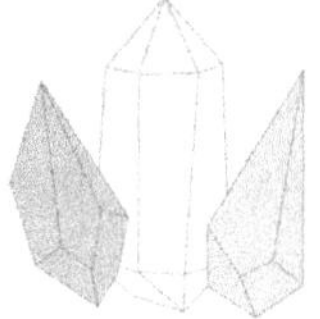

I PEER OUT THE TINTED WINDOW OF THE CAR, THE museum a few spots ahead of us. The white stone building has banners announcing the gala bookending the tall arched windows, which cast yellow light outside. People dot the steps leading to the museum, all in suits or fine dresses. The car inches its way up the street as part of the procession. I feel bougie, and we're not even inside yet.

When we do pull up, an attendant standing at the curb opens the passenger door. Rosier steps out first, offering me his hand as I step out of the car. Kas follows and hands the attendant our tickets. As we walk up the steps, I stand between them, holding onto Rosier's arm while Kas accompanies us. I can't help but look at the other guests, searching for my Father. I don't know what he looks like, but I'll know him when I see him. We have the same eyes, after all.

The museum foyer is packed with people all mingling and drinking, waiters darting between them. I'm more focused on the building itself. When I was a kid, I would stand and stare up at the skyline, wondering why every roof wasn't made of glass. I wanted so badly to go at night, to lie on the marble floor and stare up at the stars under the cover of glass, surrounded by the industrial style murals. Even now, I'm tempted to lay on the cool floor and admire the night sky in the comfort of the museum.

But I keep walking, almost dragging Rosier with me. He leans down to whisper in my ear, "Where are you taking me?"

"I want to enjoy the first floor of exhibits before we have to be cordial."

"I thought you'd be excited. This is like all of your books."

"It is..." I agree as we pass the Native American section of the museum. "But you know the heroine usually isn't excited. She's worried about her debts or about running into an old lover. I guess I'm worried, too."

Rosier slides his arm down mine, taking my hand in his and giving it a squeeze. I glance down at our interlocked hands, then back at him.

"You know you can't rip my Father's head off if things go south," I caution.

"Of course not. I have no interest in taking what's rightfully yours."

My given right to kill my Father... How dreamy.

We round a corner and come to the little limestone chapel built into the museum. I never understood how or why a little corner of a French chapel ended up in Detroit, but I do appreciate workmanship, the stained glass painting the corner in kaleidoscope colors. Tonight, moonlight shines through the glass, illuminating the floor.

Holding Rosier's hand, I step into the little chapel, then look back at him. "Are you able to stand in here?"

He rolls his eyes before taking a big step onto the limestone, though not yet standing in the chapel proper. "What did you think would happen?"

Before I can answer he takes a step into the chapel proper. We enter the alcove, and red and blue hues dance across the floor, across our bodies. Rosier releases my hand before burying his hands in his pockets.

"Is there a reason you brought me here?"

I chuckle. "Yes, I think it's very funny to have a devil standing in a chapel." It's a joke, but I do also have a reason... even if I didn't realize it till right now. "I want a contract."

To my delight, Rosier doesn't groan or swivel his head around his neck. He looks at me intently but doesn't speak.

"Are you going to give me what I want?"

He shakes his head a little, chuckling. His eyes settle on the golden altar encased in glass in the center of the chapel. I follow his eyes, the image of a Mother holding her child greeting me. These faces mean nothing to me; I never went to church. Some coven members use saints in their rituals, but I never learned the figures' names. The Mother holds her child close to her face, their eyes almost touching, flat yet somehow filled with love.

"I want a peaceful death." I can sense his eyes on me, but I'm still focusing on the golden image before me. "Regardless of the risks I take, of the danger I put myself in, I want to die painlessly. Quickly, if possible." Rosier clicks his tongue. Finally, I look at him. "You can do that for me can't you? Just promise me when my time comes, it'll be easy."

"And then Hell awaits you. So what does it matter if your death is simple?"

"It matters to me," I tell him.

"Because of the curse."

It takes a second for the shock to hit, to let it really fester within me. I never told him the details of the curse, I never even told him about it directly, but it sounds like I never had to.

"You'll die young," he reminds me. "Young and in pain. Yet you're only trying to avoid the pain? How unlike you, Minnie. Your appetite for pain is one of the things I admire most about you."

The inferno is already starting, embers beneath kindling, spilling out of the hearth but not yet evident. I turn my head, lifting my chin to look up at him. I ask again, "Will you give me what I want?"

He doesn't even hesitate. "No."

"*Why?*" I shout, my voice bouncing off the stones. "Why won't you take me?"

"I won't damn you. I won't damn *us* for eternity."

"Why do you care?" I shake my head. "You need souls. You've got mine."

He huffs, scratching his eyebrow with his thumb, avoiding my gaze. "Does the *why* matter?"

"I'm not your Mother!" I snap.

He laughs at me, a deep good-hearted chuckle.

"I chose this! No one damned me except myself." I stand up on my toes, wishing I was eye level with him—as if that would make him listen to me *for once*. "I'm not a little mortal girl for you to weep over. I never have been." I fall back onto my heels and storm out of the chapel, my shoes clicking against the stone.

Rosier grabs my wrist and pulls me to him, holding me against his chest. "You said to me that first night, you want retribution for your Mother." I writhe against his body. I try to get away, but his hold on me tightens, pushing all the air out of my lungs. "You've turned your mourning into revenge." He kisses the top of my head. "Revenge is a sword forged in the blood of its wielder. I want you to mourn and be reunited with the ones you love."

I stop struggling, his hands now running up and down my back. He holds me like he did the other night in bed, and I let him believe whatever fantasy he has in his head, just long enough for it to hurt when I push him away. I take a few steps back before hissing at him, not like a cat or even like a snake. It's like something not of this world.

The rage inside me fuels my words, steam practically pouring from my mouth. "You've gone soft."

As I march off, I reflect on everything that's occurred between us: touching, bonding over books, strong cups of coffee. All this time, I naively thought these were seedlings of love. But it's been pity and remorse. Of all the emotions he could gravitate towards, why those?

He was right from the very start. I'll always be something lesser to him. Like everyone else, he sees me as some poor lamb *he* led astray. *Everyone* seems to think I'm incapable of deciding my fate. What a privilege this is, a chance to weave my own story. Who cares if the pattern isn't a family design? My Mom would have wanted me to live. Regardless of the strings that came with it. Let the world weep for me. I'll still be standing at the entrance of Hell, confident as ever.

I find Kas and a good chunk of the party goers in the mural hall. Kas lifts a brow, holding a flute of champagne. "Trouble in paradise?"

I ignore him and snatch the glass from his hand before downing the drink–or, at least, attempting to. The taste of bitter grapes makes me gag, and the bubbles go straight up my nose. I choke a little and Kas reaches out.

"If you get champagne on this dress Chanel will kill me," he reminds me. "Slowly."

I manage to swallow back the drink, the liquid heavy in my throat.

Rosier joins us but says nothing, his eyes narrow and distant. Kas looks back and forth between us, waiting for one of us to break and give some explanation. But it never comes. Especially not after I've recovered from choking on bubbles and make eye contact with a familiar figure across the hall.

"Oh, you've gotta be kidding me..." I lament.

Alexander is standing there, his brows furrowed, seeing me next to the big, naked guy he found in my apartment a week after we broke up. Not a great look for me.

"Quite the company," Kas says his words slow and pointed.

A man walks up next to Alexander, a woman with mousy brown hair on his arm. They're talking, and I can tell from Alexander's body language that he wants to impress this guy. His shoulders are back, but his neck is craned low, trying to balance standing up straight while not standing at his intimidating height.

Kas continues, "Wasn't expecting to see Seira here."

Rosier sounds intrigued. "With her walking bank account."

"The very same—hey, where are you going?"

Rosier looks over his shoulder as he walks away. "To make a contract."

Before I can follow him and toss the rest of the champagne in his face, there's a commotion behind us. A woman in a large powder blue ball gown approaches the hall with her entourage: a man in a plain black suit who looks to be a bodyguard, a woman with a museum badge who's talking her ear off, a girl with corn silk hair that reaches her midsection, and a familiar blonde man with glasses who's holding her arm.

My blood goes cold. The group walks past us, and the woman with the museum badge gushes. "We're always so grateful for your donations Mrs. le Fay."

Kas leans down. "Your Dad's genes are strong, Lance and him could be twins."

"I don't think that's my Dad. I think that *is* Lance's twin." My voice shakes and I grip the base of the champagne flute so hard I think it will snap in my hands.

All this work, and he's not even here. If I want him to get my message, it'll have to be relayed through his spawn. I wonder if this twin will call me sister, too.

CHAPTER TWENTY-TWO

MINNIE

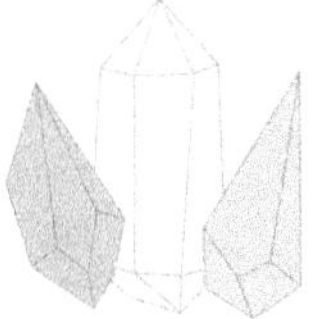

My fingertips have gone pale from holding onto my glass so tightly, but I hardly care, watching as Guine le Fay schmoozes with other donors and socialites. The two accompanying her, both blond and pale, look like bored teenagers dragged out by their Mother.

It occurs to me that I can't curse out Guine and her family–not when everyone here is fawning over them–but I certainly can cuss out Rosier. Maybe he'll get turned on by it, and we can have hate sex in the bathroom. I'm upset with him, sure, but last time I was this upset he spanked me, and I felt better. Better than using any kind of *healthy* coping mechanism. Sex is kinda like meditation, if you don't think about it for too long.

I hand Kas my empty drink and march after Roiser, finding myself on the makeshift dance floor, only for a lanky figure to step in my path.

"Care for a dance?" Alexander offers me his hand.

I look up at him, bending my neck all the way back and wondering how I ever enjoyed this painful position I had to contort myself into so I could look at his face. Saying no to his offer is obvious. Boring.

So I take his hand. We dance in silence before the peace is interrupted.

"I just don't get it, Minnie," he blurts out. "I wanted to give you a nice life. I really thought about us getting married one day. And then you break up with me out of the blue."

"I wanted those things, too," I admit. "That's why we dated, and that was the problem." A house, kids, a husband–that's the dream. Or, at least, it was before the curse and the consequences of my own actions.

"How is wanting the same things a problem?"

"I never wanted you, Alex, I wanted everything surrounding you." If I could stab the words into his heart, I would.

He stops shifting his feet but still holds my hand. "So you were using me? You spoke to my parents. We talked about moving in."

I step back, freeing my hand from his grasp. I'm sick of being an idea in people's heads. "I wanted a house and in-laws. I wanted a family. It didn't matter *whose* family."

His mouth opens, then shuts. I take my chance to escape, but once again, someone steps into my path.

He's the same height as Lance with the same dirty blonde hair, but it's shorter and slicked back like it's the 1940s. "We should talk." He offers me a hand. I look at it like it might reach out and grab my neck. "It's only a chat, Minerva. A chat and a dance."

Every muscle in my face strains to create the deepest frown, but in the end, I take his hand.

We've only taken one step when I spit out, "You've got a lot of nerve–"

"*I'm* the one with nerve?" His eyes snap to me, glowering. "I've been attending this gala since I was a teenager. You're the one who's trying to make a scene."

I catch myself in the reflection of his glasses, my face heavy with wrinkles as I scowl. "Why would I need to make a scene anyway?"

"I don't know." He shrugs rather casually as we dance. "But I've never understood dramatics. I assume you've decided to embarrass my Mother. If I'm right, then I request you not."

I'm taken aback by his request, my expression faltering. I glance over at his Mother, her features sunken from age, her large eyes empty, like a doll's. I have to look away.

"Minerva?"

I try to find the anger I had before, stoke the cinders in my stomach. "*Request?*" I eviscerate the word. "Say it again; I need a laugh."

He leans down and grips my hand. I can't tell if it's an attempt to intimidate me or if his cool persona is slipping. "Hurting my Mother won't get you what you want."

"How do you know what I want?"

"I don't. But my Mother isn't a direct line to my Father's heart. Hurt her, and it ends there. You'll leave an old, already broken woman more damaged than before. But maybe you're right, and I'm wrong. Maybe that's *exactly* what you want."

I stiffen. "I'm not cruel like the rest of you."

"Yet here you are," he breathes. "Do you even know my name?"

"Lance never mentioned it."

"Oh, good. You two have reunited." His voice is dry and brittle like grass in the summertime. "I'm not surprised he neglected to mention us–Arthur and Nim."

I lift a brow. "You're also Arthur?"

"And still you think you're at the center of our Father's cruelty." He rolls his eyes. I want to smack his glasses right off his face.

"Are we done? I don't have any interest in your Mom. I only care about ruining Arthur le Fay."

"Ruining him?" He stops our little two-step dance. "Your ambition is admirable, if not poorly planned. My Father never comes to events like this. Even if he did, he'd be more embarrassed by the doting guests than by you." He releases my hand. "So long as I don't have to deal with Mother's tears, we're done here."

He returns to his Mother, who spots me. As her gaze lingers, I blink, wondering for the first time if she knows about me. Does she see me and know I'm a result of her husband's infidelity? Or is she staring at me, wondering why this stranger has the same eyes as her sons? She's so hollow, ghost-like despite the liveliness around her, so unlike my own Mother, who was walking sunshine.

Guine looks away, and I take a breath, my lungs burning after being deprived of oxygen for too long. The gnawing at my chest continues, the pain starting to spread. I have to get out of here.

I flee the dance floor, not caring where I end up. Eventually I find a quiet spot in one of the galleries and brace myself against the wall, my head heavy and hanging beneath my shoulders.

What a fucking disaster. Like my pride couldn't be stomped and kicked enough tonight.

Rosier sees me as some poor, desperate little girl. My half-brother doesn't see me as a threat, more like a troublesome witch trying to appear intimidating. Who knows what the rest of the family thinks of me—if I'm even worth their time. I shouldn't care. Just like how I shouldn't care what Amber thinks, what Alexander thinks, what my coworkers or strangers on the street think of me and my own business.

Tears prick at my eyes, and I lift my head, desperate to not let my makeup run. The painting in front of me catches my attention. It's famous and haunting: the image of a woman, splayed out in bed with an impish looking creature resting on her chest. The imp looks inquisitive, staring right at me. *What are you going to do, Minnie?* it seems to ask.

I try to focus on the woman, her mouth agape and her eyes shut. But she doesn't appear dead; her cheeks are too rosy. She doesn't appear to be in pain, either, yet I wouldn't want to be in her position, even though it feels like I already am.

Footsteps echo behind me. I groan, blinking and catching my tears on my thumbs before they can ruin my makeup. "I'm really not in a place to talk right now," I say, expecting it to be Kas that's followed me. A figure stands beside me, and through the tears, I can see short, blond hair.

"I own a Fuseli," the man says. "Can't say it's very good. Nothing but muddy colors and strange poses."

I let the tears fall down my cheeks so I can see clearly. I was right about one thing tonight; I *do* recognize Arthur le Fay on sight. Lance and Junior take after him–similar heights, same hair color. The three of them could be mistaken for brothers, which is the first thing wrong with him. His eyes are green, as expected, but they're overtaken by large black pupils that suck the light out of his eyes. He makes my stomach churn, and when he turns his head, I look away.

"Where are my manners?" he says. "My name is–"

"I know who you are." I focus on the painting, paying particular attention to the pale eyes of a black horse in the background. "What are you doing here? You never come to events like this."

"I came to see you." He practically sings, laying on the charm thick. "Let's talk, Minerva."

CHAPTER TWENTY-THREE

ROSIER

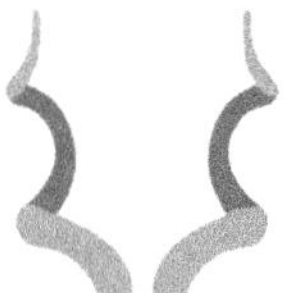

THE CROWD PARTS FOR ME AS I WALK, A SORELY NEEDED reminder that while I appear human, I am far from it. I am meant to command and control–two things I've forgotten thanks to Minnie. *Thanks to!* Damn that woman. It's worse than I thought. I've learned–bile bubbles in my throat at the thought–manners.

I make it to the other side of the room, Richard's companion spotting me first. Seira narrows her eyes but says nothing. Richard takes notice of her glare and follows her gaze. We make eye contact, and his thin lips curl into a subtle smile.

Before I can say anything, his bold voice echoes. "You must be that devil I've heard whispers about."

I look around, careful not to actually move my head, concerned about mortals overhearing our conversation.

"The devil himself," I confirm, a little leary now that it's clear he knows more about me than I do about him. "I didn't realize my reputation precedes me."

"Seira informed me a devil had crossed onto the Mortal Plane. I didn't believe her at first. The last time I heard of someone successfully summoning a devil was over a century ago in Europe."

A century of solitude, then Minnie decided, "I think I'll summon a devil to solve my problems," and now I'm stuck wearing stupid fucking clothes talking to this slimy vampire. I resist the urge to look over my shoulder and check on her.

"I don't currently have plans to leave," I inform Richard, slipping my hands into my pockets.

I've read enough books to know this is a casual sort of gesture. I'm not sure why, but it appears to work. Richard's subtle smile becomes sharp, exposing his knife-like teeth at the corners of his lips.

"A permanent resident from Hell? In our city? Hate to be a downer, but I might have to inform the council about this."

I raise a brow. "Council?"

"Apologies, I'm a member of the Vampiric Council. Have been for a few decades now. Seems my reputation does not precede me." Despite his apology, he's obviously rather amused by all this. My ignorance does give him an excuse to brag.

"Is my presence an issue?" I ask.

"Why exactly *are* you present?" Seira steps a little closer to Richard who wraps an arm around her waist. "You never mentioned what you're doing here."

Her body is so lithe, lacking hips or breasts, skin tight across her chest like a corpse. She seems impossibly pale, almost the same shade as Richard. Her light green eyes are so empty, she appears more like a demon than anything infernal.

"What would you expect a devil to do in my situation?" Her eyes narrow some more, but I return my attention to my target. "We should speak in private."

Richard's hand slides off Seira's skeletal body. He steps closer to me, his back now to his companion. "Meet me on the second floor." With that he walks away—or starts to but stops when he realizes Seira isn't following. She's too busy glaring at me with a locked jaw. "Sara!" Richard calls.

Both Seira and I blink, recognizing that Richard has said the wrong name. Close but not quite. I know this, and she knows it better than I do, but Richard is oblivious. Seira's body becomes even more corpse-like, stiffening as she turns to join Richard. The two of them disappear behind some pillars.

Now alone, I give in and turn to check on Minnie. She's dancing with fucking Alex of all people. I can recognize that gangly frame from any angle. I focus on the both of them, trying to hear their conversation, but there's too many other people talking. Minnie looks about as happy as she did looking up at me in that fucking chapel. I should go over and push aside her companion, soak up her ire while we dance in circles.

Instead, I ask a waiter how to get to the second floor. He informs me the second floor is closed off to party goers. "Really?" is all I have to say before he explains there are several staircases around the hall that will bring me upstairs, stuttering as he does so.

"Thank you." I walk off, only grasping what I've said when I'm halfway to the second floor.

Minerva *fucking* Morris, I look forward to the day I can torture you in Hell.

The second floor is made up of closed off rooms, but I spot Richard and Seira near one of the exhibit entrances. Stepping in, I find we're on a balcony overlooking the first floor. A few party guests mingle about below us, oblivious to the three of us above. Richard is studying a bronze statue encased in glass.

"Not exactly private up here, Richard," I mutter.

"Sound travels up," he says, not looking away from the statue. He rocks back on his heels, slipping his hands into his pockets. A *very* casual display–overdoing it, really. "So, let's work backward. What do you want from me?"

"Your soul."

"That's all?"

"Assuming you bloodsuckers have one."

Richard tilts his head in thought. "I can't imagine why we wouldn't. We are sort of undead, yes, but no one has ever died and *come back* as a vampire. I was very much alive when I was turned, and I'm alive now. In a sense." He looks over his shoulder at Seira, who has her arms crossed. "Do you think I have a soul, dear?"

Seira scoffs, and I expect–nay, *want*–a snarky rebuttal. Instead, she responds, "I feed off you, and you're capable of both vice and virtue. I highly doubt soulless people can make such distinctions." Her tone is half mocking, and she's looking right at me. The other succubi I've worked with aren't thrilled by me, either, but Seira seems especially pissed off by my presence.

"Then we're settled. You want my soul? Have it." He opens up his arms as if offering himself. "Didn't even realize I had one 'til now."

"You haven't even told me what it is you want," I point out. "I'm not a thief. This is an exchange at the end of the day."

"It's funny... *I'm* looking to gain someone's soul as well." He smiles, exposing his fangs. "Not literally. Not as literally as you, at least. But there's this girl–" Seira flinches behind him. "She was mine for a long time, but she slipped through my grasp, and now she wants nothing to do with me. It's like being turned a second time, over and over again."

I try to keep my face neutral. What he's asking for isn't uncommon–everything is so overdone. Undying fidelity from one person. Simple, yet I feel uneasy. "Enlighten me. Why don't you try to seduce her? You've succeeded once before."

Richard scoffs then runs his fingers through his black hair. "Like I said, she wants nothing to do with me. Threatens to kill me every time she sees me. It's not an empty threat, either. She's a werewolf, could kill me easily. You understand?"

There's some woman out there with a fire inside of her that I have to extinguish. Which, now that I think about it, why do I care? I don't know her. Even if I did, she's *one* person. I'm over-thinking this, like I did with Minnie. And look where that got me.

"So that's all?" I ask, making sure I have the measure of things "You want this girl to love y–"

"To *crave* me," Richard interrupts. "I want her to need me like water, just as I need the blood of others."

For the first time I understand him. Utter devotion. The object of your desire beneath you in every manner, clinging to your essence. "Tell me more about this girl."

Richard goes on and on about his Sara. I need to know her name and age, make sure the contract is talking about the right Sara–which, when her name is older than me, can get a little complicated. I asked him what she looks like: light green eyes, light brown hair, light skin, light body. Uninteresting, except for the part where all I can picture in my mind is Seira.

Yet, he's not satisfied. His desire for Sara is so pervasive it turns into need. For a vampire, he's got a devil's heart.

"Well?" he asks.

I'm standing with my arms crossed, humming to myself. "I need some time to think. Do you mind?"

"Please." He waves his hand. "I'm immortal; time has no value to me."

"Not immortal," I point out. "Trapped in time, so I see why it has no value."

I leave and wander through the galleries, still not quite grasping this whole art thing. All the figures look the same, with their big dresses and military uniforms. Sometimes, there's a horse. The chapel downstairs, while much too righteous for my taste, at least painted Minnie's face in brilliant colors.

She's the only art I've seen thus far.

In one of the galleries, a voice interrupts my solitude. "Do you find this art strange?" I look over my shoulder and find Seira stepping toward me, her heels clicking against the floor. "You're not one of them, you know."

"What?"

"You're not mortal. You're not even half-mortal like me."

"You don't know anything about me," I remind her.

Richard probably wouldn't care if I slapped her, but I would take no pleasure in it. Hitting Seira would feel like hitting Leaf—needlessly cruel. And while her words are exasperating, I am curious about her thoughts.

"What makes you think I want to be mortal?" I ask.

"Isn't that what we all want deep down? To feel the things they feel?"

I consider all the mortal emotions I shouldn't be able to tap into. Empathy, kindness, selflessness... love. I'm not sure if manners count, but what about guilt? Is that why I can't bring myself to take Minnie's soul? Can one feel guilt without a desire to be kind?

"I've stumped you," Seira says, a hint of pride in her tone. "Don't hurt yourself, Prince. I'm not here to give you an existential crisis."

"A what?" I've heard that term before. Amber said Minerva was having the exact same crisis.

"A very mortal crisis of faith." She rolls her eyes and rolls her wrist. "What is my purpose? What is anyone's purpose? I know my purpose well. To feed. Which is why I need you to not make that contract with Richard."

My brows furrow. "Here you come, waltzing in, calling me emotional, and now you want my *mercy*? A bold choice, Seira."

She bites her lip. "If you make that contact, I'll have to find someone else, and he... Well, all he ever thinks about is what *others* have. Be that the council or his mortal coworkers. But most of all–"

"He thinks about Sara. If someone else has won her heart."

She nods. "It's delectable how he yearns for her. He looks at me–" She touches her collarbone "–and sees her. But he knows I'm not her, and it drives him mad."

"Is your name even Seira?" I ask, unable to resist.

"It is, actually. But I didn't look like this before I met Richard. Most succubi settle into a mortal appearance." She runs her fingers through her long hair, the brunette shade turning to a vibrant red. "But I never could." Her green eyes catch mine, and I see they're a much darker shade. More like Minnie's. I blink, not sure how she would even know, curious if she has some way to sense others' desires.

She approaches me, still sickly pale but now ginger with deep green eyes. "Perhaps... if you do make a deal with Richard, we could *also* come to an agreement? I know you've made an arrangement with the other succubi."

I snort, my lips curling to a snarl. "You can't feed off me," I remind her.

"No. But I could help you recruit." Her fingers ghost along the edges of my suit. "I will be what you want me to be."

I shake my head, scoffing. "Like you are with Richard?" I walk past her. "I'd rather agree to the contract and be done with both of you."

I'm halfway across the room when she calls to me, "So you're going to let me starve? Even if I find someone else, I don't know if it'll be enough. I've been at his side for a year now and I... I..."

"You crave him the way he wants Sara to crave him." I click my tongue. "How unfortunate. For you, of course. Richard doesn't seem to realize when he has a good thing going. First, he lost Sara. Now he's going to lose you. And gain..." My head teeters back and forth. "Well, for him, perhaps it will feel like genuine love from Sara. I wouldn't know."

"Don't take him from me," she breathes.

Something about her plea makes me pause. Seira is nothing, a succubus begging to keep her meal ticket. I have no reason to even acknowledge her. If I'm going to listen to her talk, I might as well make it entertaining. "Do you love him?"

Seira blinks. "We're incapable of that."

"Fuck off." I turn around to face her again. "You're standing here, begging me to let you keep him. As if you own him. You desire him *because* he doesn't desire you. I've read it a hundred times." She raises a brow but doesn't question my words. "So tell me, do you love him?"

"If I say yes, will you leave us alone?"

Her question gives me all the answers I need. I turn on my heels to leave. "I won't be seeing you or Richard."

I make sure to use the stairs farthest away from the exhibit Richard is still waiting in. I've already had one person inconvenience me with talk of contracts, and he's not nearly as pretty as Minnie. If he does find me tonight, I'll inform him he should pay more attention to the sniveling cunt he already has on a leash.

I return to the first floor, walking past a few partygoers, when I spot Kas, looking around frantically. He catches sight of me and bolts over so fast, I think he'll rip his pants.

"Where have you been?" he demands. "Fuck it, doesn't matter. Minnie is missing."

I huff. "She's probably off pouting somewhere."

"No, Rosier, listen. She danced with her brother, right? And then, yeah, she probably did go off to pout or cry or something–nice work by the way–but she never came back."

I huff, "How is this my fault?"

He groans. "Like teenagers in love–no, worse, *tweens* in love." He's still catching his breath. Every word he says is so pressed it's like he hasn't stopped running to catch up to me yet. "But listen, the le Fays? They're gone. Just up and left out of the blue."

I raise a brow. "I don't understand."

Kas looks over his shoulder. "I-I don't know. I saw the misses leave suddenly with some museum person trailing behind her. Then I went to look for you and–Hells, they're probably gone by now."

"Where is Minnie?" My interest in the le Fays is bound by her incessant need for revenge. Though I do want her to succeed.

Kas stutters. "I don't–"

"Useless." I storm past him. Wherever the le Fays are, that's where Minnie is, I have no doubt. If they're gone, I'll have no choice but to tear up the city looking for them. Looking for her...

Little witch doesn't need a contract. Clearly.

CHAPTER TWENTY-FOUR

MINNIE

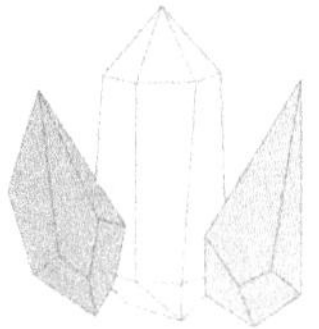

I'm in the very position I hoped my Father would be in when I finally confronted him: caught off guard, brain scrambling, trying to think of something clever. We're alone, which also isn't great. Kas and Rosier were supposed to be my backups, flanking me like loyal hounds, but better just us two than the whole le Fay clan.

Arthur is looking right at me, but I face the painting instead. *No, I need to do this*, I tell myself. I've wanted to confront him for so long, and now I have my chance.

I lift my chin and turn to him.

"I always regretted not taking you in as my own," he says.

I'm going to be sick all over Chanel's nice dress.

"Your Grandfather," he continues. "He convinced your Mother I would be a bad Father."

Gramps was right, not surprising.

"So I had no choice but to let you live apart from the rest of your kin. Shame, too. Guine always wanted a daughter."

"You have a daughter," I point out. Not that I would have ever accepted Guine as my Mom anyhow.

"Nimue is... difficult. Especially for Guine. Takes too much after me. But let's not linger on the past–"

"Actually, let's. You abandoned my Mom."

"I told you, your Grandfather–"

"She died, scared, confused, and in pain." My jaw is so tight, I'm surprised I can even speak. "I've heard about your obsession, how you want to become immortal. Are you?"

His eyes flash with pride, but I'm not sold. "I'm only as powerful as my bloodline, Minerva. To tell you the truth, I thought you would be weak. But I heard about what you've summoned. Clearly I missed something–perhaps your Grand-father has witch ancestry."

Gramps is 100% human, ancestry be damned. There are more normal humans than there are witches and plenty of intermingling between them.

"You can do great things, Minerva. Let us help you reach your potential. Accept your birthright."

I scrunch my face, trying to look as mean as possible. "I'm powerful because I worked for it. I studied harder than you and your kin–put more effort into my spells. I wasn't born better than you; I *became* better than you. Birthright is bullshit."

He lets out a good natured chuckle, like I'm a child throwing a fit in front of him. "Better than *me*? Well, you are my child. Whatever magic you have is my gift to you."

"You still haven't answered my question. Are you immortal?"

Finally, his smile disappears, and his lips fall into a hard line. "Yes."

Liar. "So you could have saved my Mom."

"Minerva..." He spreads his arms like he wants me to hug him. "A curse is a heavy burden and difficult magic to break."

So he knew about the curse, another reason to hate his

guts–as if the way he carries himself isn't enough of a reason to punch him in the face.

"You couldn't save her, is what you're telling me?" I tilt my head as if confused. "So you're not as powerful as you claim."

He drops the oh-so-charming Father act. "Your Mother was a *waste*. No magic, not even latent. Yet she stood shoulder to shoulder with the damn Supreme. A charity case taken too far." He shakes his head. "Unlike you, who have grown into an advantageous nature. And unlike the rest of your siblings..."

"What's wrong with Arthur and Nim? They take after you, don't they?"

"And they're desperate to prove it to me. But you, you're your own person. You don't kneel to a coven or even to me." He cuts the space between us, stalking toward me. "You could surpass me, Minerva. Let me teach you what I know." I'm afraid he might try to touch me, and I won't be able to keep a neutral face. "Join the family you were always supposed to be a part of."

His pupils are so large, I see myself reflected in them like an obsidian mirror. "Lance told me you need blood magic to survive." His eyes bulge. "I know you're going to siphon me, use me so you can patch yourself up. You're rotting from the inside out, aren't you? I can see it in your eyes."

He grimaces, baring his teeth like a scared dog. "You think much too highly of yourself."

"I guess that's the *real* gift you left me." I grab my purse, knowing full well I can't cast a fast, flashy spell but ready to use my materials if needed.

To my dismay, he starts laughing again, this time his soft chuckle turning heavy and sinister, almost cartoonish.

"I was wrong about you, and wrong about your Mother. What's the saying?" He pulls something from his breast pocket. "Third times the charm? You belong to me now—"

I smack him in the face with my purse and then kick him in the shin. There's no time to watch and see if my attacks are effective; I book it out of there. Thankfully, it's not the first time I've run in heels, and I'm not going very far, just to the next gallery, where I hide behind a display and start rifling through my purse.

A rose quartz and some sticks of chalk spill out, clattering against the marble floor. My panicked breathing isn't exactly quiet either. With shaky hands, I grab one of the pieces of chalk and start drawing sigils around the quartz, for once not concerned about a perfect circle or if my lines are exact.

"Isn't this adorable?" Arthur growls. "Chasing you around like the child you are. Daddy is done playing hide-and-seek, Minerva."

I whisper the incantation as quickly as possible, my heart thudding in my ears, a ceremonial drum accompanying my spell. The chalk lines start to hiss and smoke. Last time, that meant it was working.

The tip of a black Oxford comes into view. Arthur looks at me, disappointed. "I'll let that little outburst slide and give you one—"

A baseball sized creature flies into his face, leathery wings flapping right in his eyes. I should bolt, but I'm too stunned by the creature. Furry and round, its head is nothing but a cluster of fly-eyes that open and close like a latch to reveal a row of teeth. I snap myself out of it and start running, making sure to grab my purse as I go.

I need to get back to the party; there's no way he'll confront me in a room full of people. At least, he wouldn't have before I sicced a tiny devil on his face.

Rounding a corner I slam into a body. Before I can push off, arms wrap around me, pinning me in place. I struggle against whoever it is.

"Let me—"

"Vexing little thing," Rosier purrs. "You gave Kas a conniption. He was convinced the le Fays got you."

"Well, if they weren't planning on doing that before, they're going to do it now."

His voice is like thunder. "As if I'd let them."

Another voice interrupts us. "You think we'll kneel to you?"

I look over my shoulder, my concerns about the le Fay clan now realized. Arthur has scratches across his cheekbones that he takes in stride, his tongue reaching for a droplet of blood running down his cheek. Flanking him is Guine, the emptiness in her eye replaced by hatred—directed right at me. Near her is Nim, holding the little devil by the scruff, the poor thing struggling while she holds a curved knife to its gut. Arthur, Jr., is there, too, but just like in the main hall, he looks like he'd rather be anywhere else.

Arthur asks, "Do you know what happens to a devil when they get stabbed?"

Nim then pierces the devil's stomach with her knife, the creature crying out and smoke rising from the wound. She then pushes the knife deeper before dragging it down and eviscerating it, yellow-brown blood and guts falling to the floor.

He answers his own question. "The same thing that happens to everything else."

"Nim," Guine breathes, exasperated. "Your pretty dress."

She looks at her mother and frowns before holding the creature with both hands to snap its neck, more blood splattering on her hands and dress.

Rosier holds me tight, but I push his arms aside. Again, he tries to grab me, but I shoot him a look and he yields.

"Who told you I summoned a devil?" I demand. "How'd you even know I'd be here?"

Arthur gestures to Guine. "My wife is the best living

diviner. I've had her check on you from time to time. I've always *cared* for you, Minevera."

Rosier snorts. "If she's so good at divining, why didn't she see you fucking other women?"

"You be quiet!" Guine shrieks, stepping forward. "That slut seduced my husband!"

"Your husband was trying to kill her," Rosier points out. "I bet he fucks his meals, too. Anything before fingering your dry cunt."

Guine looks like she might cry. Or spontaneously combust.

"You know it's the truth," I say to her. "And if you're so good at seeing the future I'm sure you know what happened to my mom."

Guine's anger falters, her grimace slipping.

"Unlike you all," I continue, "I don't want bloodshed or power. I want an acknowledgement. I want an apology for my Mom."

"An... apology?" Her voice is breathy, reminding me of actresses in old black-and-white movies.

"All this," Junior groans, "for an apology."

Arthur's thin lips have almost disappeared, they're so tight. I don't know what upsets him more, the request itself or the fact this is happening in front of his whole family.

Guine touches his shoulder. "You could apologize. And then... maybe she could be family."

"*Seriously?*" Nim screeches.

"Oh, he's trying to kill me, too," I inform her.

The claim that she's the most powerful diviner grows weaker by the second, but the way she touches and looks at Arthur makes me think she has a glaring blindspot when it comes to her husband.

"I don't need magic to tell me he'll use me the same way he uses all of you," I add.

Nim still holds the limp, lifeless creature like it's a plushie. "Why don't we speed up the process, use you up right here?" She points the knife at me.

Rosier steps in front of me. "I like my chances against that tiny thing."

"Nimue," Arthur snaps at his daughter. "Put that away."

She narrows her eyes, the knife tip still pointed in our direction.

I hear footsteps and turn, hoping to see security or even Kas. Instead, the bodyguard that arrived with the le Fays is sprinting toward us. I step aside, and the guard goes right for Rosier, putting him in a chokehold. Rosier grabs the back of his head and effortlessly slams him to the floor. As soon as the guard is on the ground, Rosier punches him, his fist coming back bloody. I refuse to witness the damage and grab Rosier's wrist, once again running through the galleries.

"We can't keep running!" he barks at me. I try to get us to the main hall, but Rosier tugs me right back into a corridor that leads to some bathrooms. He grips my shoulders. "What happened to confronting them?"

"He's not going to give me what I want." I shake my head. "And I embarrassed him–that's enough."

"No, it's not," he growls. "His head should be on a pike for the world to see."

"Oh, okay, let me just grab my pike from my purse." I wave the tiny bag in his face.

Rosier furrows his brows. "You summoned that imp, didn't you?"

"Is this a lecture?"

"It's a reminder, a request." He pulls the purse from my wrist.

"We do not have time for you–"

He grasps one of the large golden pins at the front of my dress and yanks it, tearing the dress.

I grab his hand. "Use your tongue for something other than petty insults, you worthless Prince!"

Rosier glances at my hand holding his before leaning in, his cocky smirk right in my face. "This time, you'll summon something bigger. A beast of burden for me to command. A proper monster."

"I can't." I tell him, but I know that's a lie. "I shouldn't."

"All this magic, and you're holding back?" Still holding the golden safety pin, he reaches into my bag and pulls out a piece of chalk between two fingers. "Hesitation will grant us nothing."

I take the chalk and pin before getting down on the ground to start drawing another circle. "What if I–"

"Focus," he encourages. Rosier takes the two other stones left in my purse and sets them in the center of the circle.

"If it fails–"

"It won't."

Summoning the imp feels like ages ago, when it's only been five minutes. I hope Hell doesn't rate-limit summoning spells. Even without interplanar interference, I'm nowhere near as confident in my magic as Rosier. It figures; when I need to be impulsive, I can't bring myself to do it. The magic circle complete in front of me, I struggle to find the words, the incantation as distant as my family magic.

Rosier joins me on the ground across from me. His hand cradles my chin and lifts my face. "You summoned me." His gold eyes sparkle. "You, Minerva, need no one but yourself. You've said it yourself. Prove to the le Fays they're weaker than you. Tear them apart. Inflict the pain your Mother felt onto them tenfold."

So this is truly how he sees me.

I start the incantation, the words flowing as easily as a familiar song The runes begin to glow and steam as someone shouts, "Found her!" Still I keep chanting, looking at nothing but the center of the magic circle. The gold and crystal offerings start to give off plumes of smoke. Then, nothing.

I'm yanked back, sharp pain radiating across my scalp. The cold blade is flush against my throat. Rosier looks like he's about to leap across the circle, but Nim's girlish voice taunts, "One slip up, and her throat is bye-bye. I would stay right th–"

The sound of tearing metal interrupts her. I look down, careful to only move my eyes and not my head. A dark-clawed hand clings to the edge of the circle like whatever's attached to it is climbing out of a manhole.

Rosier almost coos, "Come out, Udtuk."

CHAPTER TWENTY-FIVE

MINNIE

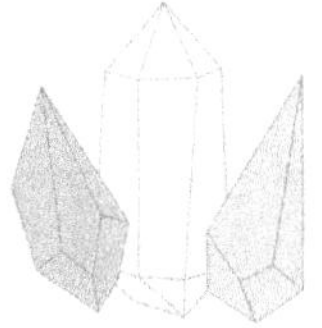

FROM THE STILL SMOKING CIRCLE, CLAWS DIG INTO THE stone floor, cracking it like an eggshell. A lion's head slowly rises. Well, at least, it has the mane of a lion. The rest of its face is scaly and flat with white pupilless eyes. A permanent, painful-looking smile shows off rows of sharp, shark-like teeth. As terrifying as the creature is, impending steel against my throat takes precedent.

Udtuk looks at us with those soulless eyes as if awaiting instruction.

"Let go of me," I say to Nim. "We don't both have to die."

"Shut up! I'm thinking!"

"Planning your funeral?" Rosier offers. He stands up, and Udtuk does the same, climbing out of the circle. The rest of its body is patches of matted hairs and flaking scales. It steps back to stand beside Rosier before sitting like a dog, though its knees are as tall as its shoulders.

Nim's grip on my hair tightens, reminding me just how potent spite can be. "Your hair is ugly."

"Your eyebrows take up half your head," I shoot back.

"You–your dress is ugly!"

It's scary how easily we bicker like sisters.

Rosier crosses his arms. "Udtuk, when I command, you'll go for the pale blonde one. Start with her head and work your way down."

I know the creature won't hurt me, but the command makes the blood drain from my face.

The knife clatters to the ground, and Nim scurries away, first on all fours before eventually getting to her feet. I take a slow, deep breath, appreciating the simple freedom of breathing without fear. Though my relative freedom is short-lived before Rosier is once again on top of me.

He pulls me from the floor, my feet dangling as he holds me to his chest. "Minnie–"

"You're being clingy," I tell him.

Before I can push him away or tease him he explains. "I'm only protecting what's mine."

I roll my eyes, though he can't see. "Clingy."

As my eyes roll about, I spot the abandoned knife. I kick my feet, hoping that will get him to set me down. He complies, though he still holds my waist. I bend down and pick up the knife, gazing at my warped reflection in the blade. Arthur le Fay won't give me what I want, but it's not entirely his fault. I've been denying myself, trying to outsource my desires to Rosier, lying to myself about what it is I truly want. Revenge against Arthur le Fay seems impossible.

So he's no longer my target.

Rosier brushes my cheek with the back of his fingers. "Minnie?"

My hand flexes, holding the hilt of the blade tighter. "I'm going to kill that bitch who called my Mom a whore."

"By yourself? I could have Udtuk do it."

I look past him at Udtuk, whose glassy eyes and aimless

smile make my blood run cold. Yet, I can't turn away from him, looking like a mascot costume left out in the elements and hanging up to dry. He doesn't even breathe.

I close my eyes to break the trance and shake my head. "What happened to what is rightfully mine?" His face softens, and I add, "It has to be me. There's no point in having it be anyone else." I pull myself from Rosier and start marching, hunting once again for the le Fays.

The clicking of Udtuk's claws against the marble echoes behind me, and Rosier appears at my side. "You know I would–"

"Rosie. Let me do this, please."

He snorts. "Still so civil, even when you're on a murderous rampage."

"It doesn't matter what I say. I could tell you to fuck right off, and you'd still follow me around like..." I look over my shoulder. "Like Udtuk there."

He hums. "It seems even without a contract, you've bewitched me. I am your loyal servant, Minerva."

"Would have been nice to know that a week ago."

We're getting closer to the gala itself, the sound of idle chatter like accompaniment. We find the le Fays all in a circle, hissing at each other, clearly trying to form a plan. Thankfully, Guine spots me, and jumps back, quite literally clutching her pearls as she looks past me.

"What is *that?*" she asks in horror.

Arthur le Fay speaks up. "Still clambering for an apology, I see, Minerva. Well, I'm so sor–"

"That offer has been rescinded." I hold the sharp side of the knife between my thumb and forefinger, showing it off as if it's on display. "Actually, I'm not even interested in speaking with you at all, Arthur."

Guine is still looking at the beast behind me.

"A life for a life seems fair," I say acutely.

Guine blinks, then snaps her attention back to me.

Junior steps between us. "Minerva, don't do this."

"Oh, so now you want peace? Like your brother?"

"My Mother is not–"

"She is absolutely the problem, or a part of it–I don't really care at this point. I lost my Mom..." My eyes narrow. "So why should you get to keep yours?"

I reach over and take Rosier's hand. He jumps, maybe surprised by the tender gesture amidst all this rage, but he holds my hand in kind.

"Have Udtuk take care of those three," I order. "Guine is mine."

Rosier squeezes my hand. "Whatever my witch desires." He turns his head. "Udtuk, dispatch of these witches. Do with them what you will."

Guine bolts, but not away from us; she rushes right into my space. I raise my hands defensively–a reflex, really–but I know I only have to swipe at her once to get a good cut in. I wonder if she's sacrificing herself for her children. The thought makes me hesitate, and it's enough opportunity for Guine to tackle me to the ground. I cling to the knife, but my head hits the ground first, and I drop it in the recoil.

There are stars in my eyes as Guine holds the knife above her head.

I force myself to breathe, and it feels like I'm inhaling smoke. My dress is wet and sticky, clinging to my body. The knife in my shoulder doesn't register, not even when I see the hilt sticking out of it from the corner of my vision.

Guine is gone, Rosie standing above me in her stead, his lips moving frantically. I wish I could hear him, but silence plugs my ears. I try to reach for him, but the pain becomes even worse. The edges of my vision start to darken, like a slow transition at the very end of a movie. I'm weightless, no longer on the floor. I rest my cheek against something soft. Over the metallic smell of blood, there is the faint, comforting smell of lavender.

The shock dissipates, and I can hear Rosier now. "*Please,* Minnie. I said *please,* so you have to stay with me."

I will is what I want to say, but all I can manage is a soft moan.

Blood curdling screams and crashing glass swell to a crescendo around me. I close my eyes, not wanting to see the mess I've made.

Rosier speaks through gritted teeth, "I should have told that devil to stay close."

From the way I'm being jostled about, I can tell Rosier is running. The screaming continues. There is so much fear; I can feel it in the air like the static before a lightning storm. My eyes shut tighter, trying to tune it all out, focusing instead on my heartbeat, faster and heavier than when I was running away.

"We have to take her to a hospital." Kas' voice carries over the terrors. "No, wait, shit, the hospitals will be crawling with people. We might... Shit."

Amber. I try to tell them. *Amber will help.* She's too good a soul to let me die like this.

"You're going to be alright." Rosier's nose is pressed against my forehead. "I'll burn this city... Hells, Minnie..."

I'm going to be alright is all I can focus on, a mantra to keep me alive 'til Rosier can save me. He refused me a peaceful death. If he's not careful, tonight we'll both reap what we've sowed.

CHAPTER TWENTY-SIX

ROSIER

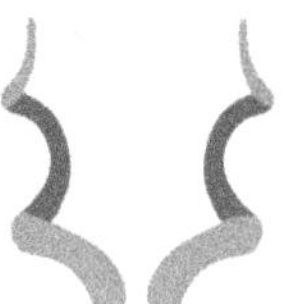

Of all the figures before us, the frail and soft-spoken Mother of the le Fays was not my pick for bloodshed. Yet she descended on Minnie like a predator, held the knife with such ease, it made me realize this is not the first time she's killed for her family. For Arthur fucking le Fay. Once the knife is embedded in Minnie's shoulder, Guine's and my eyes meet. Hers are sunken and pleading, as if asking me for forgiveness.

Instead, I choke out a command. "Kill them now." Udtuk descends upon the three le Fays, but it's Guine that shrieks. She follows Udtuk, chasing after her family, though I can't be fucked to watch them scurry about.

Minnie is on the ground, crimson spreading across her dress and chest. I take her in my arms.

"Minnie?"

Her eyes are half open. My hands linger over her wound, not sure how much blood she has left, scared if I pull out the knife I'll subject her to more pain.

"Minerva!" I shout her name, but there's no reaction. It's impossible to look away from her parting lips and glassy eyes.

There's screaming in the distance.

"Minerva, Minnie, say something." I hold her against me, her blood staining my clothes. "Please." I grip her arms as if holding her tighter will keep her here. My voice betrays how desperate to keep her alive. "*Please*, Minnie. I said *please, so* you have to stay with me."

A groan leaves her lips, and I fear that is her last breath.

Useless on my own, I start running.

Kas runs right into us, brown eyes wide and wild. "The fuck happened?! I can't leave you two alone for a moment!"

"Minnie is dying," I choke. "Do something!"

"I'm not a doctor! Shit–" He pulls out a phone and presses a few buttons before putting it against his ear. "Pull up–no, not up front, out back. We need to get the fuck out of here." Still holding the phone, Kas glares at me. "Follow me."

I do, though as we run, I catch sight of the destruction wrought by Udtuk: broken glass like piles of gems, abandoned shoes, abandoned limbs, blood...

It's nothing I haven't seen before, but for the mortals of this realm, *this* is Hell.

More and more people start to appear around us, splattered with blood like Minnie. No one bats an eye at us as we run to a door labeled EMERGENCY and step into the night. The car we arrived in screeches to a halt, and we get inside it.

"We have to take her to a hospital." Kas says to someone, me or the driver. "No, wait, shit, the hospitals will be crawling with people. We might..." His eyes dart around in their sockets like he's reading a map as fast as he can. "Shit."

"The Coven," I offer. "Witches can heal, can't they?"

"Oh, they're gonna *hate* you." Kas pokes his head between the front seats, speaking frantically with the driver.

My gaze falls to Minnie in my arms, her eyes still open but hazy. My whole body starts to shake. If I had agreed to her contract in the chapel... A painless death is all she wanted, and I refused her out of pride. Or guilt. Out of my selfish desire to be humane. Fuck me–if I had agreed to her first contract, if I had only said yes, none of this would have happened.

I kiss her forehead. "You're going to be alright. I'll burn this city..." I wince, recognizing my rage can't save her, same as siccing Udtuk on the gala didn't save her. "Hells, Minnie... I'm not ready to say goodbye."

Several screaming, illuminated cars barrel past us, heading in the direction we came from. When Kas settles back in his seat, he doesn't look at me. His only concern seems to be whoever he's talking to on the phone.

"Stop being paranoid for one second," he says to whoever's on the other end. "We're going to Lucky Witch if you need us." His phone is only away from his ear a few moments before he's blabbing again. To whom, I don't really care.

The car pulls over, and through the dark glass, I can see Amber and another woman standing by the door of the shop. The driver opens the door, and as soon as I step out, Amber is beside me, her face almost as washed out as Minnie's. She doesn't ask any questions, just takes Minnie from my arms and utters something under her breath. I follow her the way Leaf follows Minnie when she has a can of food in her hands.

Inside the shop, my nose immediately starts twitching, a sweet smell burning my nostrils. Kas is behind me, and he sneezes before grumbling, "Juniper."

Walking through the shop, it feels like a bigger version of Minnie's apartment: books, crystals, and wands everywhere I look. It's comfortable, minus the damn smell.

Amber disappears into a stairwell. I move to follow, but the other woman steps in my path and grabs my shoulder. "This is as far as you go." She must be Amber's sister with how similar their features are, that warm brown skin and those dark, slender eyes. I look at her hand still gripping my shoulder, then scowl at her. She grips my shoulder tighter.

There's so much energy in the shop, it's hard to know where it originates from. Yet, the longer I stand here, it dawns on me the energy isn't from the random stones or ceremonial bowls. It's all from this one woman. Magic surrounds her, kneels at her feet.

Her hand slides off my shoulder. "Leave if you must, but you will step no further into this house." She brushes past me and grabs a jar off a wall behind me. Kas and I watch as she spreads a mixture of salt and some other herb across the threshold of the stairwell. I stifle a cough. Kas sneezes again. Then she's gone, and as I expect, the magic in the room settles and fades.

"We're so fucked," Kas whines.

"Do you think they'll save her?"

"I think they're going to send your ass back to Hell in a handbasket."

I grimace, trying my damndest to keep Kas focused. "I wouldn't fit."

"For fucks sake, Rosier!" He throws up his hands. "What were you thinking? Summoning a... what even was that? A shaved manticore?"

My expression falters as I huff. I fucked up. From the very start, I fucked all of us.

Kas sighs. "The things we do for love, I guess."

"I'm incapable of such a thing. My hubris, my pride, those things are why we're in this mess. Why Minnie is..."

I refuse to say it. Dying. Because of me. And all she wanted in the end was a peaceful death.

I pinch the bridge of my nose, recalling how diamonds fell from her eyes when she spoke of her Mother. I wish I could cry, I wish I could feel an ounce of her pain.

Kas groans and throws his head back. "Come on, Rosier. Don't tell me you believe that shit?"

"Love is a mortal experience," I snap. "I would think a person who feeds on lust would understand that better than anyone."

Kas crosses his arms. "Well, I don't. For one thing, I love people. Lots of people over lots of centuries. Sure, I also fucked them, but those aren't mutually exclusive. Sometimes they are. But like, Tim... bad example–Chanel! I love her."

"She doesn't strike me as your type."

"My type is very fluid, but you know that's not what I mean." My confusion must be plain to see because Kas elaborates, "If something bad were to happen to her, I would feel bad–devastated even. That's part of love."

Maybe. When I look at Minnie, I do feel some sort of love. I know it's not purely lust. Seeing her dance with someone else made me feel all sorts of things: envy and rage and maybe a touch of broken pride. That can't be the components of love. I think about Richard and how he wants his old lover to run back to his arms, to desire no one else. I want Minnie–but not like that. I want her to choose me. I want her to be able to desire others and still choose me. I want her to wake up next to me and smile at me like it's our first morning, over and over again.

I shake my head. "I've seen plenty of devils get upset over their coffers being burgled or a paramour scorning them in favor of another. That can't be love."

I'll suffocate her with my greed until she's hollow, or we'll bicker until we hate each other. Nevermind her still wanting to make a deal and give up her spirit, the *true* thing I admire most about her.

"Well, whatever it is, I hope it was worth that mess at the museum." He pulls his phone out again and makes a gagging sound. "I don't even want to guess how the news is spinning this. Maybe something escaped Belle Isle–nope, not thinking about it!"

Minnie's face, draining of color, rests behind my eyes.

"Not thinking about it..." I grumble.

———

HOURS PASS. Kas and I both discard our jackets and neck bows. I also toss out my frilly shirt, the white permanently marred by blood. I crack open a book while Kas paces up and down the shelves, both of us occasionally sneezing and coughing. In the long term, I wonder if simple juniper can do me any real harm. I search the books for an answer, but I can only find information on healing, physically and spiritually.

Kas yawns. "When can we leave?"

"You can leave whenever you like. I'm staying."

He groans and leaves for the door. "I'll be back; I need fresh air."

The bell on the door chimes cheerfully yet feels ominous. A few moments later, the woman who met us at the door appears from the stairwell. I glance at her over my book before going back to reading about mugwort.

"You are a very strange devil."

"So I've been told..." I shut the book. "However, I disagree. I'm right in assuming you've never met a devil before me. So how would you know if I'm as strange as I seem?"

She chuckles and smiles at me, an act that, much like the bell, feels foreboding. "You're correct. I only know of devils through stories, same as fae and angels."

"And demons?"

"Unlike the rest, demons never stopped arriving on this Plane. Unfortunately, I've dealt with many demons."

"How do they compare to devils?"

She *tsks*. "Your little show at the museum makes that a hard question to answer. People are dead." She glares at me as if I killed them myself, then keeps staring like she's expecting me to say something.

"People do tend to die," I point out. "Pretty universally."

Her eyes shut, and she hums to herself, the magical objects in the room humming as well.

"Who are you, anyway?" I ask.

"You will call me Madame Albe during our short time together."

I lift a brow, and the bell on the door sings again. Three women walk inside, all different shapes and sizes, all dressed in bright dresses. They walk in a line and fall behind Madame Albe. I try to catch their gazes, but each woman looks away from me before we can connect.

"Rosier," Madame Albe speaks my name like I'm already dead. "We do not condone bloodshed within our ranks. Do not make us act against you."

I set the book on the shelf behind me. "So you gathered your friends to do what? Braid my hair?"

"We're going to send you back." She hides her hands, and I wonder which one of the three women is armed. I've yet to see any brutal displays of magic from anyone, but a knife would cut me all the same.

"That's it? You'll just send me back without any punishment?"

"How could we possibly punish you in propriety? We do not know what the victims would have wanted, and your death will not help those in mourning. Not to mention the politics of killing a being from another Plane. That, I'm sure you understand."

"You think the Archdevils would be upset if you killed a Prince of the Hells?"

"I think I'd rather not take the risk. Once you're back in Hell, you can cause no further harm."

I keep my eyes on the women, though my mind is anywhere but this little shop. I hoped to stay longer. Everything ends. It would be nice to take home a token of my time here: a potted plant, a paperback, Leaf. Things that will only remind me of her.

I can already hear her objection if I said goodbye. She'd say, *"I decide when you leave; we haven't formed a contract, so you can't do this to me,"* all while pushing her bottom lip into a pout, her eyes alight with rage. I'll take my memory with me; it will last longer than paper or plants.

"Fine," I huff. "Send me back. Make it easy for all of us."

Her eyes on me, Madame Albe speaks over her shoulder. "Prepare the circle. I'll watch him." Each woman squeezes Madame's hand before walking to a door that leads below the shop.

Once again, it's me and her. I slip my hands into my pockets. "What's going to happen to Minnie?"

"Hopefully, she lives a full and peaceful life."

"We both know she's going to die soon."

"The length of a life does not determine its impact. She is loved, she will be missed." There is a heaviness to her voice. I can't tell if she believes her own words.

I snort. "That's enough for you all? Pitiful."

"It's better than an eternity in the Hells or wandering the Earth as a corrupt soul. The Veil will welcome her, just as it will welcome you someday." Again, she smiles at me, but it no longer feels like a threat. "You'll see her again, in time."

"I don't need your comforting," I snarl.

"Mmm, clearly not." There's a sparkle in her eyes, like she finds me humorous.

I take a step in her direction, and her gentle expression melts, muscles tensing.

"How long is this going to take?" I ask.

"The ritual should be ready now. Come." She leads me to the door and motions for me to go downstairs first, still holding one hand behind her back.

"How do I know you're not going to stab me on the way down?"

"Hmph, you think I have the energy to carry your big body down those steps? And what terrible energy that would bring to the Coven's space." Finally, she reveals what's in her hand, an all black hilt and holster sheathing a five-inch blade. "It wouldn't be practical."

"Fine," I grumble. I'm only a few steps down when I start sneezing. "Fucking Hells, is this necessary?"

I don't get an answer, but the scent of juniper and sage from below is overbearing, making me lightheaded. I'm not sure I could put up much of a fight down here. At the bottom of the steps, I'm met with a windowless room, the three women from before standing around a now familiar magic circle.

There's an altar in the center with thick purple candles, an animal skull, and a good array of fruits, though I can't identify each one. "Is that a coconut?" I point to a yellow, waxy orb.

Madame Albe's lip twitches. "That's... a lemon." She purses her lips as if to hide a smile.

"Well, I fear I'll return to the Hells without the knowledge of coconuts."

"Shame, really, but best we make this quick." She motions for me to step into the circle. "The le Fays may want you dead, and a devil is easy to spot."

I stay still. "You swear to me Minnie will be safe?"

"We will do everything in our power to keep her from the le Fays, but if she seeks them out–"

"Right. Not much anyone can do if she decides she hasn't had a proper taste of revenge..."

I step into the circle. The colorfully-dressed women all gather and join hands around the circle, close their eyes, and begin to chant. Almost immediately, the offerings in the circle begin to burn. I pick up the lemon and watch as its yellow surface goes from red to black, disintegrating into ash.

CHAPTER TWENTY-SEVEN

MINNIE

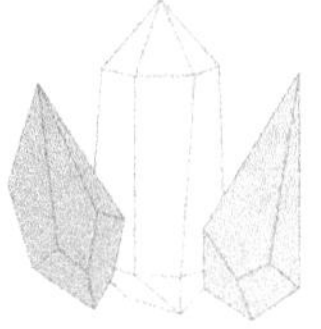

THE SHARP SMELL OF PEPPERMINT PULLS ME FROM THE darkness. When I open my eyes, everything is a blurry mess of brushstrokes. Despite the world being muddy, I make out the shape of a man with blond hair. My heart thumps once like a gong, and I sit up, gasping for air.

"Minnie–" Amber's voice is in my ear, and I shut my eyes, wondering if this is a nightmare. "Lay back down. You're going to hurt yourself."

Instead of listening to her, I open up my eyes again, blinking 'til everything is clear. Lance is sitting on the edge of the bed, his thick eyebrows close together, his lips turned down in a frown. Amber rubs my shoulder, and I remember what happened. Glancing down, I confirm the handle of the knife is no longer sticking out of my shoulder.

"Girl, seriously," Amber pleads. "Those stitches weren't easy."

I settle back into the bed, Amber and Lance now looming over me, both of their faces plastered with concern. "Do you remember anything?" Lance asks.

I remember everything; the le Fays, the devils, the whole getting stabbed in the neck thing. Well, not quite the neck, but close enough. Hurts bad enough, though. Lying here, my shoulder feels tight, like I've pulled every muscle in my right side.

"Do you have any eucalyptus?" I ask.

Amber's expression softens, and she walks away, returning with several long dark green leaves. She presses them to my shoulder, and I can better feel the stitches. I listen to her incantation; it's familiar to me, but I can't for the life of me recite the words. The pain starts to fade, and I sit up again.

"Lance..." He perks up up when I say his name. "Did your Mom used to check in on me? When I was a kid?"

Again, his brows and lips fall. "No? No, I don't think so. She told me everything growing up. I mean *everything*, and she never mentioned you. I didn't even think she knew about you."

"She's a powerful diviner."

"The sight is easy to ignore if you want to. I ignored it for the last decade."

Amber cuts in. "You talked to his Mom? You spoke with the le Fays?"

"I did." I glare at Lance. "If your mom wasn't checking up on me, how did they find out I summoned a devil?"

"I don't know—I mean, I know she checks up on me despite us being no contact for a decade..."

I blink, thinking about every time Lance and I have crossed paths this last year. He showed up at my house, caught me crying outside Lucky Witch, and then came to my apartment, where I told him who Rosier was. We stare at each other, but Lance doesn't seem to get it.

"You visited my house six months ago," I remind him. "*You told me who my Father was.*"

His hand covers his mouth, the revelation finally hitting

him. It would be cruel to say he's completely at fault but ignorant to say this wouldn't have happened without him being so sentimental over an idea, over the little girl his Father abandoned.

Amber, intentionally or otherwise, cuts us off. "Which one stabbed you?"

"I could tell you," Lance grumbles. "But since Minnie's awake, why don't you do the honors?"

"It was Guine, the Mom." Lance shakes his head like I've just poured cold water on him, but I continue, "But Arthur was the one going after me. He pulled something from his pocket, but he never got a chance to use it. Then he chased me, along with all the other le Fays. We only escaped because–"

If I tell them, it's going to be a fight. I don't remember what happened to the devil I summoned, only that it followed Rosier's command. Rosier's never shown much interest in violence or harming innocent people, but I'm not sure it's that simple.

"Minnie," Amber has her mom-voice going. She places her hand over mine. "If you summoned a devil out of self-defense... maybe this can all work out."

"Of course, I summoned it for self-defense."

Lance mutters, "Looks like it didn't get the memo."

I call him out. "We don't need to act shy. Did the devil kill Guine? Did it kill the le Fays?"

Amber shifts her body so she's blocking Lance from view. "Is that what you told it to do?"

"It followed Rosier's command."

She nods. "Good, good. Then it's not your fault."

The pain in my shoulder is replaced by a tightness in my chest. "Amber, what happened? I don't remember much after I got stabbed."

Lance's head pops up from behind Amber's shoulder. "Maybe wait 'til you're healed–"

Amber ignores Lance's plea. "The Devil you summoned *might* have killed a le Fay. People are dead. That's all the news is reporting right now."

I touch the leaves on my shoulder, ruminating on the fact I could have been one of those people as well.

"Not a lot of people," Lance assures me.

"So there aren't four le Fay corpses on the steps of the Institute of Art?" Lance and Amber are silent, though both their mouths hang open. "Shame."

"Minnie!"

"They deserve to die, Amber! Don't tell me you disagree."

"I do. I do disagree on a matter of principle. Killing the le Fays won't solve any–"

"Bullshit."

"Listen to yourself!" She's right in my face now. "What will killing Arthur le Fay change? It won't bring your Mom back. It won't bring back any of the people he killed. He must have a backup plan in case he dies, some spell to keep him alive."

"No." I start to shake my head, but the tension from the stitches stops me. "No, he's not immortal. Not even close." I lean over to get a better look at Lance. "You were right. He's not nearly as powerful as he thinks he is."

Lance grimaces. "Somehow, being right in this instance doesn't feel so great."

I hear a familiar *murp,* and a silky black coat comes into view at the end of the bed. Leaf trots over to sit in my lap. I hold his head in my hands, rubbing his cheeks with my thumbs. As happy as I am to see him, I know we're nowhere near my apartment.

"What's going on?" I ask, though I'm focused on Leaf, his eyes closed in contentment.

"You can't stay here, Minnie," Amber informs me in a grave tone. I keep petting Leaf between his ears. "The le Fays have every reason to go after you now. Not just them, either. If any other covens find out what you did, they'll want answers. And let's be real, your reasoning for summoning two devils isn't very great."

"Three," I correct. "I summoned an imp, too."

I don't have to look at Amber's face to know the exact expression she's making, the face she uses to try and hide how angry she actually is. She's always careful not to be too angry, too sad, or too much of anything that could get her in trouble. We used to check each other in school, remind each other the world isn't ready to really see us.

I want to shake that little girl and scream in her face, tell her there is no reward for being good for the sake of everyone and everything, tell her that she should scream and kick and cry—that she should make the world uncomfortable. It's too late for that child, just like it's too late for me.

"Where would you even send me?" I raise my head.

"Divination isn't perfect," Lance explains. "With some protective wards, if you keep your head down, no one should be able to find you."

Amber continues, "The sponsor for wayward supernaturals is already setting things up for you up in Ontario. We packed your stuff–"

"You went through my things?"

"That's what you're gonna object to?" she scoffs. "Us rummaging through your stuff?"

"I object to all of it. I'm not going to hide out for the next ten years and then die in a snowbank in a place you can only find with coordinates."

Amber throws up her hands. "I can't have this conversation." She steps away, going off into a corner of the room with her arms crossed.

Lance inches toward me. "Minerva, be smart about this. Is dying here really better than... dying anywhere else?"

"Where's Rosier?" The question comes out of nowhere, but once it's said, it can't be undone. If these two have already made plans for how to deal with me, no doubt the coven has plans for him. "Where is he?" I press.

Lance is trying his hardest to remain neutral, but his lips quiver. Amber is very intentionally looking away from me, focusing on the door that leads out of her room.

I bolt out of bed, Leaf leaping with me. I toss the door open and start running, realizing I'm only wearing panties and one of Amber's old shirts. My bare feet slap against the linoleum floor of the shop. It's empty, but the door to the basement is wide open, confirming my fears.

I trudge down the steps, chanting hitting my ears once I'm past the threshold, Leaf almost trips me as he darts between my legs down the stairs. My bare feet touch the cold concrete of the basement. The smell of juniper, sage, and cinder is overwhelming, and the ash the size of snowflakes swirls in the air like the eye of a storm.

Four women hold hands, all of them familiar to me—even the back of Madame Albe's head is recognizable. Yet none of them have noticed me, too focused on the spell. Past them, I see Rosier, his form wavering, turning from a solid to something else—a shadow is all I can compare it to. I hold my breath. Despite the magic changing Rosier's form, his eyes remain—his golden gaze locked on the table of offerings as they, too, fade from this Plane.

Timing is everything—I can't risk the coven stopping the spell, but I can't risk missing the moment of completion. There's no room for second guessing.

That is until Amber shouts my name from the shop. "Minnie!"

I bolt, breaking through the circle of coven members and into the magic circle. My body collides with Rosier's, and I wrap my arms around him, shutting my eyes tight. I become part of the spell, my own form becoming some sort of *other* that only exists in the sphere of magic. Despite this, it feels like Rosier is reaching out to me, holding onto me.

Then there's this sudden drop, like a rollercoaster as it races down the steepest part of the track.

CHAPTER TWENTY-EIGHT

MINNIE

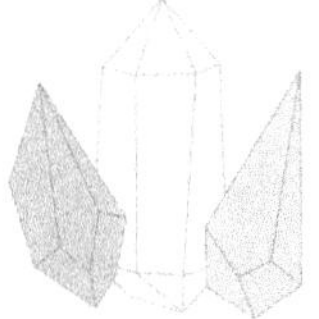

THE FIRST THING I HEAR IS A ROARING MEOW.

My cheek is pressed to Rosier's chest, and I can feel him hum. "A parting gift..." he whispers. "Memories of you in my arms." He holds me tighter, and I force my eyes to stay closed.

"It's not a memory," I tell him. "I'm here."

Silence, then another meow, Leaf nudging my ankle. Rosier's hold on me loosens. "*Minnie.*"

Finally, I open my eyes. It takes a second to realize it's Rosier looking down at me. His features are the same–tall curved nose, pillowy lips, thin piercing eyes... No, wait, his eyes *are* different. He has no whites or even any pupils, just two rivers of gold looking down at me. He still has his curls, but sticking out of them are two winding spiral horns the same night-shade black as his hair. Yet, what's most striking is his skin; it's a vibrant royal purple, like his skin is made of velvet. Not at all the color I expected of a devil, but it's beautiful.

Less beautiful is the grimace on his face, showing off thick, sharp canines on the top and bottom of his jaw. I can feel his body tense as massive wings unfurl, trying to intimidate me like a cat arching its back. I'm so used to him towering over me, I didn't notice he's even *taller* now. Not counting the horns, he's got to be over six and a half, maybe seven feet tall. He grabs my arms, and sharp fingernails threaten to tear my skin.

"Minnie, what are you doing here?" he demands.

I open my mouth to speak, but no words come out, not a single sound.

He leans over now, getting his teeth right in my face as he hisses. "Minerva, you shouldn't be here!"

The tension is cut by Leaf chirping. Looking down, I see him reaching up to bat at a fluttering toy. But it's not a toy. The flat, heart shaped ornament is attached to a long, thin purple tail connecting to Rosier. Leaf manages to catch the flat end in his paws and bring it to his mouth, nibbling at it.

"Beast!" Rosier scolds, his tail flicking violently out of Leaf's reach.

I cover my mouth with my hand, but it does little to stifle my laughter.

"This isn't a laughing matter, Minnie!"

Unfortunately, this makes me laugh harder.

"You're not supposed to be here!"

I clear my throat, trying to stop the giggles. I take a breath and am finally able to speak, though my giggles accompany the end of my words.. "I wanted... to come with you. So I did."

Rosier's jaw tenses. "You shouldn't have done that."

"Well, I did."

His hand, moving faster than a viper, grabs my chin and squeezes my cheeks. A familiar situation we find ourselves in, but now the tips of his long, black nails leave divots in my flesh like homemade dimples. His wings curl around us, leaving us in shadow. Rosier leans down, all the way down, his entire back bending to reach me, his nose brushing against mine.

I watch his lips but flinch when his fangs peak past his lips.

"Vexing little thing," he curses, his fingers flexing like he might shatter my jaw.

I'm afraid. I haven't been afraid of him for a long time. "*Your* vexing little thing," I whisper.

His face falls, and I would kill to know exactly what he's feeling. "Minnie..."

A shrill voice interrupts us. "Prince! My Prince! Oh, praise to the Hell-pit you're home!"

Rosier and I both turn towards the sound, despite him still holding onto my face. I almost jump back with surprise.

The figure is about my height, with the face of a bullfrog, his moist skin the color of dry cracked earth. His lower half is hairy, covered in mud brown fur, and he has hooves. He wrings his hands, which are small and rodent-like.

"What is *that?*" My voice is pressed and panicked, especially as the thing walks towards us, its hooves clicking against the floor.

"My page, Lithobates," Rosier says, like the answer is obvious.

He finally releases my face, only for Lithobates to get right up in it. One eye blinks, then another. His sideways pupils go wide, and he jumps back with a croak. "She's alive!"

"Yes," Rosier grumbles. "Unfortunately."

"Should we kill her, my Prince?"

My voice is embarrassingly shrill. "*Kill me?*" I look up at Rosier, who has his arms crossed like he's considering it.

Lithobates hops from hoof to hoof. "Torture her? Throw her on the stakes beneath the castle?"

Rosier's wings open wide, then he grabs my hip and pulls me to him. His wings flap, a gust of air pushing Lithobates to the floor. "She is much too precious to harm. Understand?" From the ground, Lithobates nods vigorously. "Minerva here is a guest. Treat her as you would a Devil of the highest caliber."

Lithobates lets out another croak. "B-but she's not–" Rosier opens his wings wide again, and his page stutters, "Y-yes, my Prince. Of course, my Prince. She is our most honorable guest!" He gets up and starts clopping out of the room into a massive hallway. Leaf chases after him. "Make way for our esteemed guest! Minerva Minnie!"

Close enough, I guess.

I crane my neck to look up at Rosier, who isn't moving to follow Lithobates, though he's looking straight ahead like he might. Or maybe he's avoiding looking at me.

"Rosie?" I say in the hopes he'll turn to me.

Instead, his grip on my body tightens before he starts running. His wings flap, and we're soaring off the ground. The ceilings of the hallway are lofty and wide, Rosier gliding beneath them with ease.

Meanwhile, I'm not too happy to be ten feet off the ground. My fingers grab at his muscles, trying to find a secure grip. We pass Lithobates, who's still announcing mine and Rosier's arrival to the palace. I struggle to take it all in as we fly. The palace is completely made of red sandstone, with pillars reaching towards high ceilings like an ancient temple.

Rosier flies through an archway, and I don't immediately recognize we're outside, the sky blood red and the air hot and sticky like the worst days of summer. I look back over Rosier's shoulder to see the palace in full. It's built into a cliffside, made of the same stone as the mountain itself. The top floor is deco-rated with spires, while the second floor where we came from has several open archways. The bottom floor is the complete opposite, closed off with only small windows to the outside and no obvious entrances.

My stomach feels the drop first as we start to fall. I scream and dig my nails into Rosier's skin as the palace becomes smaller and smaller. But then he opens his wings wide, and we start to soar. I still cling to him, my nails leaving crescent-shaped reminders of his little prank.

"Jerk," I mutter into his chest.

His body rumbles as he chuckles. "Look down."

"I'd rather not." But of course, I look.

A flowing river cuts through the mountains. At first, I think the water must be deep because it's practically black, but the more I look at it, I realize it isn't water flowing. I can see wide, moaning mouths and eyes transfixed in fear. The ghastly expressions roll and bounce against each other. I can hear the river, and I tell myself it's the normal sounds of rushing water, though in my gut, I know it's a chorus of agonizing screams.

It would be easy to say those people deserved what they got, that they must have been terrible people to end up here. Except I'm here. Though maybe I'm not an exception but the rule itself.

Rosier's wings snap down, propelling us back up towards the palace. He only has to flap his wings a few times before we're settled on a balcony on the second floor. Rosier tries to set me down, but I refuse to let go, pulling myself up and trying to wrap my legs around his waist.

"Good, I've finally scared you." He holds my hips, his very sharp nails poking my stomach as he holds me so my feet dangle off the ground. "Now do you regret coming here?"

"I told you..." I snap my head to look at him. "I want to be with you. You can't scare me out of that." I kiss the curve of his nose. Then his lips and cheekbones. I kiss every inch of his face, slowly and methodically.

"I should know better by now to try and talk you out of anything."

"You should," I agree. "I'm staying. I don't know for how long, but I'm here. You're not getting rid of me."

"That's the last thing I want," he admits. Rosier shifts so we look out over the cliffside at the world dripping in red. "Welcome to the Hells, Minnie."

CHAPTER TWENTY-NINE

MINNIE

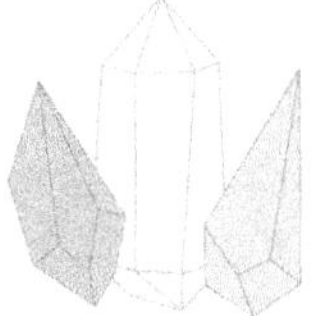

WE STEP INTO THE PALACE THROUGH ONE OF THE OPEN
archways and are surrounded by people. Well, not people per
se–devils of all different statures and shapes. Some of them look
like Rosier with horns and tails and skin the color of jewels,
though no shade is nearly as vibrant as his. Others are like
Lithobates, hybrids of sorts, both familiar and upsetting. The
devils all bow their heads as we walk past, Rosier carrying me
in his arms like I'm a princess.

As we step deeper into the room, we come across devils
dripping with chain armor, sharp teeth and tusks accompanying their horns. One of the devils snorts before stepping to
greet Rosier.

"Prince, if we may–"

Rosier shoots him a look, his gold eyes narrowing. The devil
steps back, bowing his head and saying nothing further.

That doesn't stop me from speaking, of course. "Where are
you taking me?"

"What did I tell you before?" His tail swishes with delight.
"I want to fuck you in my true form."

We walk deeper and deeper into the castle, into the mountain where it resides. A hallway leads to a massive set of double doors that Rosier opens with his back.

Instantly, my eyes are drawn to the room's dome ceiling, decorated with thousands of gemstones of all different colors. It reminds me of the stained glass at the museum but *more*. It's certainly more expensive than colored glass. I'm so enamored with looking up that I don't notice the large bed 'til Rosier sets me on its edge. This thing is like two king-sized mattresses pushed together. Rosier crawls on top of me, grinning from ear to ear.

"What happened to being all grumpy I came here?" I tease.

"Grumpy? I wasn't grumpy; I was furious." He kisses me, then, his fangs brushing along my lips, threatening to rip them like paper. His tongue teases mine, and I feel the split down the middle. Still holding my bottom lip he slowly pulls away. "So I'll have to punish you, then..."

He curls a finger around the neckline of Amber's old shirt and tugs, his sharp, scissor-like nails cutting the fabric straight down. He bends his head and runs his tongue from my clavicle down between my breasts. When he reaches my stomach I notice his tongue is forked like a snake's. Goose pimples rise all along my torso.

"Does my true form frighten you?" His nail teases the elastic of my panties. "Are you afraid?" he asks with glee.

"You're beautiful," I tell him. "Just like you were before. But... yes, some parts of you are scary."

Same as my shirt, he snips my panties from my body. "Am I what you imagined?" He opens my legs and kisses the edge of my knee, working his way up my thighs.

"No." My voice shakes.

Horns, wings, and a tail were to be expected, yet he's still not what I imagined. His horns are much longer, his tail more lithe–every part of him is *more* than I thought possible.

"The purple is a nice surprise," I say, watching his tail flick back and forth behind him. It reminds me of Leaf, and I have to stifle a giggle.

Rosier lifts his head. "What?"

"Nothing," I assure him before reaching down to stroke his bottom lip with my thumb. "Would you prefer I was afraid of you?"

Rosier answers by snapping at my thumb, holding it gingerly between his teeth. Still holding my thumb in his maw, he crawls forward, looming over me once more.

He takes my thumb in his mouth, the tip of his forked tongue fluttering against my thumbpad. I feel it all through my entire body, between my legs especially. Finally he releases my digit.

"You make me so soft, Minnie." He grabs my thighs, pulling them apart. "But I won't be gentle. I'm going to give you that pain you crave so dearly."

I reach over and tug at his tuxedo pants. His cock springs forward, and my lips part. His girth is as massive as the rest of him and purple as well, but that's not what surprises me. His shaft is covered in bumps and ridges lined up like scales. I reach for him, wanting to feel them. Rosier's chest heaves as I stroke him ever so slowly, feeling along each bump. I know I'm about to feel every little bit of him more intimately, but I like familiarizing myself with his true form. As I stroke him, his cock becomes slick, my hand gliding with ease.

Which is a relief, I'm going to need all the help I can get when he's inside me.

Roiser hisses through his teeth, "Touch yourself."

I reach down between my legs with my free hand and start

stroking along my clit and folds. touching both of us with gentle yet effective swipes.

"I need you ready for me," he purrs.

"I thought you said you would give me pain?" I ask innocently.

To be honest I'm not sure I can handle the pain—not when he's thick like a water bottle and his nails could shred me like paper.

"I could rip you in half Minnie," he tells me, as if he's read my mind. "But I don't want to break you. I want to *make* you: foster your rage, your masochism, your wicked ways..."

I slip my fingers inside my cunt, fucking myself on his words. My hold on his cock tightens as well.

Rosier shuts his eyes, and his head rolls back. "You're my Queen, Minnie."

He takes my breath away, and we've only just started. "Kiss me," I order him, and he does, his forked tongue exploring my mouth.

Pinning me down with his lips, he grabs my arms and holds them against the bed, but only for a short while before he grabs my thighs and spreads them open. The head of his cock rub against my cunt, and he moans into the kiss.

I keep waiting for him to thrust his hips, to feel him inside me, but he teases me with the head of his cock over and over. His wet ridges running over my clit are better than any toy. Slick pours past my folds and down my cheeks, my body practically begging for him. His lips are still locked on mine, and I whimper, begging for him to take me.

Rosier grabs my hips and flips us around, laying flat on his back while I'm straddling his hips, his cock flush against my stomach.

"I want to watch every inch sink inside you."

I shiver. "What if I can't take it all?"

Despite my hesitation, I lift my hips and guide him to where I want. The head slips inside me no problem, and Rosier and I both hum with pleasure, practically harmonizing. I slide further down, starting to feel the bumps along his length.

"Such a perfectly wet cunt," Rosier praises.

His words urge me to sink further down. Soon, I'm stretched more than I've ever been before. I slow my descent, worried I'll tear something, afraid I'm not going to make it despite the pain not being any worse than when he'd spanked me. Rosier takes a hold of my hips, his fingers digging into them. It reminds me of when I rode his knee till I orgasmed, something I also thought was impossible.

"Relax," Rosier warns me, his voice breathy.

I sigh, letting my shoulders and hips ease. Roiser pushes me down and lifts his hips, pressing further inside me.

My bottom lip quivers, and Rosier smiles at me like I've said something clever, like I've done something amazing. One of his hands releases my hip and goes between my legs.

"Careful," I squeak, his claws still making me uneasy.

He balls his hand and then extends a closed finger, rubbing my clit with the backside of his digit. My body grips around his cock, and I can feel every bump and curve as wavering moans leave my lips.

"Already I feel like I could finish," he admonishes. I tilt my head to try and see how much of him is left to take inside me, but he's faster, grabbing my chin and forcing me to only look at his face. "Move your hips," he commands. It's an order I only need to hear once before I start rocking my body against him.

Rosier's lips part as heavy, hot breaths make his chest rise and fall. The head of his cock rocks against my sensitive spot, his knuckle rubbing me in deep circles, and his nails threatening to pierce my cheeks. Then there's a sharp slap against my ass, the sound of flesh against flesh. I gasp as another slap makes me double over, bracing myself against his chest. My eyes strain to the corner of my sight, barely seeing Rosier's tail sway cheekily, before smacking me again.

This time I let out a sob. "Don't stop," I beg him.

"Never."

My whole body feels like it's burning up, and I love it. I don't even realize how close I am 'til I sink a little lower down his cock and feel a new row of ridges.

"Fuck," I breath as my thighs shake.

He keeps touching me through my orgasm, not letting up even as I whimper and shut my eyes. I push my thighs together, rubbing the girth that isn't yet inside me, trapping his hand against my clit.

"Good girl," he coos. "That's what I want to see."

His knuckle presses harder into my clit, and the hand around my chin slips down to my neck. I start rolling my hips again, whimpering and crying openly. Rosier squeezes the sides of my neck, and my voice become hoarse. I wrap my hands around his forearm to steady myself as my hips buck, now hungry for him, no longer afraid of any possible pain. The tip of his tail draws little circles on my ass, outlining my bruises.

Rosier growls, and his head rolls back into the mattress. "I'm close–" He curses, and I smile. His grip tightens around my neck. "Fuck, Minnie, look at what you do to me."

He releases me, and I gasp, a tingling wave of relief flowing from my head down the rest of my body. The relative peace only lasts a moment, though, before Rosier pushes me back down onto the bed with him on top of me.

It's his turn to move his hips, grinding against me slow but deep. He dips his head between my neck and shoulder and bites down. I scream, a mix of fear and pleasure, his fangs piercing my skin like needles.

"Rosie, please!" I don't know if I'm asking him for more or

asking him to be gentle. Either way, his teeth release me, and he starts sucking at the wound, sure to leave a nice frame for his mark.

He grunts against my skin and warmth fills my cunt. I gasp and cling to his shoulders, pulling him closer to me as he finishes inside me. We both shudder in the aftermath. "Don't pull out–please," I whimper, my bottom lip trembling.

Rosier's cheek rests against my shoulder, and he pushes some sweat-laden curls from my forehead. "You want me to stay inside?" he asks. His voice is heavy with lust, but there's a hint of genuine confusion as well. He runs his nose along my neck. "What is it, my Queen?"

I try and fail to avoid his gaze. "No one's ever finished inside me," I admit.

Rosier hums with pride. "You really are mine completely. Body and soul, cunt and mouth..." He kisses the underside of my chin. "The only one to fill you like this. No wonder no man could satisfy you. Your needy cunt wanted this, didn't it?" I bite my lip as he says, "Just aching to be fucked and filled. I'm going to pull out, Minnie." I whimper, and he shushes me. "I promise you, I will give you pleasure."

I nod, trusting him completely.

He pulls back, his textured length making me moan as it leaves my body. Within seconds, his face is between my legs and his forked tongue deep inside me. I gasp and reach for the back of his head. Rosier's nose rubs against my clit as his tongue slides deeper inside me, deeper than should be possible. I realize he must be tasting the both of us, his cum mixed with mine. I want more of him, grabbing the base of his horns to pull him closer to my cunt. Rosier makes a little sound of surprise followed by a deep chuckle as he continues to dine on my cunt.

"Y-you're so good at this," I moan.

Why didn't I sit on his face as punishment when we were

on the Mortal Plane? I suppose there's plenty of time for that now... and he's got that long, forked tongue to tease me with.

"You like my cunt, Prince?" I ask, and Rosier moans in reply. I crane my neck to look down at him. "You like cleaning me up after ruining me?"

His yellow eyes snap open, and he looks at me with reverence.

"Take responsibility." My head spins, making it hard to speak "For what you do to me." The image of half his face shoved between my legs, using his horns like reins, is one I never want to forget.

His tongue darts in and out of me, and another orgasm builds inside me, this one culminating in a scream of pleasure. My thighs crush Rosier's head as I call out his name over and over. I'm so wracked with pleasure that I hardly feel him bite the soft inside of my thigh, the sharp pain complimenting my pleasure well.

My body relaxes, but Rosier stays between my legs, kissing and lapping at the fresh wound between my legs. I look up at the ornate ceiling, a mosaic of uncut gemstones.

"You taste amazing..." Rosier whispers.

"Are you... talking about my blood or...?" I'd hesitate to say "my cum" under any circumstances, but my brain is so foggy with lust that it's nearly impossible to form sentences.

The bed creaks as he crawls to lay beside me. Something wraps around my hips, but I can feel both his hands around my shoulders, one hand resting on my breast. I glance down and see it's his tail. Once I'm properly tied to him, he presses his chest against my back. He kisses my shoulder, sore from his bite and hickey. As I lay there, my body starts to ache more and more.

"I don't know if I'm going to be able to walk tomorrow," I lament.

"We won't leave the bed." I huff, and he adds, "I'll carry you, Anything for you, my Queen." His arms slide down my body resting on my stomach above his tail.

I start to fade as he whispers sweet nothings in my ear. I don't process his words at first, and even when I do, I doubt if I've heard him correctly.

"My body and soul. My cunt and mouth. My Queen, my Minerva."

CHAPTER THIRTY

MINNIE

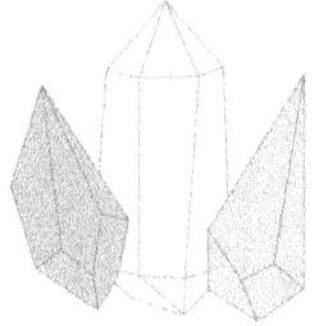

It would've been nice to wake up slowly, to take in our first morning together.

Instead, we're both woken up to a shrill screeching in Lithobates' unmistakable voice. "*MY PRINCE!*" He clops over to the bed, wringing his rat hands and pacing back and forth like his heart will stop if he stops moving. "*MY PRIN–*"

"Shut. Up." Rosier curses before burying his face in my neck. "I'm going to punt him through a window..." he grumbles against my collarbone.

"I won't stop you," I admit as I reach back to touch his hair.

A much more familiar voice is what really pulls me from my slumber. "Ugh, you two are so darling!" I sit up, seeing a figure with ashy pink skin and black hair down to his shoulders grinning ear to ear. "Hey, Minnie! I like your accessories." Kas drags a hand along his left shoulder.

I pull the bed sheets up to my neck, glaring at him.

Kas starts laughing maniacally. "Pretty swanky place our Prince has here, huh?" He flops down on the edge of the bed. Up close, there's a hint of purple to his pink hue and little devil horns poking out just below his hairline. A tail swishes behind his back, but he lacks wings. "Gotta say, Minnie, you lucked out. Rosier is one of the better looking devils down here."

Rosier is still resting against his pillow. "I should throw you in the river Styx."

"*Why?* That was a genuine compliment!"

"Um..." Lithobates shivers. "Baphomet is here my Prince! They wish to speak with you!"

Now Rosier sits up. "What? Here? Now? Why?"

I've never heard him speak so urgently.

"Yes, my Prince, they are waiting in the throne room for your audience."

Rosier grits his teeth, and his tail tightens around my waist. I touch his shoulder. He takes a deep breath and then asks Lithobates again, "What are they doing here?"

"I, um..." Lithobates' voice trills. "I-it's an honor to have an Archdevil visit, my Prince! So much so, I... I did not inquire..."

Rosier's tail glides around my waist as he gets out of bed, "Useless. Let's go." He grabs my wrist and pulls me upright. "Do you need me to carry you?"

I blink. "I'm *very* naked," I remind him. He lifts me up, carrying me in his arms like a princess again.

We pass a golden mirror, and it makes me want to crawl back into bed and hide till this Archdevil is gone. My hair is a mess and, as expected from Kas' comment, I have a massive bruise on my shoulder, a yellow and purple halo around two puncture wounds. My other shoulder isn't much better, stitched up and red like a fire siren.

I smack Rosier's shoulder. "I look terrible! I am *not* going out like this! And put me down!"

Rosier grumbles but does as I say, letting me stand in front of the mirror. There's a sharp gasp, and I see Lithobathes standing with his mouth wide open like a fish on a hook.

Rosier barks, "Fetch the crown jewels!"

As Lithobates trots off, Kas comes to my side. "Honestly, the nude look suits you." I glare at him, and he shakes his head. "But if you insist..."

He snaps his fingers, and two other figures appear out of thin air. One is pastel like Kas, with black hair that extends long past her body, pooling around her feet. The other is a dusty red, with thick, broken horns growing out of his forehead.

"I'm still pissed about the dress." Chanel's vocal fry gives her away. Kas hands her a sheet from the bed, and she drapes it over me, gathering the fabric around my hips as Kas hands her some pins. "Timaios, you wore togas, help me out here."

Tim frowns. "Did you use my full name? And I am not a handmaiden!" Despite this, he comes over and starts helping Chanel with the makeshift dress. I try not to think about the fact Rosier and I fucked on these sheets a few hours ago...

While they assemble the dress, I glance back at Rosier, who's leaning down as Lithobates lifts chains over his head, careful not to catch any of the links on his horns. Gold cascades across his chest, each link leading to a cut and polished gemstone. Lithobates slides gold bangles onto his wrists as well, the color stunning against his purple skin but hardly as impressive as his chest piece.

The dress is done and it, unfortunately, does look like a toga. But beggars can't be choosers—which means after this, I'm going to have to demand a better dress. I'm about to step away from the mirror when I bump into Lithobates, who's holding out a necklace encrusted with amethyst. Same as Rosier, I lean over and let him thread the necklace over my head.

Rosier bends down to pick me up again, and I almost stop him, something about an audience making the gesture feel less wholesome. Except when he holds me, I can see his face properly, and I tower above the other devils, making me feel like I'm something precious worth protecting.

So he scoops me into his arms, and I avoid looking at Kas, Tim, and Chanel, though it's painfully easy to picture the expressions they must be making. We all leave the bedroom and head down the long corridor to the throne room.

I can't keep my questions at bay. "So, is Baphomet a big deal? He's a big deal on Earth."

"Exactly." Rosier nods. "They are one of the nine Archdevils and have been for a very long time. Their reputation is a good source of power. I've witnessed Archdevils lose their title in part because their names no longer hold as much weight."

"Do you know Baphomet?"

"In name only," he admits. "I've never had the honor of meeting them myself. That was a role reserved for my Father."

"Maybe they just want to meet you then?"

Everyone is staring at me, a not-so-subtle reminder that I'm a mortal surrounded by the infernal. Of course an Archdevil isn't here to say hello or drop off brownies like a housewarming gift: *Congrats on the whole heir to the throne thing!*

"Do you have any idea what they could want?" I ask.

"You," Rosier deadpans. Before I can properly panic, he continues, "Let me do the talking." I must make a face because he looks at me with a soft expression. "I know that mouth of yours could get us in trouble. Let me talk with them, and we can finish this quickly. Please."

From up high, I can see Lithobates's mouth is hanging open even wider than in the bedroom, no doubt reeling over the fact his Prince is saying please. It's funny, sure, but it's also a reminder of the weight of his words.

I nod. "Alright."

Rosier kisses my forehead. It's then he notices Lithobates

staring, and his soft expression burns away, replaced with a snarl and a heavy brow. *"What?"*

Lithobates croaks and starts prancing down the hall. We reach another grand set of doors. As Lithobates' presses his hands against them, his feet comically slide along the floor before the doors start to open with a groan.

Even with the doors open just a hair, Baphomet is unmistakable: naked and tall with a goat face and the torso of a human. Their skin is the color of chalk. A set of red goat eyes are watching the door we're entering through, then a second set of eyes pop open below the first set.

"Is this... the witch we've been waiting for?" they ask.

Surrounding Baphomet is an entourage of human figures, pale and naked like the Archdevil they serve. I try to make eye contact with any one of them, but their eyes are glassy, like animals mounted to a wall. Beyond their ashy skin and dead eyes, each person is unique, a few of them with markings on their bodies I recognize as runes.

Rosier takes me to the throne carved of stone in the center of the room. I'm surprised to find Leaf has settled into the seat, curled up in a ball and looking content. Lithobates rushes over, hissing and shooing, before pushing Leaf off the throne. Rudely awakened, Leaf goes after Lithobates furry leg, chasing him behind the throne. Rosier ignores the violence and sits, keeping me in his lap.

The room is quiet, save for Leaf and Lithobates' scuffle behind us. Then Rosier asks, "You seek an audience?"

Baphomet steps forward, their entourage of human figures following like ants, each person in sync with the next.

"We have quite a lot to discuss, young Prince." Baphomet's lips don't move as they speak, their voice a gravely whisper. "Your Father's death was quite sudden."

Rosier waves a hand. "My Father's death is not your concern. Nor is it mine."

"Yes, a tragedy. Or a comedy, perhaps? No matter. I hear you were summoned to the Mortal Plane. Is this true?" Baphomet's four eyes shift from Rosier to me.

"It is true, yes." He places a finger under my chin and lifts it ever so slightly, like I'm a prize he's showing off. "She summoned me. Minerva. A most powerful and feared witch on her plane."

"Some hundred years it's been since a witch summoned one of us to the mortal realm," Baphomet muses. "I was beginning to think we were unwelcome. Then again, mortals are so *touchy* these days. Quick to start wars and drop bombs, less quick to scheme and plan. But I digress..." An explosion of red eyes erupts all over Baphomet's body, each one looking in a different direction. "This witch still lives," their voice booms.

I cower, digging my nails into Rosier's thighs, clinging to him. Thankfully, he's unphased by Baphomet's display and my scratching. "She was in danger on the Mortal Plane. She fled here, without my permission. But I've since *punished* her for such transgressions."

There's no way Baphomet can tell he's talking about sex, right? I don't think I want the goat-devil knowing about my sex life.

"Dear me, a punishment is wholly unnecessary. Minerva is not the first living mortal to wander the Hells, after all." Baphomet holds their hands in a pyramid shape as their eyes flutter shut, except for the two arguably normal eyes on his head. "All of this is a delightful development. It's been so long since we've had a living mortal visit. Not to mention the new contract—"

"We never made a contract," I say.

I think if it weren't for the Archdevil, Rosier would spank

me right here. But it feels weird just sitting here, everyone talking like I'm incapable of understanding what's going on. Then again, I *don't* really know what's going on–the full weight is lost on me.

"My soul is not his by, um..." I settle on the word that makes the most sense to me. "Law."

"Oh..." Baphomet tilts their head. "The heart of a witch is a very valuable thing."

There's smirk on Rosier's face, proud of himself or me, I don't really care. Something snakes up my arm, and I manage to stay put, realizing it's Rosier's tail moving up my arm. It starts to wrap around my neck, not tight, not even pressing the gold and amethyst against my skin. The flat side of his tail rests against my cheek, and I shamelessly lean into it.

"And he has mine," I breathe. "He has all of me."

Baphomet is silent, taking all of this in. Holding my breath, I see the dozens of humans at his feet, dying to know if they've ever been held in Baphomet's tender arms.

Lithobates screams and everyone, even the glassy-eyed humans, turn to see Leaf clinging to his furry hide. "My Prince! Compel the witch to control her familiar!"

"He's just a cat," I remark.

"COMPEL HER TO CONTROL THE CAT!"

Rosier shakes his head. "The cat has no master, not even me."

Baphomet hums. "Truly, you have surprised me, Rosier, Prince of the Hells. You may have ushered us into a new age."

Rosier covers my mouth with his tail before I can ask questions. His caution is fair, but I don't appreciate the gesture.

"Flattery will only take you so far, Baphomet," he says smoothly. "Why should I share my plunder with the rest of the Hells?"

Baphomet clicks their tongue several times. "We will

certainly reward such an accomplishment. Perhaps... you are more a King than your father was."

Rosier's jaw is tight, and he bares his teeth. "Your empty offerings mean nothing! Come back when your bite has some teeth. Make me a King of the Hells, then you can have an audience with *my* witch."

Baphomet's eyes open once more, slowly this time, blinking at different intervals. "If that is the case, I will take my leave." They walk backwards along with their skirt of mortals, moving closer and closer to the edge of the throne room. "I will return, *Prince*." He hisses the title. "And Minerva... Ah, such a powerful name for a powerful witch." They're at the edge of the throne room now, some of the humans falling off the edge. "I plan to see you again soon."

With that they fall as well, but down to where, I do not know.

CHAPTER THIRTY-ONE

ROSIER

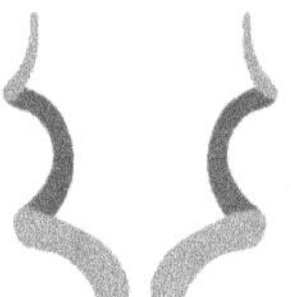

All I need is Baphomet to think Minnie is obsessed with me, not I possessed by her.

She plays her part well, acting almost as brainless as Baphomet's own court of souls. A question haunts me–if any of them were ever like her brash, arrogant, and intoxicating instead of existing solely for the purpose of their master. I fail to picture Minnie ever being fulfilled by me alone or that I could replace her books and her magic. I don't want to supplant these things.

Even as Baphomet takes their leave, I fail to relax. My misgivings are vindicated when they say my title–mocking it, reminding me I'm beneath them despite having what they want. They plummet into the Hells, and there is a welcome silence.

Only for a moment, though, before Kas starts squealing. "We're moving on up!"

He and Chanel hold hands and start jumping together, giggling and laughing. Tim has a ghost of a smirk on his lips. When Kas is finished celebrating with Chanel, he grabs Tim's face and gives him a kiss. The gesture is unremarkable, except when Tim leans in to press his forehead against Kas'. Lithobates holds Leaf, who kicks and bites at his hands, but my page still looks pleased.

I slam my fist on the arm of the throne. "Nothing has changed!" Everyone is taken aback. "You're all so desperate that you celebrate a hypothetical. Until I am made a King before the whole of the Archdevils, we are all in the same spot."

"*But*," Minnie chimes in, holding up one finger, "I didn't get kidnapped by a goat-devil." Her soft smile makes me feel foolish for my outburst.

"Yes," I huff. "That is a victory to be sure." I pinch the bridge of my nose. "Now we only have to deal with whoever else decides to *grace* us with their presence."

"Grace *us*? They're coming to see me." She plays with her curls and rolls her eyes before falling into a fit of giggles.

Warmth stirs in my chest, blooming like a flower. I consider bringing her back to the bedroom, to find new ways of making her scream with pleasure. But I know there's something else I can show her to make her scream. I hold her in my arms and spread my wings before flying off. Minnie wraps her arms around my neck, and Kas and Lithobates calling after us, unable to keep up on foot.

I bring her to the bottom floor of the castle, the most secure, with few entrances or exits. It's where our coffers are stored, where our prisoners are kept, and, most importantly, where one of the few libraries of Hell resides. There are only a few other learned places, and all of them are impossible to gain entry unless one receives permission from the devil who owns it.

Minnie doesn't have to ask permission. I want to see her spend her hours here among her favorite things.

The library entrance is simple, inconspicuous. Minnie looks at me with a raised brow.

"Close your eyes."

She pouts but does as I ask with a sigh. I open the door, the smell of paper and ink unmistakable. My Father had several witches under his tutelage, and as such, the library is enchanted to be much larger than should be possible for the space. Books line every surface save for the floor. Even the ceiling holds volumes upon volumes, and it tickles me to imagine Minnie asking for help reaching those very books.

"You can open your eyes now," I tell her.

She does, her eyes going from half lidded to wide and enamored in a matter of seconds. Her head keeps tilting further back as she looks for the end of the tall bookshelves. She says nothing, but she lets out a breath that tells me more than any of the tomes here ever could.

"I'm afraid you won't find many romances or epic tales here. Most of these are histories of the planes, a few magic books penned by dead witches, I'm sure you'll find–"

"Put me down right now."

I stifle a laugh as I set her down. The second she can reach the floor, she's off, rushing about the room and its many alcoves, her head practically spinning round and round trying to take it all in.

Then, Lithobathes arrives, huffing and puffing. Leaf is at his heels and bounds into the library.

"Be gone," I tell him before shutting the door. Leaf keeps running, and I follow him to find Minnie already curled up in an alcove with a book.

I lean against the entryway, the warm feeling inside my chest continuing to blossom. She makes me feel mortal. So long as that is kept between us, we should be fine. Devils are known to fall from pedestals of power; why should we not also fall in love? At least, I think that's what this is, the pride and excitement that comes with looking at her.

Finally, I join her in the alcove, tilting my head to see what book she's picked up: *Hells Omnibus: Volume One*, detailing a conflict between the Archdevils of old and several of their reaped souls attempting a coup. The book is about as big as her.

Footsteps alert me to another's presence. Kas waltzes in, looking rather proud of himself.

"Get out," I growl and he turns around as if he's attached to a wheel.

Minnie perks up. "Wait, Kas."

Kas keeps walking away.

"Kas," I grumble. He stops in his tracks. "Come back."

Again, he turns on command and begins marching back, his proud expression replaced with a grimace.

Minnie holds the open book in her lap. "What happened to the le Fays?"

"Well..." He breathes and puts his hands on his hips. "The vampire council of all people took control of the scene you created. They're notoriously secretive." He finds a bookshelf and leans against it. "It would take someone *very* charming and clever to get any sort of details about what happened there that night."

Minnie and I look at each other. She rolls her eyes and speaks his name with a slow drawl. "Kas..." He smiles. "What information did you get with that silver tongue of yours?"

He practically giggles. "Sad to say, the le Fays got out of there without harm. My guess is with magic, same way Arthur le Fay got *into* the gala."

Minnie tilts her head. "Teleportation magic?"

"You would know better than me. Anyway, Udtuk didn't make it, shot by a security guard and probably mounted and stuffed on some vampiric council member's wall. Though I shoudn't be so harsh. The council compelled enough people to forget the details of the event that there's not even a hint of monsters or magic to be found in the news."

For the sake of other witches, Madame Albe and Amber's kin, that's good news. Still, Minnie sits there frowning. "Thank you, Kas," she huffs.

"*Weird* hearing that phrase in Hell."

"Let me rectify that strangeness." I wave my hand. "Fuck off."

In an instant, Kas has his back to us and is gone from the library. Minnie's brows knit together, head tilted down ever so slightly, looking at nothing in particular.

"Disappointed?" I offer.

She blinks, and her expression softens before she looks at me. "Rosie..." She shifts her body so there's room for me to sit behind her. I do so, and she leans back, situating herself in my lap. "I want the le Fays dead, and I'm sure the feeling is mutual. But I'm here now, on a completely different plane. It would be a waste of time to think of them when Baphomet might make you a King."

I snort and shake my head. "They'll taunt me with the possibility for a long, long time." I wrap my arms around her shoulders, realizing we don't have an eternity together. "Minnie..." I feel embers rise in my throat.

"And I'm still cursed..." she reminds me. "I know time works differently here, but I doubt it will allow me much of an extension..." She nibbles her lip, and I realize she's been thinking aloud, working through the issue at hand. "Those people with Baphomet..." She rubs the thin parchment between her thumb and forefinger. "Those were his reaped souls, people he's made contracts with."

"Yes. It's possible he has even more, considering his age and his influence, but it's hard to say." I purse my lips. "I don't want you to lose your free will. I'm not sure if there's a way to tie your soul to mine without making you hollow."

She sets the book down and rolls her body so our chests are touching. "Is that the only reason?"

"I spoke my truth in the museum. You deserve to see your family."

"And I will one day. And when that day comes, they can meet you as well." She climbs my body enough to kiss my chin. Something in that little gesture reminds me how much I need her, how *she* is my vice.

Holding her face like the precious gem she is, the compulsion I felt at the museum returns. "Minerva, I..." The embers are back, this time burning my tongue, making it hard to speak. "I..." The words catch in my throat–if I even have the words I want to say. They float through my mind like the souls in the river Styx, incorporeal and impossible to catch.

"You don't have to say anything." Her smile is brighter than diamonds. "I think you've already told me in a few ways." She shakes her head, still smiling. "You can deny it all you want, Rosier, Prince of Hell." She says my title like it's the name of a fool at court. "But I know the truth. Despite all your moaning and groaning that devils can't care or show kindness, I know better. And I'm going to exploit that."

She lifts her chin, and I lean down so our noses can touch. "Exploit me all you want. Plunder my father's coffers. Curse my name; spit in my face." She laughs, but I continue, "You, Minnie, are my hubris, the chink in my armor. Perhaps, even, my downfall." Her laughter fades to a giggle, and I can't help but kiss her. "I like kissing you," I whisper against her lips.

"Then don't stop." Before I can act on her request, she presses her finger against my lips. "But maybe not until after I finish this chapter."

She rolls back around and picks up the book once more. I read over her shoulder, saying, "Maur loses the war and is tossed into a crevice as a traitor, where he still resides to this day."

"Spoilers!" she hisses.

"It's history."

She settles further into my lap, wriggling her body, getting comfortable. "Shush."

I hold her, forgetting where we are. The plane we're on doesn't matter. So long as I have her, I feel powerful—not from might or wealth, nothing to do with the leverage we hold. Her companionship is all I desire.

If that is to be my downfall, so be it.

EPILOGUE

Minnie

ROSIER SITS ON HIS KNEES, LOOKING UP AT ME WITH complete admiration while his lips are curled in a cocky smile showing off his fangs.

I stroke the hair between his horns. "You've been very sweet today."

"Am I not sweet every day, my Queen?" His tail swishes behind him.

I giggle, both at his eagerness and at the plans I have in store. "Would you like a reward?"

"Yes, my Queen."

I bite down on my smile, dying to know what he's picturing in his head. Maybe me riding him or me struggling to take all of him in my mouth. I'm half tempted to abandon my plan and do both. But I stick to my resolve.

"Stay put."

I walk over to the drawer where I've stashed the object I commissioned from the court blacksmith. Kas had to help me a little. I wasn't sure what metals would work best for a toy like this, but of course, Kas did. (*"You kids have it good with silicone. Back in my day—"*)

"Close your eyes," I tell Rosier. Peeking over my shoulder, I can tell his golden eyes are shut tight. He's pretty obedient when he knows he'll get a reward.

I take the leathery straps made of I'm-too-scared-to-ask-what, but they feel nice against my skin and do a good job of holding the metal toy between my legs. I return to Rosier, holding the base of the metal cock.

"Open up now."

"*Oh,*" he breathes. His smile grows, becoming properly devilish. "I *have* been good."

I giggle. "So very good. I'll even let you decide what I fuck first."

Rosier lets out a little groan like he always does when I say "fuck." *I want you to fuck me. Fuck me harder and deeper. Fuck you're so good...*

"Do you want me to pleasure your ass first?" I run my thumb along the slit at the head of the metal cock. "Or your dick?"

Rosier responds faster than I expected. "Mouth."

"O-oh." My cheeks start to burn. So much for being some stone-cold femme top. Though, I have my reasons. "It's... are you going to chip a tooth? On the metal?"

"I would never use teeth on you like that Minnie," he assures me, as if there is any way this little game could possibly harm me.

His forked tongue laps at the toy's tip. Then, to my surprise, it wraps around it, starting at the head and working all the way down the shaft, like a ribbon.

He looks at me, clearly wanting some approval. "Cute trick. Too bad I want to see you choke."

Rosier's tongue unfurls around the cock slowly. Once his long tongue is back in his mouth he opens wide. I slip the tip in first, then stroke his hair. Rosier wraps his lips around the metal cock again and holds it in his mouth dutifully.

"So patient," I praise.

There's a sparkle in Rosier's eyes. I grab the base of one of his horns, my hand stroking his hair, which trails to his nape. I grab a fist-full of hair and pull on his horn, dragging his face forward and down on the toy till he chokes.

"Such a polite devil deserves a reward."

A silver bell rings, snapping me out of the mood, my desire to see Rosier vulnerable and whimpering replaced with a new excitement.

"Oh!"

I pull my hips back, and Rosier leans forward with his tongue out, clearly wanting more.

"I'm sorry, uh..."

He looks at me with pleading, puppy-dog eyes.

"Tim must have gotten the component I needed."

"Minnie," he whines. He folds his tongue back into his mouth and whimpers. "Can't it wait?"

I start undoing the straps around my thighs. "Sure, but I want you to see it!"

He leans back, his hands catching him, his hips lifted, displaying his half hard cock. "See what cruddy little stone Tim has gotten for you so you can summon granola bars?"

I glare at him. "So, it's cute if I starve?" Once the straps are off, I place the toy on the edge of the bed and go grab my clothes.

It may not be customary to dress in the Hells, but I'm uncomfortable with the whole castle staff and our visitors seeing me nude. The outfit still shows off plenty, my top made of sheer white fabric that climbs from my wrist up to my neck and flows like a waterfall down my torso, making me feel like I have wings while I walk. A damned soul tied to a lesser devil of Rosier's tutelage was a revered seamstress when she lived and stitched sigils I designed along the hem of the coat. My pants, tight as they are, are black and opaque. So, leggings, basically, but it's not basic when you're in Hell.

I grab Rosier's shoulder and try to pull him from the floor. "Come on!" He sits there, making me strain. "How can you be so obedient one moment and absolutely childish the next?" His lips twitch. "Maybe I'll use that new toy on myself while you're tied up in litigation with the other Princes of the Hells, how's that?"

He pouts. "Fine."

As he stands, I take his hand. It's a funny sight, trying to hold his massive clawed hands in my small palms.

We take the steps to the bottom floor, where it's easy to hide. I've got my own little mortal oasis there: water, food, and books, all of which I've been able to summon thanks to the collection of texts in the library. Damned souls can't cast magic, so I guess writing it down is the next best thing. Plus, it's such a taboo on the Mortal Plane, finally getting it all out on paper must feel cathartic.

That's what I tell myself, anyway.

We enter my little home-away-from-home, the magic circle I've been working on mostly prepared. Sitting on a table is a bundle with a note attached. I recognize Tim's handwriting–*Minerva's Magic Mess*. Kas and his trio of succubi help me get whatever I need for casting. I unwrap the parcel to find several sticks and smile to myself.

Rosier looks at the magic circle with furrowed brows, as if he's trying to figure it out. I take his hand.

"Careful," I tell him as I step around the chalk outline and the little offerings of unpolished jewels placed inside the circle.

"This took a lot of trial and error. A lot of smaller circles to make sure I could summon what I wanted to this plane. If this works, so much could change."

Standing in the center of the circle, Rosier's face is scrunched, somewhere between concern and anger. "If you're about to send me to some other plane–"

"*Why* would I do that?" I ask, lifting a brow.

He shrugs. "So you could usurp me and take the throne for yourself. It would make all of this quite the betrayal, a long and arduous scheme. I respect it."

"You plopped in the middle of the Fae Realm would be funny, but no. This is a summoning circle. You should know that."

Rosier tilts his head ever so slightly, but the gesture is made more apparent by his horns. "I'm not at all proficient in magics, Minnie–regardless of you, my Mother, and the various texts in our library."

There's a little flutter in my chest when he says *our* library. I bend down and arrange the sticks the way I want them. "Do you trust me?"

"I have no reason not to."

I hum, now wanting to build the anticipation for as long as possible. "It's not against your *nature* to be trusting?"

Rosier groans, rolling his head back. "You trust me, and I trust you. It's an exchange."

"Wow."

"And I trust you more than anyone, Minnie. More than other devils, more than Kas..." He looks back down at me. "Now show me what this thing summons... please."

I blow him a kiss from the floor before I start the incantation. Within moments, dust and a sparkling mix of chalk and minerals encircle us like dancers at a ball. Yet Rosier and I only look at each other as the circle and its offerings fade and form a new shape around us, lush and cloud-like. The dust has settled into something new, something living, something purple and green. Rosier finally looks away from me and takes in this new surroundings: lilac bushes.

His gold eyes go wide, like Leaf when he sees unsuspecting Lithobates turn a corner. "These are..." He keeps looking at them, as if they're multiplying before his eyes. "I don't think anyone has ever brought plants to this plane."

"Nope! I'm the first." Humility won't win me any points here. "Hang on." I exit the makeshift garden, grabbing a blanket, two goblets, and a bottle of water. I return to the bushes and lay the blanket out on the ground, sitting. "Don't stand around, come on."

Rosier huffs, but the corner of his mouth reveals a smile. He sits down on the blanket, still so much taller than me and the lilac bushes. But down here, their smell is impossible to escape, so much cleaner and crisper than the sulfuric and stagnant smell of the Hells.

I pour us both some water and catch Rosier out of the corner of my eye reaching for one of the blooms, letting a bustle of lilacs rest in his palm. I offer him the goblet of water, but he doesn't take it, only looking at me with those pupiless eyes that can be so hard to read.

I'm about to ask him what's wrong when he pounces on me, knocking over the water and pulling me to his body. He kisses me, violently, his tongue halfway down my throat. I grab onto one of his horns and yank his head back. We both pant now that our lips are free.

"I love you, Minerva."

I breathe even deeper. It's the first time he's said it. I know he loves me, but I also know those are words he's never said to anyone, words he didn't even think he was capable of saying.

He leans on his side, hand still wrapped around my hip. "You know the hardest part of loving you–"

"*Careful*," I warn him.

"Is the fear of losing you." He grumbles, "No wonder devils deny themselves the terrors of love..."

He pauses, and I realize there's something eerie about being surrounded by nature without the accompanying sounds of life.

He presses his forehead against mine. "Do you..." He doesn't finish his sentence.

It takes me a second to catch what he's asking.

"Of course, I love you, Rosie."

I chose to be his, and in the end, he chose to be mine. And when I remember that everything feels possible. I kiss the tip of his nose. Then his lips. And we lie there, in the first and only garden in Hell, holding one another.

Perhaps for eternity.

PLAYLIST FOR CRYSTALS AND CONTRACTS

Cashmere - Tkay Maidza
A Dark Place for Somewhere Beautiful - Nova Twins
Take Care of Business - Nina Simone
High Beams - Tkay Maidza
This Hell - Rina Sawayama
No More Lies - Thundercat feat. Tame Impala
The Parton Saint of Liars and Fakes - Fall Out Boy
Wish I loved - KIRBY
Demolition Lovers - My Chemical Romance
Body And Soul - Billie Holiday
Miracle - Paramore

ACKNOWLEDGMENTS

A most gracious thanks to the various editors who worked on this novel: Sharina Wunderink, Kelsea Reeves, Alexia Howell, and Gabriel Hargrave. All your feedback was insightful and your comments wonderful.

Additional thanks to beta readers Marat Earendel and Lita, both devilishly wonderful people.

To Clanky who has been my cheerleader since Teeth and Tarot and who does so much to support the indie author community. All the love to Monster Manor a discord server where I continue to meet the coolest, strangest little freaks.

To Sophie aka dextrose.png who deserves infinite flowers, coffee, and cats. Her art always blows me away and she's the most hardworking person I know. Much love also to Savannah whose line work is to die for.

A final note to my partner, my bear, who supports me through my artistic angst. I love you to Hell and back.

ABOUT THE AUTHOR

Arin was born and raised along the American east coast and has called the city, the shore, and the country their home. They've come a long way from writing anime fanfiction in their bedroom and even have a BA in creative writing. When they're not writing Arin enjoys playing tabletop games, drinking coffee, and collecting bits and bobbles. They currently live in Stephen King's backyard with their partner, cat, and lizard.

Crystals and Contracts is their second novel.

www.ingramcontent.com/pod-product-compliance
Lightning Source LLC
Chambersburg PA
CBHW072103300726
48975CB00003B/684